OUTLAWS

Outlaws

Aidan Phelan

While this story is a work of fiction, it contains references to historical events, people and places. All efforts have been made to approach such subjects with sensitivity.
The author acknowledges the First Nations of the land in which this story is set. This book was written on the land of the Wurundjeri people of the Kulin Nation.

Cover design by Aidan Phelan

FICTION

Paperback: 978-0-6489572-9-4
eBook: 978-1-7642152-0-6

 A catalogue record for this book is available from the National Library of Australia

Dedicated to those who kept going, even when it looked like there was no way out.

THE PEACOCK GANG

LATEST PARTICULARS

From *The Bendigo Gazette*:— The notorious Peacock Gang, led by the murderer John Cooper, have not been seen since their brief and chaotic appearance in Heathcote, during which the leader drew a pistol and levelled it at the local constable before his party fled. A party of police was sent in pursuit of the bandits but were unable to locate their tracks. It is believed that the government is being inundated with requests for police reinforcements in the region, but the Premier has not yet committed to any provision of significant additional manpower.

The transgressions of this band of marauders are well-known to our regular readers. The bailing up of Mr. McKenzie's run, which has been stated as the genesis of the formation of the Upstanding Citizens League that has been so vocal in advocating for the apprehension of these criminals, was of a daring manner, but paled in comparison to the monstrous attack on James Churchley and his wife. Churchley, a respected man throughout the district, was murdered and his wife cruelly maimed by the bushrangers when their house was invaded, and although the widow Churchley has recovered admirably from the hideous wounding, it has left her without her right hand. Despite this hardship she continues to attend to her late husband's affairs with zeal and remarkable aptitude.

These depredations are only part of a long string of offences that has unfurled in recent months, which includes horse theft and highway robbery under arms, and most recently the callous murder of Constable Bowen and the wounding of Harold Henley, J.P., near Rochester in the north of the colony.

The gang is reported to be comprised of five members. In addition to the aforementioned Cooper, there are two women by the names of

Ellen McReady and Lillian Brook. McReady was, until recently, considered to be a decent and respectable woman of Myers Flat, whose husband had died of heart failure leaving her to be the sole occupant of their meagre farm. Lillian Brook, a woman of around nineteen years, was a servant of the Churchleys and has been named as the person that fatally shot James Churchley and so cruelly deformed the widow Churchley. The remaining banditti are two unidentified men described in the first instance as a tall, thin man with long light brown hair, and in the second instance a man of average height with black complexion and two fingers missing on his left hand. It is unknown how these disparate individuals came into each other's company, but the results have been nothing short of catastrophic for the law abiding and hardworking people of this respectable community.

As we go to press, a reward of £2000 has been offered for the capture of these offenders, living or deceased, who have been dubbed the Peacock Gang for the large peacock feathers they wear in their hats. A reward of £100 has additionally been offered to persons who provide information that leads directly to the apprehension of these dangerous outlaws.

One

Murchison, a town that had enjoyed great growth in the preceding twenty years thanks to the vineyards and the gold rush, lay in the north of the colony of Victoria, along the Goulburn River and not too far from the New South Wales border. There was a brick flour mill outside of the township and in the dim light of dawn a gang of riders moved past it from the south, heading north.

At the front of the group was a young man with light brown hair and the scruffy beginnings of a beard riding a chestnut mare. On his back he wore a bundle that contained a small canvas tent. Close to him was a young woman with her curly blonde hair let out and bobbing with the movement of her horse. She was pregnant and riding a palomino mare. Behind them was a man of African descent on a black stallion. He was not much older than the man in front, but it was difficult to tell. His left hand was tucked into his coat, but if it had been exposed then witnesses would have noticed the pinkie and ring fingers missing. Next to him was a woman with blonde hair hastily tied into a loose bun that was slowly losing integrity, dressed in a man's frock coat and trousers, and riding a bay gelding. Bringing up the rear was a man with longish black hair, a short black beard, dressed in rough clothes stained with blood, riding a grey nag. These were the members of the notorious "Peacock Gang": Owen Brady, his wife Lillian, Dan Thatcher, Ellen McReady and Jack Cooper.

Up until very recently, Cooper had been the leader of the gang and remained its most noted member as far as the press were concerned. However, a drunken crime spree had left a police officer dead, and a Justice of the Peace badly wounded, so the rest of the gang had voted to strip him of his position. Leadership was now shared between Owen and Ellen.

They rode onwards to the town, following roughly the same route as the river. Their mission was to reach the border at Echuca and cross into New South Wales. They were fugitives – bushrangers – and getting out of the colony was their only hope of avoiding the hangman's noose. The police presence on their original route had forced them to widen their path, setting them back several days.

They rode past the cemetery and into the town. As they moved along the road, past dwellings on small blocks, they approached the police paddock where the old Aboriginal Protectorate Station had been and the bridge that would get them across the Goulburn River. Thin fog rose ominously from the soil in the cold and gloom. Tensions were high as they came closer and closer to the paddock and the very real risk of being spotted by the police. It might lead to a shoot-out, or it might lead to nothing, it was impossible to tell at this point.

Cautiously they approached and sighed with relief that there were no police out and about in these early hours. It was a good thing for them that the local troopers were too fond of bed to be up to greet the dawn.

They continued along the banks of the Goulburn River, which had been reduced at this point to little more than a string of pools due to the ongoing drought conditions. This made it easier to get the horses across as they headed west towards the Balaclava Hill gold mine.

The gang had become accustomed to long stints on horseback, but the constant movement was taking a toll on their constitution, as well as the horses, by this point. Lillian, the youngest member of the gang, was already struggling with the effects of her pregnancy on her body, but riding for close to eighteen hours a day was making things excruciating. She was now somewhere between her second and third trimesters, and it was showing.

The gang's short-term goal was to reach Shepparton, which they soon discovered would require them to head north-east from where they were when Owen finally had enough light to consult his map. Navigating by night was proving to be difficult, especially with everyone being so exhausted. After a brief consultation the decision was made to set up a small camp in the scrub and rest. It was sweet relief, but they needed to remain vigilant.

While the others tried to sleep through the excruciating aches in their muscles and the hunger pangs, Owen kept watch. He felt his newfound responsibility was a huge weight on his shoulders and he struggled to allow himself time to rest.

"You must rest," said Lilly, who had emerged from the tent to check on him.

"I have to figure out the route from here," Owen replied, gesturing at the map.

"You're no good to us exhausted. The rest of us can take turns keeping an eye on everything. Please, even just a little nap."

With great reluctance, Owen gave himself permission to head into the tent to relax and get some sleep.

**

After midday, the gang resumed their travels. It took them until well after nightfall to reach the outskirts of Shepparton.

"This is it for now," said Ellen, "we will make camp here and, in the morning, I will go into town with Jack to replenish our supplies for the next leg."

The bushrangers dismounted and lit two oil lamps that they had been carrying. The tents were not pitched as it was too dark to be searching the scrub for appropriate branches to use as the frames. The horses were hobbled and left to graze while the gang slept under the stars. Dan took up duty as the sentry, assuming his position with a bottle of overproof rum to help him stay warm in the frosty night air.

***

Shepparton had started as a squatters' haven full of sheep and cattle farms built on land that had been "extrajudicially" acquired. The man credited as the founder of the settlement was a puntman well known for his predatory business practices as he fleeced prospectors crossing the Goulburn River on their way to the goldfields. For years it was known as McGuire's Punt because of this important feature, but more recently the locale had been renamed in honour of one of the most prominent landowners in the area. It was a small but turbulent place where crime was common, and squabbles were often settled violently. Burglaries, arson, stock theft, dog poisoning and quarrelling were the kinds of things one would expect in Shepparton. In fact, it had only been recently that the proprietor of one of the hotels had burnt down his competitor's business, and the local pound keeper was accused of stealing cattle to impound, effectively holding them ransom.

Jack and Ellen kept their wits about them as they went into town. They headed into the Prince of Wales Hotel and went to the bar. The barman nodded to Jack but did a double take with Ellen, who was dressed in men's clothing: a green overcoat, purple waistcoat and scarf, loose trousers and tall boots. He thought to say something but decided against it.

"Gentlemen, what can I get you?"

"A couple of ales will do," said Jack.

"Right you are," said the barman as he fetched two pewter tankards and pumped ale into them from a swan-necked tap. Jack tossed some coins on the counter to cover the cost.

"Say," said Jack, "have you heard about those bushrangers?"

"The ones that been murderin' folks down near Bendigo? Yeah, I heard about 'em," said the barman.

"Do you know anything about where they are?"

"Lotta folk reckon they'd be heading up to cross the river into New South Wales if they know what's good for 'em, but nobody knows anything much. I haven't noticed any more police about, despite the local troopers saying the government is sending people up here to find the bastards. You looking to get the bounty, are you?"

"We're more interested in giving them a wide berth if we can manage it. Helps to know where they might be," said Ellen, attempting to make her voice gruff and masculine.

"Smart," said the barman. "The way I see it, I don't care much about them so long as they leave me alone. Plenty around here I wouldn't shed a tear over if they ended up on the wrong end of a bushranger's bullet, though."

Jack and Ellen finished their drinks and went in search of a store.

"Sounds like we need to be on the lookout for extra troopers as we go," said Jack.

"They will tend to back up their numbers if someone has been gunning troopers down," Ellen replied tersely.

"It was self-defence, Nellie. If you had been in my position, you would have done the same."

"I doubt that very much, Jack, and don't call me Nellie. What's done is done and now we all have to help you carry that cross. Let's grab what we need and get going."

The shopping trip was brief but efficient. The pair left the store with simple provisions that would last them a few days – flour, tea, salt beef and sausages – as well as some information about the machinations of the police that would prove useful. Jack had picked up a new Crimean shirt, coat and scarf and, after putting them on, discarded the bloodstained ones he had been wearing in a caged fire that was burning outside the store

Ellen noted the strange looks aimed in her direction as they passed locals, most of whom were men who seemed to be employed in smoking pipes and propping up walls with their backs.

"Turning a few heads," said Jack.

"Not in the way that I would like," replied Ellen.

"Perhaps we need to rethink the way you dress if we're going into towns from now on?"

"I will dress however I like. This happens to be an effective disguise as well as far more comfortable to be riding in all day. Would you prefer I be in a hoop skirt and riding side-saddle?"

"That's not what I meant."

When they regrouped with the rest of the gang, the decision was made to head out towards Tallygaroopna station and camp nearby. As they rode, they kept their heads down.

They had been on the road barely half an hour when they spied a group of horsemen riding towards them totalling four in number. Each man was armed with a revolver and either a carbine or shotgun that was slung across their chest. There was no doubt that these were police in bush clothing returning from a hunt for the bushrangers. There was no way out of it now – either they could continue their course and be recognised and possibly be shot at, or they abruptly turn and ride into the bush and raise suspicion immediately, likely resulting in a chase and shoot-out. Regardless, there would be gunplay.

The horsemen exchanged glances and motioned towards the gang.

"Let them make the first move," Ellen said to the others.

The horsemen drew their revolvers.

"Stand!"

"Get to cover," Owen shouted.

The gang dismounted and scrambled for hiding places as their horses scattered. The police opened fire and bullets whizzed around them. The bushrangers drew their weapons and prepared for battle.

Ellen and Dan went behind a boulder, Jack behind a log, and Owen and Lilly behind some thick-trunked trees. They checked their firearms. Jack, with the Colt Navy revolver he had stolen from the policeman he had murdered, took aim at the foremost rider and shot him. The man reeled and lurched in his saddle from a shot in the chest, but he was not fatally wounded as the bullet had merely grazed him.

Dan peeked over the boulder and fired his revolver at one of the men at the back, putting a bullet through his hat. He received a bullet in reply, but it merely zipped past his ear, clipping it very slightly. It felt like a bee sting but was nothing serious, despite the blood.

Ellen cocked her repeating rifle and fired at the same target as Dan had: a stocky man with a large moustache dressed in hunting tweeds and a floppy felt hat. Her shot struck him in the shoulder, and he screamed.

With two of the police out of commission, the remaining two paused. They fired off one more shot each before turning tail. The others, although wounded, followed.

The bushrangers came together once the area was clear.

"That was too hot," Dan complained, pressing his fingers to his wounded ear.

"Did anyone see where the horses got to?" Owen asked. This prompted a ten-minute search in the scrub for the gang's horses, who had been spooked by all the gunfire.

Upon recovering their mounts, the gang continued towards Tallygaroopna station without stopping. There was no time to waste processing what had just happened. The land in this area was very flat and open where it had been industriously cleared to make way for pastures, which meant there were fewer places to stay hidden. This was farming land, and Tallygaroopna station was one of the bigger stock farming establishments in the region. Luckily for the gang there were still some dense clusters of trees that were kept as windbreaks, which were useful for gathering branches to use for the tents and campfire. Thus, it was here that they set up their camp, far away from the paddocks. When it grew dark, they built a small fire on which they cooked the sausages knowing they would spoil otherwise, hoping the darkness would hide the smoke. They would not be here long.

Once night settled in, Lilly retired to the tent with Owen. The air was cold, and they warmed each other up by stripping off their clothes and huddling up as close as possible under the blankets. Owen spooned Lilly and gently stroked her round belly as he hummed music to her.

Ellen kept watch as Dan and Jack slept in the open. She layered herself up with her coat, blanket and the kangaroo skin she kept on her saddle. The chilled air hurt her lungs, but mouthfuls of cheap rum warmed her belly enough to distract her.

The expanse of the pastures was pallid in the moonlight, and the sky seemed to be alive with twinkling stars. The milky way streaking across overhead made Ellen feel small. She was alone with her thoughts and began to ponder about the mystery of life. Her husband Wallace, in the early days of their marriage, had always told her that whenever she felt lonely because he was out on the road for work, she should look at the stars because he would be looking up at the very same stars, which would remind her that he wasn't really so far away after all. But there she sat looking up at the stars knowing that he would not be doing the same and it made her feel more alone than ever before. She wished with all her heart that Wallace was there to talk some sense into her about this ridiculous bushranging life she had gotten herself into, but she could no longer rely on his counsel. Her sorrow felt like a lead ball dropping from her chest into her stomach and she realised that she could not even muster tears or a wail from such a depth anymore. It was silent sorrow.

Her thoughts turned to her children. They were not children anymore, of course, but to her they always would be *her children*. She had one daughter, Cate, who lived with her husband in England, another, Susie, living with her family in Campbelltown near Sydney, and a son, Terry, who had seemingly vanished from the face of the earth while away from home working on the railways. She wondered what they would have thought about her falling in love with Jack Cooper, a man much younger than her who had convinced her to follow a life of crime and had thereafter proven to be not only unreliable but dangerous when she was already too far down the path to turn back.

She looked down at her hand. The skin was rough and calloused in parts, and her veins seemed more prominent. These were not a girl's soft and dainty hands. These were red-knuckled hands that had tilled fields, slaughtered livestock and mended her house. With age came wisdom, with wisdom came the burden of knowledge. She felt foolish that she had allowed herself to fall for Jack and throw her honest life away. She had been so desperate for a way out of the struggle to survive that her judgement had seemingly frittered away, but there was a creeping realisation that perhaps all Jack had offered her was an excuse to be who she always secretly was. She could have turned those bushrangers away from her door, but instead she saw an opportunity and seized it without stopping to think about consequences. Regardless, now she was on the run and trying to avoid an appointment with the hangman. This was no life for a woman who was a mother and grandmother, but it was her lot, and she only had herself to blame.

**

The gang moved on from Tallygaroopna, heading west along the Goulburn River. They could tell they were getting close to their goal as the dry plains began to give way to verdant farmland and orchards. A couple of days travel at a leisurely pace saw them finally reaching the outskirts of Echuca where the Goulburn, Campaspe and Murray rivers converged.

Echuca was a fairly modern town, boosted economically by its position on the Murray River, which allowed easier trade, and had grown incredibly fast as a result. Beautiful brick buildings stood along the river, paddle-steamers carrying huge bails of wool moved gracefully like swans along the Murray. There were factories, a butcher, a baker, blacksmiths, doctors, sixty hotels, a railway station and, importantly, a punt and a floating pontoon bridge across the river.

On the New South Wales side of the river lay Moama, a town that had been built on its reputation as the largest cattle market outside of Melbourne but had since begun to shift focus to boat building. This was where the gang set their sights. If they could get over there, then the police wouldn't be able to chase them because they would need permission to enter the neighbouring colony. By the time the ink would have dried on the paperwork, the gang would be long gone.

As they moved through the streets of Echuca, they were very conscious of the sheer number of people everywhere. They were not far away from the riverside when they noted the presence of a small army of men from the Volunteer Rifle Regiment, dressed in neat green uniforms with kepi caps, long woollen trousers, and tunics decorated with chevrons and brass buttons. These men were all armed with percussion rifles, and they patrolled the border to prevent the bushrangers from escaping. A small cluster were at the bridge, blocking access to all who were not approved to cross. The colonial government was prohibited from forming its own formal army, but provisions adopted in 1854 allowed them to create volunteer armies and in the little over a decade since then a number of them had been created. Many of these volunteers had military experience but were too old for active service in Her Majesty's armed forces. Since most of the regular army had been shipped off to New Zealand to fight the Māori, the Volunteer Rifles had stepped up to the plate to assume their responsibilities.

Though there had already been police out looking for the bushrangers in the area, in response to the gang's attack on the party of police near Shepparton days earlier these soldiers had been loaded onto a train and taken straight up the new railway from Melbourne to Echuca to guard the border crossings while police hunted them in the bush.

There were now charges of multiple murders and grievous bodily harm on top of the many robberies to their names, but only three of them had been formally identified. Jack, Ellen and Lilly were the only ones named in the reward notices, but Owen and Dan were listed as men "whose names are unknown" and described. The volunteers were expecting armed resistance and were ready to use deadly force.

The gang, upon seeing these riflemen, paused to collect their thoughts.

"Alright, Brady," said Jack, "you're the boss now. What do we do?"

"You could always go up and ask to look down the muzzle of their rifles to see whether they're loaded," Owen snapped back. Ellen hissed at them, irritated.

"We should find somewhere to spell the horses while we get a closer look," she said.

The gang rode through the town until they found a boarding stable at the back of one of the scores of hotels that seemed suitable. Each of them paid a few shillings to put their horses in the stalls to rest and feed. The bushrangers convened outside and tried to stay out of sight as they debated.

"I will go up and see if I can find out how many of these volunteers there are. Lilly will come with me," said Owen.

"What about us?" Dan asked.

"You and Ellen lay low. You're not exactly inconspicuous. Jack, I need you to see if you can get some more supplies. We're probably going to have to keep moving along the border if we can't cross here."

"As you wish, milord," Jack said sarcastically with an exaggerated bow and flourish of his hand.

Owen and Lilly began walking deeper into the town towards the river. As they walked, they noted several of the volunteers wandering around town in uniform with rifles slung across their backs. As Lilly was dressed in a simple pleated dress, and Owen was dressed in much the same manner as a stockman, they did not arouse suspicion as they strolled hand-in-hand.

They saw a volunteer walking towards them and Owen felt his heart race. He tried to keep a calm exterior and gestured for Lilly to enter a sweet shop as they passed. They swiftly passed through the door as the volunteer casually strolled past them. They were in the clear.

"Can I help you?" the confectioner asked from behind the counter. The walls were decorated with shelves of glass jars full of boiled sweets, candied fruits and other delectable treats.

"You have quite the assortment," said Lilly.

"Oh, yes indeed. I have some exquisite chocolate drops from Mr. Giraud in Melbourne. There are sugar plums, comfits, lollipops, peppermint lozenges, rock lollies. And a fresh batch of jujubes made with silver wattle gum by Messrs. Dillon and Burrows has just been brought up express by train from Melbourne."

"Well, my dearest," said Owen to Lilly, "how about you pick out some sweeties to take with us?"

Lillian began to peruse the inventory while Owen approached the counter.

"It's pretty busy out there today,"

"No more than usual," said the confectioner.

"It has been a while since I was here last. There are soldiers about the place – that's new."

"Oh, yes. There's about a dozen of those volunteer riflemen up from Melbourne. Supposed to be protecting the place from bushrangers, but if you ask me, they ought to send someone to protect us from the blasted volunteers."

"Oh?"

"They swan about the place like Wellington back from Waterloo, but most of them couldn't find their navel with two hands let alone shoot straight. There's one chap who would have to be no younger than sixty years old!"

"I saw some up at the bridge," said Owen, moving the conversation along.

"Yes, only about three or four, I think. Most of them are patrolling the riverside. Frankly, all the bushrangers would have to do is pass through the middle of the town and head a little up the river if they wanted to cross into New South Wales without being bothered."

"You think so?"

"Oh, certainly. Even though Swan Hill is only about a day west of here I very much doubt anyone thought to reinforce the police out there. It would be no inconvenience at all, I think, to anyone desperate enough to want to go north of the border. It's what I would do."

"I reckon you're on the money. They're useless, aren't they?"

"My word! It's no wonder all that lawlessness from over the border has taken a hold down here if this is the best they can do – old men and portly butcher's boys playing soldier."

After some superficial conversation, Owen and Lilly left the shop with bags of sweets and walked towards the river once more.

When they got within view of the pontoon bridge, they took careful note of the men guarding it. There were three men guarding the approach, two older and one younger. The eldest was a man with a long white beard and eyes like tiny blue glass beads; the youngest was short and overweight with a fluffy beard strategically shaved to imply a jawline that wasn't really there. The other was tall and gangly and made up for his lack of chin with his surplus of nose. It would not take much to overpower them if it came to it.

Lilly scanned the surrounds and spotted three other soldiers scattered along the riverside, including the one who had passed them in the street, none of whom seemed to be too fussed about keeping an eye out for bushrangers.

"Pretty docile bunch," said Lilly.

"They seem like it, but I bet they'd be eager to get some shots off."

"What do you think we ought to do?"

"Well," said Owen, "let's catch up with the others and work out a plan. The shopkeeper suggested Swan Hill was a good place to cross, so my bet is on that."

"Could he have cottoned on that we were the people they were sent to guard against? Maybe he was trying to trick us into walking into a trap?"

"No," Owen replied, "he seemed more interested in airing his grievances than anything. I doubt he cared much about who we were as long as we were listening."

"I hope you're right," said Lilly, rubbing her hands together nervously.

***

By the time the gang had gathered it was almost evening. They elected to stay in the hotel overnight, convinced that their presence in town was not known yet. Luckily there were two rooms free. Owen and Lilly took one, the other three shared a room.

They met in the bar for tea, retiring to the dining room to eat. Roast beef was the only thing on the menu other than beef stew, but they were happy to finally have some decent food.

"What's the plan, boss?" Jack asked Owen. Owen glared in reply.

"Owen thinks we should head west and cross at Swan Hill," said Lilly.

"I spoke to a shopkeeper who said that the government had only sent about a dozen of the volunteers up and most of them are guarding the river here in town. We can slip through the town and up to Swan Hill without any real risk of being interfered with, then take the punt across the Murray there," said Owen.

"The shopkeeper I spoke to said he reckoned the volunteers would be gone in a few days," said Jack, "if it were up to me, I'd have us linger here and wait for them to take off then we can just go over the bridge at our leisure."

"What do you two think?" Owen asked Ellen and Dan.

"I'm tired of being shot at," said Dan, "Swan Hill sounds like a safer option. That's where my money is."

"Both plans have merit," said Ellen. "On the one hand, the longer we stay here the more chance there is that we'll be spotted. On the other hand, I don't know how much more riding I can take right now. I'm exhausted and would love to lie low for a few days. I'm sure Lilly feels the same given her condition."

"We could split up," Jack suggested, "half stay and try our luck with the pontoon bridge, the rest head to Swan Hill, and we meet up in Moama in a few days."

After some contemplation, Ellen was the first to respond.

"I agree with Jack, splitting up could be an effective way of getting everyone over the border safely. Think about it – they're looking for five of us. If we split up, they won't know where to look."

"I suppose there's some logic in that, but there's strength in numbers," said Owen.

"I reckon I'm heading west with you, Owen," said Dan.

Lilly stared at her hands, which were clasped on the table.

"Well," she began, "now that I'm thinking about it, I want to join you boys, but I just don't know if I can ride all the way there and all the way back to Moama. I need time to rest properly. I'm in a lot of pain as it is and hours and hours in the saddle is just making it intolerable."

"So, you're going to try the pontoon bridge here with Jack?" Owen asked.

Lilly sighed and nodded, avoiding Owen's gaze.

"I will take my chances with the bridge also," said Ellen.

There was an uncomfortable moment of silence. Owen nodded to himself.

"Alright, if that's what you think is best," he said sadly.

"Don't be like that," Lilly said, giving him a little kick under the table.

"No, you've made your choice. Dan and I will head west. Hopefully we will see you all in Moama in a few days."

Jack smirked.

"Not so easy as it looks to be the decision maker, eh?"

Owen stood up and left the room.

"What did you say that for?" Dan snapped.

"He reckons he can lead better than me. Now he sees that when it comes down to making the hard choices it's tough work. That's come-uppance," said Jack.

Dan scowled.

"Unlike you, Owen has enough faith in us to make our own choices. I'm just surprised that you ladies didn't back him up."

Lilly gazed at the floor. Ellen shifted uncomfortably.

"We're not taking sides," said Ellen, "it's not about Jack versus Owen. It's about what we think will work."

Dan grunted and left the table, taking a bottle of rum with him and shaking his head.

"You need to stop with this," Ellen said, turning to Jack.

"Stop what?"

"This childishness. You only have yourself to blame for losing your status. You want to be the big boss man; you bloody well earn it."

"I earned it by keeping their bloody necks out of the noose. I made the decisions they couldn't. Same goes with you two. You want to stick with me? You gotta do as I say. That will keep us alive."

"I don't want to hear any more of this," said Lilly as she got up from the table and left. There were tears welling in her eyes.

"You want to storm off too?" Jack asked Ellen.

"And leave you here to wallow in self-pity?"

"Self-pity?"

"Yes. You're acting like a spoiled child who got his bottom smacked for being mean to the other children. That's not the man I fell in love with."

Jack frowned and wriggled in his seat.

"I will go with you on this, Jack, but I won't let myself be tricked into making myself vulnerable to you ever again. My Wallace was an honourable man. He never raised a finger to me, and he gave me respect. If he were here now, he would have laid you out."

"Yeah, well, where's he now? Where'd that honour get him?"

Ellen shot up with a look of utter contempt broiling in her eyes. She walked over to Jack and grasped his face in one hand to make sure he could not look away.

"You know what hurts the most? I threw away any hope of dying in my own bed at a ripe old age for you. I would have died for you. In return, you lied to me and hit me, and now you insult my dead husband. You talk a lot about loyalty and looking out for each other, but you wouldn't know real loyalty if it bit you in the balls."

With that, Ellen turned and left Jack to reflect.

Two

Owen and Lilly sat on the edge of the bed in their room holding hands. Owen was greatly downcast.

"I think you need to reconsider going with Jack and Ellen. I have a gut feeling that something is going to go wrong if we try crossing that bridge, and we need to steer clear of this town. It's not just the soldiers, but I can't put my finger on it."

"I know you've got my best interests at heart, but you need to try and look at the situation from my perspective. Being saddle sore is bad enough without having a little one in you making you need to stop all the time to pass water or feel like there's a fire in your gut and your throat is the flue. I'm tired, I'm in pain, and I need rest. Having at least a few days here might give me time to gather my constitution for the short ride over the river."

Owen sat in thought for a moment. In his mind he tumbled around all the possibilities he could muster to convince Lillian to go with him. He finally settled on an option he felt would work.

"What if I got a buggy?"

"What do you mean?"

"What if I bought a buggy or a gig, or some such conveyance, and you could ride in that instead of on horseback? Would that make it more comfortable for you?"

Lillian thought.

"I suppose it might. But how are you going to get one of those?"

"I still have most of my share of the gold escort money tucked away. If I find a vehicle that you can ride on would that change your mind?"

"If you could do that, then I might rethink my stance."

"Alright," said Owen with a grin, "it's a deal. Tomorrow I will go out to the wheelwright and see what I can do."

***

The next morning Owen dressed in his cleanest attire and rode into town from the hotel with a valise in his satchel containing £200. He figured that any small vehicle and the appropriate gear could not have been worth more than that.

It did not take him long to find a shop matching the description he was in search of, and fortuitously there was a sign out front that read: *Waggonettes, Dog Carts, Buggies and more at reasonable prices.* Owen entered and sought out the man in charge, who was a wiry looking man of around thirty years of age.

"Morning, sir," said the wright.

"Good morning. I suspect you're the chap I should talk to about a buggy?" Owen asked.

"Aye, what are you in the market for?"

"I'm looking for something small, reliable and affordable."

"Ah, I think I have what you want out the back here," said the wright gesturing for Owen to accompany him to a yard at the rear of the workshop.

In the yard was a wide selection of wheels and conveyances. Some of the vehicles were new and were painted and polished to a high sheen.

"Old or new?" the wright asked.

"If I can pay for it with what cash I have with me, I don't really care too much. I just need something with a comfortable seat and room in the back for the shopping."

"Well," said the wright, "if you're looking for something like that, I have a couple of older ones here that might do you if your purse strings are tight."

They moved over to a pair of slightly shabby looking vehicles that were designed to be smaller and speedier. The first was an English-style dog cart with two large wheels and a padded seat that could cater to a single driver in front and a passenger in the back *dos-à-dos* with the driver, facing in the opposite direction. The second was a two-horse gig with a padded bench seat that allowed two people to sit next to each other, but not much else, and looked far worse for wear than the other, with tears in the leather, rust on the wheels and scuffs along the woodwork. Owen's eyes gravitated to a light, four-wheeled wagon. It was in less-than-perfect condition, but it had a bench seat, plenty of room in the back and only required a single animal to pull it.

"How much for that wagon?" Owen asked.

"That's one of those American things. It used to belong to a little Chinaman who used it for delivering vegetables in town. She may look a little rickety but she is as sure as mud after the rain. I can do that one for... hmm, let's say £70."

"Is that the best price you can do? It's pretty rough."

"Well, they're in high demand these ones so they go pretty quickly. If you don't get it, someone else will."

"It's not exactly your fanciest option, though, is it? Surely, you can knock a bit off the price given it's already got some miles on it and possibly some rot given the state of some of those panels."

"Alright, alright. I'll give it to you for £60. How does that sound?"

"I will give you £40 if I can leave here with it right now," said Owen confidently.

"Fifty and she'll be all yours."

"Have you got all the tackle?"

"I do, and I can do you a bargain on that too."

"What are we talking?"

"£10."

"Five."

"Five? Heavens above! Are you trying to rob me?"

"Me? Rob? The thought never crossed my mind," Owen smirked, "Alright, ten it is. It had best be in good condition."

The men shook hands and retired to the counter in the shopfront to do the necessary paperwork. Once everything was signed off Owen took the new collar and tackle out to Ruffy and prepared her while the shopkeeper brought the vehicle around. Ruffy, who was used to hauling wagons and carts after being raised to work, was hitched to the new wagon and Owen rode back to the hotel, giving the wheelwright a cheerful wave.

As Owen drove the new cart down the street to the hotel, he noticed Lilly resting against the fence in front of the stables. As she saw Owen pulling up her eyes lit up and she jogged out into the street.

"Oh, my goodness!"

"My dearest, I present to you your new chariot," said Owen proudly.

"How much was it?"

"Never you mind. Now, do you know how to drive one of these?"

"Um, not really."

"Well, no time like the present to learn."

Owen hopped down and moved around to help Lilly up into the seat. He climbed back in and handed her the reins.

"Now, it's not too much different than when you are in the saddle, but it will take some getting used to. You can't spur her on, so you've got to give a flick of the reins to let her know when you want her to go. Give a tug this way to pull her away from the footpath and we'll go for a drive."

Lilly held the reins up and tugged with her left hand, which made Ruffy turn her head and start plodding out into the road. The horse had taken to the wagon well and Lilly found it easy to steer her and control her speed. They rode through the streets, Lilly giggling with joy as she got the hang of driving.

***

At midday, the couple returned to the hotel to meet up with the others. Once more they ordered meals and withdrew to the dining room. Jack, Ellen and Dan did not seem to be in the best mood.

"I take it you did not sleep well," said Owen.

"You could say that. It was a bit… chilly in our room," said Dan.

"Oh, you poor thing. It must have been so uncomfortable for you and Ellen sleeping like babies while I had to spend the night on the floor like a dog," Jack said sarcastically.

"Well, there's an update to our plans. Lilly will be coming with us, Dan."

"What?" said Ellen.

"Owen used up his savings to get a wagon so that I'm more comfortable when we're on the move," said Lillian.

"And how is that going to go if the traps catch up to you and you have to ride fast?" Jack asked.

"The trick, which you may come to learn eventually, is not to draw attention to ourselves in the first place," said Owen.

"Very well to say that now, but where was that advice when you caused the commotion at the stud farm, or when you blew Jim Churchley to Kingdom Come?" Jack retorted.

"Will you let that go? A lot has happened since then and it is possible for people to learn from their mistakes," Lilly snapped back. "Besides, we're not the ones who got drunk and went on a rampage when we were almost clear of the traps, are we?"

Jack slunk back into his chair, pouting.

"Moreover," said Owen, "the wagon will be useful once we're over the border because our plan is to give up bushranging and try to make a clean start. I'm tired of this life and I have a good reason to give it up now."

"Is the plan still to meet in Moama?" Ellen asked.

"Of course. That hasn't changed, although we wouldn't object if you wanted to come with us," said Lilly.

"We're setting off at first light so we can make good time and get to Swan Hill in about a day. Once we're across the river it should take about two or three days to reach Moama," said Owen.

Ellen nodded.

"Alright, let's aim to meet up in Moama in three days. That will give Jack and I time to plan a way across."

"What do we do if you aren't there to meet us?" Dan asked.

"If we're not there within two days of the rendezvous then it means we're not coming. That's your signal to get moving as far away from there as you can get because there is probably going to be troopers on the lookout," said Ellen, "we will assume the same in reverse order."

"Sounds like this might be our last hurrah," said Dan.

"It's only a few days. Not the end of the world," Ellen replied.

"Still, in case something does happen I say we make this night a good one."

***

That night the gang ate well and drank plentifully. The liquor mellowed the men out and Jack took Dan and Owen onto the veranda with cigars for a smoke.

"My boys," said Jack, "you've stuck by me through many adventures and now you are spreading your wings. Let's have a smoke and reflect."

"Where did you get these?" asked Dan.

"I picked them up the other day. I had a feeling we might have occasion to celebrate getting over the river, but it seems a good idea to indulge in them now, just in case. Puff them slowly. Savour them."

Jack used his pocketknife to slice the ends off and handed a cigar to Dan and another to Owen. They lit matches and ran the flame over the end of the cigar until the tobacco caught it. Soon the air was filled with grey plumes of rich-smelling smoke.

"So, Owen," said Jack, "when Lillian pops, are you going to be Da, or what?"

"That's Lillian's call," Owen replied. "It is my desire, but it's not my place to decide anything on that front. I will do what I can to help her bring the child up well regardless of her views."

"It doesn't bother you to take on all the work and have had none of the fun beforehand?" Jack asked.

"That's not exactly the truth of it," said Owen blushing slightly.

Dan laughed and gave him a playful punch in the arm.

"My good man," Dan chuckled.

The next hour was spent talking about the old days when they were a trio, committing bold robberies without anyone knowing who they were. They drank much whiskey and soon they became sentimental.

"Gentlemen, whatever happens over the next few days, let us remember this night when we sat on this veranda in the quiet part of town, smoking cigars and whiskey bought with the proceeds from our gold escort robbery. This is what it's about. What we're doing right now sends a message to those who are hunting us. We are not afraid, we know we're smarter and will outwit them. Bad laws are meant to be broken. Greedy men must be made to share their wealth," said Jack.

"Rob from the rich; give to the poor. And there are none poorer than the likes of us," Dan slurred as he knocked back more whiskey.

Inside the hotel, meanwhile, Ellen and Lillian sat by the fireplace in the women's parlour. Ellen had decided to wear a dress for the evening in an effort to keep unwanted eyes off her. They reclined in elegant armchairs and enjoyed the quiet ambience. This hotel, although grand, was not popular and this suited the gang's purposes just fine.

"Do you think you'll be alright out there on the road?" Ellen asked.

"The wagon will make things a lot easier. A seat is far more comfortable in my condition than a saddle, and I've some kangaroo skins to plant under my backside to soften it up. Owen and I went for a drive so that I could get the hang of things. I think we'll be fine."

"I understand that, but, like Jack said, what if you come up against some police? Will you be able to get yourself to safety?"

"Owen knows what he's doing. He hasn't let me down yet."

Ellen sat silently for the next few moments. She did not doubt that Lilly had reason to be optimistic, but she also felt nervous about allowing her to go off with the men without her. She felt protective over the girl and was on edge at the prospect of having no control over what became of her in the coming days. Despite this, she had no intention of changing her own plans as she still felt taking her chances with the bridge was the best option.

"Do you think you'll ever patch things up with Jack?" Lilly asked.

"No... I don't think so. It's pretty hard to bring myself to forgive him for what he did. If he can be weak enough to do that once, he'll do it again. I have very little faith in the unfair sex after my experiences. Maybe if he could prove he had learned his lesson..."

"But you care for him, don't you?"

Ellen stared into the flames.

"I do. In spite of what my mind is screaming at me, my heart is still in the same place. I can't quite bring myself to believe that's who he really is. How foolish I must have been to believe he was anything else."

"Is that why you agreed to stay and try the bridge?"

"No. I still think it's our best chance. We have been in town for three days, right under the noses of the men who were sent to gun us down, and nobody has recognised us. I think we'll get across that bridge without so much as a hair out of place."

Lillian nodded with a knowing look in her eye.

"Still, you're saying there's a chance that you could mend the rift," said Lilly.

"If he can show me that he's changed, then there's a chance."

"You had some fun, though."

Ellen relaxed into her chair.

"Yes," she said, "we had some fun."

Lilly smirked.

"I know that look, Lillian."

"I said nothing!"

"I know what you're thinking, though."

"Oh, do you?"

Ellen narrowed her eyes at her young friend.

"I was thinking about when I first joined you lot and I spied Jack in the creek having a wash," Lilly continued.

"What of it?"

"Well, I've had a little more experience now, and I was thinking about the difference between Jack and Owen."

Ellen arched her eyebrow.

"What differences?"

"Well, Owen is bigger."

"What has height to do with anything?"

"I was referring to his dick."

Ellen spat out her drink.

"Lillian Brady, you shouldn't be talking like that!"

Lilly cackled.

"You are incorrigible," said Ellen with a leer.

"Are you jealous?" Lilly said with a look on her face like the cat that got the cream.

"Why would I be jealous?" Ellen leaned over and spoke in a quiet voice, "a big prick is a nice thing when all is said and done, but what can he do with his mouth?"

Lilly looked confused.

"What do you mean? Kissing?"

Ellen made a V shape with her fingers then stuck out her tongue and waggled it in the gap. Lilly blushed bright red.

"I'm sure I don't know what you mean," said Lilly bashfully.

"Don't forget the fingers too," said Ellen as she curled her index finger up in a come-hither motion as if scratching an itch in a hard-to-reach spot.

"Oh, my God, you let him poke around inside you?" Lilly said, wide-eyed.

"Yes, I did, and it felt *wonderful*," Ellen replied with a mocking cackle.

Lilly averted her gaze and sipped her lemonade. Ellen broke out in a loud belly laugh.

"What's the matter, Lil'? You started the conversation."

"I shan't be engaging in any of those larks while I've this belly. What if Owen pokes the poor tot in the eye!"

"Well, then," replied Ellen, "Just make sure you give yourself time to recover after the little one comes out before you give it a go. Trust me, you won't be in haste to have anything big or small going back in there for a spell."

Ellen sipped her drink.

"Still, it feels pretty good when a man cares about your pleasure and not just his own," she said, "I felt like a different woman after I laid with Jack. He seemed to enjoy seeing what I liked. He can be unselfish when the mood takes him, believe it or not."

"I can believe it, I suppose."

"I had never before considered that it was possible to feel pleasure in such a way. It's almost as if it's forbidden knowledge for we of the fair sex."

"Why do you suppose we're made to feel like our only purpose is to please men and not ourselves?" asked Lilly.

"Selfish men love selfless women because they always get what they want without ever being asked for anything in return. I believe the word for a creature that takes what it likes for as long as it likes without giving anything back is called a parasite. The problem with parasites is that they tend to destroy the things they feed off eventually."

"I'm sick of being made to feel ashamed for being a woman," Lilly replied, "and I hate men who only think of their own pleasure and see us as things to be used up and disposed of."

"Me too, Lilly. Me too."

"From now on I'm going to make sure I get what I want."

A brief moment of calm floated down between the women.

"I wish you were coming with us," said Lilly.

"I know," Ellen replied.

"I hope nothing goes wrong and we all meet up on the other side of that river in three days like we planned. I don't think I would be able to live with myself if anything happened to you on that bridge. I love you and I want you to be with me when the babe finally comes."

Ellen leaned over and grasped Lilly's hand firmly.

"Don't you worry about that. It's only a few days. All you need to think about is yourself, your darling husband and that beautiful baby that you will be bringing into the world very soon. I will do my best to make sure you're all safe."

Lilly thought to herself for a moment then spoke.

"Ellen, I was thinking perhaps it might be a good idea to do a swap."

"Swap?"

"I could take Old Tom to pull the wagon, and you could take Diana to get you over the border quicker."

Ellen gazed into the fire and rubbed her hands together.

"Alright," she said, "that seems appropriate, but you had better look after him. He's my good boy."

"I will care for him as if he were my own," Lilly replied.

***

After the bar closed, the gang returned to their rooms. Owen was clearly buzzing from all the alcohol and tobacco he had consumed and couldn't keep his hands off Lilly as they entered their accommodation. He kissed her all over her neck and swept his hands over her breasts and belly.

"You smell like lavender," Owen said as he nuzzled her neck.

"Ellen got me some perfume a while back and I was saving it for a special occasion."

"I like it," Owen said giving little kisses on her throat.

"You're in a good mood."

"I'm just very lucky to have a wife such as you. I just want you to know how much I appreciate and admire you."

"You are drunk, Owen Brady," Lillian giggled. She could feel the bulge in his trousers and knew exactly what he was in the mood for.

With all the hormones coursing through her in recent weeks she frequently found herself becoming quickly aroused over unusual things. Her breasts were so engorged and sensitive that even Owen accidentally brushing against them at night as they lay in the tent was often enough to get her excited, but embarrassment or fear of being heard usually quelled her desire. Little looks that Owen gave her as he rode beside her made her hot and bothered, which only served to make her frustrated because she couldn't act on her impulses. There had been a moment only a few days earlier when she had positioned herself in the saddle slightly awkwardly, which had given her a little thrill and for the rest of the afternoon she thought about what she would have liked to be doing with her husband under the blankets.

The feeling of Owen's lips pressing gently on her throat triggered her body to prepare for action. It was like a rush of warmth through her body and a prickling sensation in her loins. She helped Owen disrobe, taking time to run her fingers over his body. She felt herself getting wet, so she ordered Owen to help her remove her own clothes as quickly as they could manage. Owen fumbled with buttons and hooks but the adorable look of concentration on his face only served to heighten Lilly's feelings. Layers were clumsily peeled off until she was standing in front of her husband completely nude. She guided him over to the bed.

The structure creaked as Lilly climbed on and reclined against the bed head in a half-sitting position with her legs apart. Despite being intoxicated, Owen succeeded in clambering onto the bed without falling and injuring himself. Lilly's mind went back to her conversation with Ellen and she decided to put the theory into practice.

"Use your mouth," Lilly said clasping the sides of Owen's head and gently guiding his face down to her crotch.

Owen began to kiss her engorged lips and caress them with his finger, which tickled and delighted Lilly.

"Tongue," she sighed.

As he began to use his tongue, the sensation was soft and almost soothing, which gave Lilly a pleasant tingling that spread up through her body. With her crotch already so tender and sensitive to touch between her condition and the extensive horse riding, it all felt incredibly intense, and she held her hand over her eyelids to help her focus on the sensations without vocalising. She ran her fingers through Owen's hair and clawed at his scalp as surges of pleasure washed over her. He listened intently to her heavy breathing and knew what he was doing must be hitting the right spot. Owen continued, only experimenting a little with his technique to make sure he didn't lose momentum, until Lilly's breathing became shallow, and she clutched at the bedsheets as if holding on for dear life then let out a moan loud enough that she could be heard clearly in the adjoining rooms as pleasure overcame every other sense or thought. Owen paused and looked up at her in surprise, unsure if he should stop or continue. Without looking down, Lilly pushed his head back into her crotch.

"Don't fucking stop," she snapped, her voice guttural.

As she climaxed, she bucked and writhed and clamped Owen's head in place with her thighs. When the explosion of bliss petered out, she relaxed, panting like an athlete after a long sprint.

"I did good?" Owen asked.

Lilly could only manage a nod. Her entire body tingled, like her skin was vibrating at a tremendously high frequency. The motion in her belly was intense.

Owen was filled with great satisfaction to see his actions having brought her such delicious pleasure and the salty sweet taste of her lingered on his tastebuds. After a minute of rest, they resumed love making. After the third repeat of Lilly's orgasmic operetta there was a vigorous knocking upon the bedroom door.

"Steady on, mate," came the voice of the proprietor from outside, "You're making the rest of us look like slouches!"

Owen and Lilly burst out in peals of laughter as they heard the aggrieved proprietor slink back to his room. Owen sat up and smoothed his hands over Lillian's belly. He could feel the baby inside seemingly doing somersaults.

"I think you have an admirer," said Lilly with a blissed-out expression.

"I hope to get to meet them in person soon."

Lilly gazed up lovingly at her husband. It puzzled her that he should be so excited to welcome into his life a child that was not his own when most men were vehement in wanting an 'unspoiled' bride to bear them progeny and continue their own bloodline.

"Come lie beside me," said Lilly, shifting slightly to make room. Owen accepted the invitation and snuggled in close, draping his arm across Lilly's chest.

"If it's a girl, what will you name her?" he asked.

"I'm pretty sure it's a boy."

"Alright, if it's a boy, what will you name him?"

"I think," Lilly said after a moment of contemplating, "I should like him to be Owen junior. I think that would be a fine name for a fine, young man."

Lilly looked at Owen and saw tears welling in his eyes.

"What's wrong?"

"Nothing," Owen said, trying to hide his face. "I must have just had too much to drink. Don't mind me."

They both got under the bedcovers and Lilly lay on her side while Owen nestled into her back.

"Owen?"

"Yes?" Owen replied.

"Thank you."

"You've no need to thank me."

"Well, I just did."

Her mind was a jumble of thoughts and feelings, most disconnected from each other. But underlying them all was that she was glad now that Owen had made sure that she would accompany him and Dan. She realised in that moment that she could not bear the thought of being apart from her husband. He made her feel safe, but he also allowed her to be herself. In fact, it was the first time she could recall feeling like she could truly let her guard down and be vulnerable. She felt like that with Ellen too, to some degree, but it was different with Owen. Men always made her feel threatened, but she knew in her bones that Owen would fight to the death to keep her safe.

As Lilly shifted slightly to get comfortable, she felt a little poke in her buttock.

"Good grief... Seriously?"

"Pay it no heed," said Owen, "it'll sort itself out momentarily."

***

While Owen and Lilly were fooling around like newlyweds, Ellen lay in bed in the room she shared with Dan and Jack thinking. She stared at the ceiling and acknowledged a yawning, empty feeling in her heart. It was a void only family could fill. As she contemplated her journey, she came to the realisation that going over the border would give her an opportunity to reconnect with her daughter Susie.

She expected that the New South Wales police would be unlikely to pursue them if they kept a low profile once they crossed the river, and this would allow her to make her way to Campbelltown. It was also an opportunity for Jack to prove himself to her. If he could remain well-behaved and assist her in getting to Susie's home safely, then she would contemplate allowing him back into her good graces. Having reached her decision, Ellen was finally able to relax and drift off into sleep.

***

The next morning the gang were up early. Owen hitched Old Tom to the wagon and helped Lillian up onto the seat. Provisions to last the trio a few days were loaded into the back. Jack shook hands with all three and Ellen gave them all kisses.

"You bloody well look after yourself, missus," Dan said to Ellen with a sorrowful expression. She nodded in reply as her words stuck in her throat.

"Be careful Lilly," said Ellen as she turned her attention to the buggy.

"You know me," Lilly replied.

Dan mounted his stallion, Sancus, Owen got on Ruffy, and they all began the journey to Swan Hill. Ellen waved to them until they were out of sight, then turned to go back into the hotel with Jack.

"What's the matter?" Jack asked Ellen, noticing her quiet demeanour.

"I can't quite explain it, but part of me feels like something is going to happen. Something horrible."

"You know they will be fine."

"How can you be so sure?"

"If I wasn't I would have tried harder to stop them," said Jack.

"That doesn't answer my question, Jack. How can you be so sure nothing will happen to them?"

Jack went quiet, apparently wrestling with something in his own mind.

"I did something."

"What did you do?"

"While you were all getting the wagon ready, I paid a boy to take an anonymous letter to the police. In the letter it said that the gang they were after was going to cross the border at Corowa. That's a fair way east of here. As soon as they get the letter, that's where they will send the reinforcements."

Ellen was unimpressed.

"If that was your plan all along, why didn't you tell the others? Why did you let them go to Swan Hill instead of making them stay with us?" she asked.

"I was thinking about everything last night. Even if it's only them who get over the border safely, three out of five is a success."

"And what about me?"

"You have your own mind, Ellen. If you decide to take off after them now, I won't hold it against you. But you also know I won't do anything to put you at risk, let alone myself. It would serve nobody except those who wish us harm."

Ellen folded her arms and gave Jack a scornful look.

"I made my choice," she said. "There's another thing I need to bring up."

"What?"

"When we get into New South Wales, you are going to help me find my daughter. I've decided to leave this lifestyle behind. I need to be with my family, Jack. It's the least you can do."

"Of course," Jack said with a solemn nod.

"Prove yourself to me. Show me that I'm wrong about who you really are, and that Jack Cooper is an honourable man."

***

As night fell, Jack and Ellen went for a stroll through the town. As they walked the streets, they noted that it appeared a lot of the volunteer regiment had moved on, but there were still some men guarding the bridge.

"Do you think that means the letter worked?" Ellen asked.

"It seems like it. It will be easier to get around three guards on the bridge than dealing with a whole army."

"When do you think we should make our move? Do you still want to wait a few days?"

Jack stared across the road to the bridge. There was very little traffic, but the odd wagon hauling goods across the border was still making its way. The soldiers were stopping the wagons and interrogating the drivers, but none were ever detained longer than it took to say their name and business.

"We'll do another scout tomorrow, see what they're up to, and then we will know what to do. Maybe we'll get lucky overnight."

***

That night as Ellen and Jack were in their room they lay on separate beds. There was an awkward silence as neither felt inclined to be the first to speak. Finally, Jack decided to break the tension by sitting up and lighting his pipe.

"I don't think you're allowed to smoke that in here," said Ellen.

Jack stopped in his tracks and gave Ellen the most bemused stare he could muster.

"Not allowed...?"

"Yes, you could get in trouble," said Ellen. The words had barely left her mouth when she realised the absurdity of her worry in light of everything else and cringed.

"Old habits, eh?" said Jack.

"Yes, old habits. I was a good, law-abiding woman before I met you."

"The sheep you stole and butchered might not agree with that."

"Oh, shut up," said Ellen with a slight smile. The tension began to slacken.

Jack reclined, puffing on his pipe and looking out of the window. Ellen got up and walked to his bed. She ran her gaze over him. He was dressed in his undershirt and trousers and his strong shoulders were on display as he locked his hands behind his head to soften his resting spot when he leaned against the wall. Ellen couldn't help but be reminded of the intimate moments they had shared, and how Jack had cared for her when she arrived at the cave hideout badly injured. She struggled with her feelings of betrayal at the way he had attacked her when he had returned to their room in Rochester after that drunken rampage that had jeopardised their safety and left at least one person dead. She questioned whether that one act of weakness was enough to negate all the positive moments they had shared and all of the growth she had undergone because of their romance.

"Jack," Ellen said, "do you remember what happened at Rochester?"

"What do you mean?"

"Before the gang voted to follow Owen's lead, do you remember what happened? What you did?"

Jack was silent but nodded.

"What do you remember?"

"I remember we fought. You punched me."

Jack's hand went to his cheek. He remembered the haymaker she had given him. It was almost strong enough to knock some sense into him.

"Do you remember hitting me?" Ellen asked.

"I..." Jack faltered, "No. I don't."

Ellen stood and scowled.

"I told you some uncomfortable truths and you struck me across the face."

Jack sat up and looked at Ellen with intensity.

"I wasn't myself. I was out of control. I was drunk."

"If that's what happens when you drink, then you need to cast aside the bottle. There's an old saying my father used to use: *In vino veritas.*"

"What does that mean?" Jack asked.

"It means, 'in wine, truth'. When someone is drunk the mask comes down and they show you who they truly are. What I saw from you was scary and I do not wish to see it again. Do you understand? You let drink turn you against the people that care about you, and even worse, it made you a murderer."

Jack averted his gaze as his eyes became glossy with tears.

"Can you forgive me?" he asked.

Ellen hesitated to reply.

"I can. But it will take a little time. The real question is, once you realise what you have done will you ever be able to forgive yourself?"

Jack pursed his lips, clenched his teeth and gulped, trying to swallow his emotions. He reached out and placed his hand on Ellen's arm, but she brushed it away.

"I'm going to bed now. Don't stay up too long. You need to be fresh tomorrow."

She turned and walked back to her bed, disrobed and slid under the blankets.

Jack sat in silence contemplating the conversation. There were many things he regretted doing. This was the first time he had been made to think back on them and question how justified he had truly been in making those awful choices that had such high costs.

+++

Terence McReady was nineteen years old and out in the world on his own as a man for the first time. Standing slightly under six feet tall with golden hair and green eyes, he was a striking young man. He had just spent the last six months in and around Melbourne working on the railway as a navvy and now was on his way back to his mother's home at Myer's Flat for a spell before rejoining the navvies working on the line further north around Echuca. He had not sent word to her as he wanted his arrival to be a surprise.

In his haversack he carried all his worldly possessions: a purse filled with what earnings he had left over after his expenses had been paid, some clothes, photographs of his parents and sisters, a well-read copy of *David Copperfield*, a leather-bound journal and pencils, and a bottle of wine he was saving until he got home. In his waistcoat pocket he carried a silver locket on a fob chain, inside of which was a small portrait of his mother.

As he walked along the highway, the heat of the day beat down on him and he decided to stick to the shade of the trees. He walked off the road into the scrub and continued along the same trajectory. After an hour of walking, he decided to find a good spot to sit and read. He had a flagon of water slung around his neck and he drank eagerly from it. He marched deeper into the bush where he stumbled upon a camp that appeared to be abandoned. Seeing this as an ideal place to rest, he walked into the camp and sat on a tree stump. As he rifled through his sack for the novel, he heard movement in the scrub that he dismissed as being a kangaroo or a wombat.

Suddenly there was a figure before him with a wide-brimmed hat with a red fly-veil around it and a scarf pulled up over the lower half of his face as a mask, aiming a pistol at him.

"Who are you?" the stranger demanded.

"Terry McReady," Terence replied.

"What are you doing here?"

"Resting. I've been on the road."

"Is that so?"

The man cocked the weapon.

"You look like trouble to me," the stranger said.

"I don't want any trouble; I just wanted to sit and read my book. I can leave; there's no need for violence."

"I can't take the risk. There are traps all over the place and if I let you go, you'll just go straight to them."

"I won't, I swear! I don't even know who you are."

The stranger walked across the camp to Terence and gestured for him to stand. He patted Terence's pockets down and plucked the locket out.

"Please, don't take that. It was a gift from my mother."

The stranger opened the locket and saw a coloured photographic portrait of a beautiful young woman with smooth, round features, wavy golden hair and plump lips.

"That her?"

"Yes, that's her."

"Old portrait?"

"Not very old."

"What's in the bag?"

"Nothing of value, I'll show you..."

Terence reached into the bag and grabbed the bottle. The stranger, in a moment of paranoia, mistook the neck of the bottle for a firearm and pulled the trigger on his pistol. The shot hit Terence in the chest, and he fell, dropping the bottle of wine on the ground.

"Ah, shit," the stranger muttered.

Terence began shaking and sobbing.

"Why? Why did you do that?" he repeated over and over.

"Shut up! Shut up! I thought it was a gun."

Terence calmed himself enough to ask the stranger to fetch his journal and pencil out of the haversack. The stranger complied. Terence used the last of his strength to sit up and hurriedly scribble a note on a blank page.

"T-take this... to my mother. I'm dying. I'm dying..."

He handed the book to his murderer and collapsed. In a moment Terence McReady breathed his last. There was a stillness in the air as if time was standing still. The stranger pulled down his mask and looked at the scrawled note in the journal.

Ellen McReady

Myers Flat

Love

Terry

There was a commotion in the bush, and he turned to see Owen Brady and Dan Thatcher rushing towards him.

"What on earth happened, Jack?" said Owen.

"We got found. We need to move."

"Is he dead?" Dan asked with his eyes wide.

"Yes. It was him or me. Police spy."

Jack snatched a blanket from the tent and draped it over the body before shoving the journal in the bag and slinging it over his shoulder.

"Shouldn't we bury him?" Dan asked.

"You got a shovel?" Jack replied sarcastically.

"Where are we meant to go?" Owen asked.

"Myers Flat. It's a bit further north from here. That's where we're going."

+++

Sleep had not come easily for Jack, nor had it lingered. After his third violent start fuelled by bad dreams he decided to get up and watch the dawn. *Yes*, he thought, *I'm going to write a different story for myself from now on.* He looked over at Ellen who had been restless all night. Her blankets were a mess and bunched up at her belly. She lay on her back snoring gently with one arm over her head and her breasts exposed. Jack was unaccustomed to guilt, but he felt it in spades when he looked at her.

He had to make amends. He would find a way.

Three

The morning came, and with it came inevitable nervousness as the two fugitives prepared for a possible flight over the border. Ellen had been certain this plan would go off without a hitch, but now she was second guessing herself.

They headed to the river on their initial scout. The bridge was still guarded, and as it was midweek there was a lot of activity on and around the bridge as people went about their business.

Jack maintained his cool but was prepared for trouble. He made sure his revolvers were ready to go and anything essential was in the haversack he wore over his shoulder or in his saddlebags as they had no longer had a packhorse to load up with items.

Ellen had wrapped her Spencer repeating rifle in a blanket and stuck it on the front of her saddle. She did her best to disguise it as a bundle of clothes, hoping the guards would not stop her on suspicion of carrying firearms. She wore her pleated dress to blend in better.

"Do you think it's worth taking the chance today?" Ellen asked, "we can wait another day if you're not satisfied we can get past the guards."

Jack pinched his nose and stared into middle-distance then sighed.

"I say we ride across separately to reduce the chance of the guards becoming suspicious. You go first and once they let you pass you keep riding, no matter what happens to me. If they get suspicious I can hold them back until you get clear."

Ellen nodded.

They split up so that they would be coming at the bridge from different directions. Ellen rode slightly ahead, giving her a minute of extra time to get across. As Ellen approached the bridge, she could feel her heart racing and heard the rush of blood in her ears. As she reached the blockade a middle-aged man in a green military uniform flagged her down.

"Morning, ma'am. State your name and business."

Ellen took a breath.

"My name is Eleanor Pratt. I'm heading over the river to visit my cousin in Deniliquin."

The volunteer gave the rider and her mount a once over.

"Pretty bold of you to be riding astride, wouldn't you say?"

"I had to borrow my brother's saddle. My side-saddle was damaged and I'm waiting for it to come back from the saddler."

"I don't suppose you know about the bushrangers that are about?"

"Of course. A lady must always be aware of the potential dangers. But they are still on this side of the border, are they not?"

"That's why we have to stop everyone, ma'am. Nobody is above suspicion."

"And do I look like a bushranger to you?" Ellen snapped.

The volunteer scratched his cheek and sighed.

"Alright, come through."

He waved Ellen onto the bridge, and she complied readily. The sound of the hooves on the floating bridge was nerve wracking. She tried to resist the urge to look over her shoulder and kept her eyes on the prize: New South Wales and freedom. Time seemed to stretch and the few minutes to get across felt like an excruciating hour. The bridge creaked and bobbed but remained sturdy. Suddenly she was on the other side, riding off the bridge onto New South Wales soil. She allowed herself to look back over her shoulder momentarily as she rode to the cover of a cluster of trees. Her heart was in her mouth. She made sure she was out of sight, then peered through the trees.

She could just barely see Jack riding up to the guards. Suddenly, Jack began arguing with the guards, gesturing across the bridge. He was becoming very animated. One of the volunteer riflemen grabbed Jack's arm and tried to yank him out of the saddle. Tombstone snorted and shied away. The volunteers trained their weapons on Jack who swept his coat open and grabbed a revolver from his belt. He swung his horse around, unsettling the guard who had tried to grab him. The older man fired, but the shot missed by a country mile. Jack fired at the ground and the men jumped back. Jack turned the horse towards the bridge and galloped across. The riflemen fired at him, but their aim was atrocious. One shot zipped past Jack, the other struck a duck that was flying past along the river. Jack was hunched in the saddle and kept facing forward. He raced all the way along the bridge and straight past where Ellen was waiting.

Ellen turned to look at the guards who were throwing their hands up in defeat, except for the older man who was fumbling in his attempt to reload his muzzle-loader. Ellen mounted and followed Jack. It was around five straight minutes of hard riding before they stopped. They both rode into a clearing and dismounted. The horses were foaming and panting, the riders were drenched in sweat and weak in the knees.

"Jack! Oh, my God," was all Ellen could manage as she panted. It took Jack a few seconds to catch his breath well enough to talk.

"Those bastards..."

"What happened?"

"They tried to stop me crossing. Said they didn't like my tone of voice. Bored little boys with guns."

"Are you alright?"

"Yeah. They... They couldn't hit a tree if they were in the middle of a forest."

Ellen rushed over and hugged Jack tightly. Jack began to nuzzle Ellen's neck and before either had processed what was happening their mouths were pressed together in a deep, passionate kiss. The adrenaline coursing through their bodies made them tremble and heightened every sense. Ellen frantically rubbed her hands over Jack's body. Jack pressed himself into her and began to grind his pelvis into hers while grabbing her buttocks through her skirts. Ellen let out sharp little gasps as she unbuckled his belt and unbuttoned his trousers. Dragging them down to his ankles, Ellen kissed his thighs and groin. The world was a blur of colour and noise as she grabbed his tool and pressed it against her lips, the sound of white noise in her ears drowned out everything else. Jack squeezed his eyes shut and threw his head back, letting out a small moan as he began to feel like everything was spinning around him as if he was a fish in a bowl and someone was swirling the water.

He and Ellen were both foggy eyed with arousal, yet hyper aware from the terror of the confrontation and the flames of passion. Ellen lay back on the grass and lifted her skirts, parting her legs to give Jack access to the gap in her drawers.

"Here!"

Jack got on his knees and eagerly slid his member into her, taking a moment to enjoy the warmth and the softness with a moan before his raging lust had him bucking and thrusting like a maniac. The threat of dying had only heightened the thrill of living, and the furious riding over the border had whipped Jack into a frenzy. His legs were sore and his groin almost numb from the pounding he had received from his saddle in the flight, but every sensation was tantalising at the same time. The feeling in the base of his pelvis was like flexing a muscle after lifting a heavy weight – not exactly painful but deliciously aching. As he came it was like a jolt from a galvanic battery device that shot up into his body from the tip of his prick. He gasped and exploded and saw every-colour speckles dancing in front of his eyes like explosions from a Chinese skyrocket.

As he relaxed, Ellen rolled over and threw him to the ground on his back. He stared up, dazed, as she straddled him and pushed his pulsing cock back into position. The strange warm and gooey feeling of what he had spurted inside her only added to the exquisite delight she felt as she ground her pelvis against his with such intensity that she felt light-headed and short of breath, but she could not bring herself to stop. It was like stretching after a long period of stillness, sweet relief followed by a tender burn. It didn't take long for her to climax with a drawn-out cry somewhere between bliss, agony and a feeling of total sensory overload. As she slowed her movements, every little touch on her vulva and thighs was like being jolted. She quivered and jerked with each sensation as she slid Jack's softening penis out of her with a tiny gasp of relief.

She flopped onto the grass beside Jack to catch her breath, drenched in sweat and bright red in the face. They gazed up at the sky, wanting to dig their fingers into the soil for fear the spinning world would fling them off.

Ellen began to sob, overwhelmed. It was as if the sexual release had popped the lid off the jar trapping her grief and insecurities and all the negativity she had t tried to suppress in the past few weeks, and now it was gushing forth in a flood with nothing to dam it.

Jack felt queasy and his legs were weak, shaking uncontrollably when he tried to move like his joints were jellied. He reached over and grasped Ellen's hand.

"Nellie," he said, "we made it."

Ellen could not speak, but she squeezed his hand to show she understood that they were safe now.

***

Before nightfall, Ellen and Jack used their hatchet to gather sheets of bark and strong branches to build a makeshift shelter. They ate rations and drank rum before retiring to sleep together. For the first time in weeks, they were not terrified about someone finding them. The ground was not exactly comfortable to sleep on compared to the beds that they had enjoyed in the hotel, but sleep came easily for both of them.

The next morning, they discussed what was to come next. The other three were due to reach Moama in the next day or so, therefore they needed to make sure they were in town when they arrived.

"We will rent a room in one of the pubs there until we meet up. The good thing about Moama being so close to the border is that they will accept Victorian bank notes and not question it," said Jack.

"If they don't come, what should we do?" Ellen asked.

"Well, even though we already agreed that we should assume they're not coming and continue on our way, I suppose we will go and look for them. If we head west, following the Murray, we should reasonably expect to find them along the way if they haven't been captured or killed."

It was not exactly an optimistic answer, Ellen noted, but it was realistic. At least Jack was thinking of the well-being of the others, even if he seemed to disagree with diverting from the agreed course of action.

They tried to retrace their steps and find their bearings in order to head to Moama. Eventually, with the help of a compass Jack had stowed away in his sack, they found their way and reached the riverside town. It was, like Echuca, a tidy and modern place complete with brick buildings such as a police barracks and a post and telegraph station, but perilously low and close to the riverbank. The pair rode through the streets looking for the horses that belonged to their friends, just in case, but without success.

"No fear," said Jack, "We are early anyway. We will find a place to stay while we wait for them to arrive. We'll give them time to get here, then we go out looking for them."

Ellen nodded and followed Jack to a small hotel. Something was niggling at the back of her mind and her chest felt like it was being stretched outwards and inwards at the same time. As much as she tried to convince herself that she had no reason to be anxious, the feeling wouldn't go away.

Four

After leaving Echuca, Owen took the lead ahead of Dan and Lillian. He had the map of Victoria folded up and safely stored in his saddlebag. He knew that so long as they followed the flow of the Murray River, they would find their way to Swan Hill. To their great relief, the trip was without incident. It allowed them the chance to take in the scenery, watching bandicoots zipping through the undergrowth and brightly coloured rosellas playing in the branches of the gum trees.

For once, Dan did not touch his flask or any bottles of alcohol. He was sober and doing his best to stay alert. It was not often that he had the ability to tuck his ruminations away and be in the moment, and he was determined to soak up every second as Jack had set a very good example of why it was so important to remain sober while on the run.

He had been bothered by Ellen and Jack choosing not to join them but understood that their decision was their own to make. Despite his misgivings, the fracturing of the gang had made him feel freer to some small degree. There had been such a sudden change in the gang's dynamic that it was hard to even recognise it as the same group of people who had banded together months earlier. By sticking with Owen and Lilly he realised how much of that feeling of disruption was simply from Jack's change of attitude. He wondered how much of that was influenced by Jack's relationship with Ellen.

He had been monitoring Jack's temperament and noted that his moods had become increasingly tumultuous over the course of his romance with Ellen. He had heard them arguing in Rochester when Jack eventually came crawling back from his murderous, drunken rampage and was most surprised by the fact that the sound of a punch landing and a body slamming into the wall had been Ellen's reaction to Jack slapping her. Dan shook his head as he thought about the times he wished he had laid Jack out but had abstained for one reason or another.

Lilly brought up the rear in the wagon, hitched to Old Tom. She had now gotten used to controlling it and was enjoying sitting on a soft seat for once as her posterior rested on a stack of kangaroo skins. It was only a small improvement to her comfort, but a necessary one. Life would have been far easier of they had acquired a vehicle ages ago, but it was Jack's insistence on travelling through the bush to make it harder to track them that had made the idea seem impractical. She was relieved that they were finally far from Jack's influence. She hoped the freedom might allow Owen to realise he could take charge and stop second guessing himself constantly.

As for Owen, he refused to allow himself to think for too long. Riding in silence was not an option lest the noise of a thousand intrusive and belligerent thoughts invade his mind, so he hummed, whistled and sang to drown them out. He was tired of the way that his traumatic memories and the inner voice that only existed to erode his confidence had been growing louder and more insistent since the incident at the Churchley farm. The sooner they got over the border and found somewhere to settle, the better it would be. He tried to shift his thoughts to the future he looked forward to sharing with Lilly, but it was hard to be optimistic with everything that had been happening.

***

As they entered the township of Swan Hill, Owen noted the telegraph wires suspended from timber poles along the street. The poles were topped with cross-arms that held the wires up and ceramic insulators that stopped the electric signal travelling into the wooden poles. The wires were connected to the post and telegraph office where messages would be sent and received. The telegraph meant that news could travel far faster than via the post or messenger, and although a fascinating piece of modern ingenuity, it meant that it was imperative that the outlaws kept a low profile.

The town possessed two churches — one of brick and one of wood — as well as a hospital. Beyond that it had a sleepy charm, owing largely to the small number of locals – no more than about a hundred. The trio passed a Moreton Bay fig tree as they approached the riverside. The tree had been planted in 1860 by the explorers Burke and Wills before their ill-fated attempt to reach the Gulf of Carpentaria. Having followed the story in the papers at the time, Owen had been fascinated by just how much of the country still remained unseen and untouched by white man, and the inherent dangers they faced in trying to venture into the unexploited wilderness. Life as a bushranger had only given him a taste of what Australia's wilds were capable of throwing at people who unwisely sallied forth in the name of expanding the Empire, but even that small sample left a huge impression.

They stopped briefly to rest the horses and grab food supplies from the store and the butcher. They filled the back of the wagon with their purchases and took a moment to take in the surroundings. The sun was out and sparkled on the river surface as the trees swayed gently in the breeze.

"We could stay here tonight," said Dan.

"No. We must cross. The longer we stay the more we tempt fate," said Owen.

On the banks of the river was the punt – a broad flat boat big enough to move a few horses and cargo over the river. It resembled a short jetty with railings around the outside, and at one end of the boat was a wheel that was used as a pulley in conjunction with ropes that extended across the water to move the craft. Each of the trio paid five shillings to go across the river in the punt before boarding. Once the horses and wagon were safely on the punt, the puntman and his assistant began to pull on the ropes and the boat began to traverse the width of the river. When they reached the opposite bank, a ramp was lowered, allowing the group to disembark.

Once Owen, Dan and Lilly were safely in New South Wales they took a moment to process the fact that the whole process took barely a few minutes once they had paid. It was surreal how simple and easy it had been.

They began heading east towards Moama, hoping that Ellen and Jack would have figured out how to get across the pontoon bridge and meet them in the town by the time they got there. They followed the river, knowing that it was the most reliable way to find their way back to the rendezvous point.

**

That night they pitched tents close to the river and camped. Knowing they were unlikely to be set upon by police, they were far more relaxed and made themselves a decent fry-up of the sausages, bacon and fresh bread they had procured that day.

"Do you know how long you have left?" Dan asked Lilly, pointing to her baby belly.

"When Ellen took me to see the doctor, he said I was a bit over halfway. I think that means a few more months looking like I'm ready to pop. So long as we have a safe place to live by then, that's all I care about."

Dan scratched at his beard.

"Given the circumstances of the situation, you're not thinking of, you know...?"

Lilly scrunched her nose up.

"What do you mean?"

"I mean... You're happy to keep the little one?"

"Are you asking if I intend to hand him over for adoption?" Lilly said with a frown.

Dan felt his heart suddenly begin beating incredibly fast and became aware of a slight ringing in his ears.

"I'm not judging or looking to pry. I only ask because I imagine it might be hard on you both given who the father is."

Lilly nodded and let out a sigh. She rubbed her round belly affectionately.

"I thought about that. In a round-about way, I'm taking that pain the Churchleys inflicted upon me and trying to turn it into something beautiful. I plan to raise this boy to be a better man than his father was and spite that cow he was married to."

Dan smiled.

"I get to be an uncle, then?"

"We'll see," Lilly said with a sly grin.

"I noticed that you haven't been drinking," said Owen to Dan after a pause.

"No, I haven't," Dan replied.

"By choice?"

"Yeah. After that stunt Jack pulled, I want to make sure I keep my head."

Owen nodded.

"I'm proud of you."

"Why?' Dan asked.

"Because I know the reasons why you drank and how hard it would be for you," Owen replied.

"I would be a liar if I said it was easy," said Dan.

Owen leaned across and put his arm around Dan, pulling him tight and kissing his forehead.

"You are the strongest man I know, Danny boy."

***

When everyone retired for the night, Dan slept on his own in a tent and was quickly away in the land of nod. Owen and Lilly remained awake in their tent cuddling.

"When we get to Moama, what then?" Lilly asked.

"I'm not sure. I was thinking we could head up to Deniliquin and I could try and find us a place where we can get established. We need some place where we can lay down roots and grow. Maybe, I'll get a job in the town, or I can find a farm and try rearing some sheep. I've got enough experience working on a farm, I reckon I could manage that. What I don't know I could learn."

"That could be nice. I could stand at the door to the kitchen with the babe and watch you toiling in the field. Then when you come in for dinner, I will have a fine meal waiting for you on the table. At night I can practice my wifely duties."

"That would be a good life," said Owen longingly.

He brushed his hand over Lilly's shoulder, down her arm and across to her belly. He felt a kick.

"He will have some powerful legs," he said.

"Maybe we'll send him off to boarding school and he can play rugby?"

"Rugby? I wouldn't want any boy of mine near that thuggish sport, nor a boarding school. You ever met a kid from one of those places? They make you want to slap their parents for the indecency of having perpetuated their bloodline."

Lilly didn't respond, she just interlocked her fingers in Owen's. *"Boy of mine"*, she thought, *has he forgotten that it is not his child?*

"What's the matter?" Owen asked.

"Nothing, just thinking about how much I love you."

"I love you too."

"We should turn in. None of those larks like the other night. We don't want to disturb Dan."

"Or wake the dead," Owen said with a grin.

***

The following morning everyone rose feeling refreshed. There was a sense of optimism that had been severely lacking in recent weeks, and they rode with their heads held high. Along the river was lush with vegetation, but it also felt very dry. The waterside was choked with yellow reeds and the leafless forks of limbs that had broken off trees along the river and had washed downstream. The earth of the bank was hard and the rusty colour of desert sand, the water a murky green. As the trio travelled, they were shielded against the sun by the spindly, ashen limbs of gum trees whose yellow-green leaves bobbed gently and rustled in the breeze like the elegant sweeping of a dancer's taffeta gown along a ballroom floor. Twittering could be heard in the treetops and Lilly allowed herself to close her eyes and feel the sunlight on her cheeks.

Gradually they became aware of the sound of approaching hooves and the voices of men. Owen looked back at the others and gestured for them to wait, then rode ahead a short distance around a bend to get a better look. He leaned forward in his saddle and could make out four riders. They were dressed like stockmen, but as they grew nearer, he recognised the police boots, the pistol belts and the carbines slung across their chests.

"God damn traps," he hissed.

He rode back to the others and motioned for them to turn towards the tree line. Dan responded straight away and got clear of the road. The wagon, however, was much harder to take off-road without creating a commotion. Owen lingered on the road while Lilly turned Old Tom around and tried to get up the embankment into the tree line.

"Quickly," Owen snapped.

"What do you think I'm trying to do?" Lilly snapped back.

The horsemen grew ever closer, gradually coming into view, and Owen gazed back over his shoulder. They were out of time.

"Listen, Lilly. I'm going to confront them head-on to give you long enough to get out of sight. Once you're up there with Dan, stay quiet, stay still, and stay hidden."

"Owen, stay here," said Lilly.

"I'll be right back, my love," Owen replied, blowing a kiss. He rode out into the middle of the road and waited for the police to meet him.

"Out of the way," shouted the lead horseman.

"What's that?" Owen replied.

"I said get out of the bloody way. You're blocking the road, you fool."

"Oh? Aye. So I am," Owen replied, acting obtuse but remaining in place.

The police drew to a halt in front of Owen.

"Have you taken leave of your sense, boy?" the lead trooper barked. Something triggered in Owen's brain. He scrutinised the appearance of the speaker. This trooper seemed familiar.

"What did you say?"

"I said, have you taken leave of your sense?"

Owen felt a shiver run down his spine.

+++

"Have you taken leave of your sense, boy?" said Senior-Constable Dolan.

"I beg your pardon," Owen mumbled.

"Pick up the bloody pistol and help me bring this bastard in."

Owen touched his face gingerly. The miner, powered by grog, had landed an almighty blow to his jaw and sent him flying backwards. When he hit the ground, he dropped his pistol, and the miner had leapt on top of him. Owen had fought valiantly but the speaker had got him pinned with his enormous weight. He was of a husky build, certainly, but this behemoth's weight was distributed across a body that was well over six and a half feet tall. It was Dolan who had to intervene and land a swift blow to the man's head with the butt of his carbine to get him off.

As the miner lay unconscious on the ground, Owen lay stunned next to him. It should have been a routine licence hunt, but, as Owen was quickly learning, licence hunts had made the miners incredibly hostile towards the police and there was nothing standard about asking them to prove they had paid their dues. Dolan was an old hand at handling the rougher sorts out on the goldfields, but Owen had only been on the job for a few weeks and was yet to find his strengths in dealing with these men.

The drunk was handcuffed and revived. A rope was tied to the handcuffs, and he was led like a dog on a leash back to the police camp where he was shackled to a log to be dealt with later. There were already three other men there shackled. Two were found without valid gold licences, the other had been arrested for starting a fight at a tent guised as a coffee shop where sly grog was being sold.

"Look here, boy," Dolan said, "You've got a billy club on your belt for dealing with beggars like him. Next time, bloody well use it."

Owen took a sweeping glance over the arrested men and noted the black eyes and swollen lumps visible on their heads. He expected there were other injuries hidden beneath their garb as well.

"Grab your club and show me what you can do," said Dolan.

"What?"

"I said grab your club!"

Owen complied.

"Give the big bastard a whack."

Hesitantly, Owen raised the club and struck the drunkard in the shoulder.

"Is that it? Strike harder you molly!"

Owen swung again, harder. Dolan was furious and snatched the club out of Owen's hand.

"Like this…"

Dolan swung the club with enough force to make an audible whooshing before it struck the drunk in the head. It was a sickening blow, and the man's eyes rolled back in his head and blood streamed out of his nostrils.

"You've killed him!"

"Have I? Are you sure? It was your club that hit him," said Dolan with a sneer as he thrust the weapon into Owen's hand.

+++

This trooper was flabbier, greyer, but unmistakably Dolan, who was now a sergeant — although being in plainclothes meant this detail was not something Owen could deduct. It seemed to him that being the most brutal bluebottle on the goldfields had paved the way for a fruitful career in the police force.

"Do I know you, boy?"

"Don't call me 'boy'."

"What was that? Speak up, boy."

"I said, don't call me 'boy', you bastard!"

Owen drew a revolver from his belt and aimed it at Dolan. He pulled the trigger and sent a conical bullet through Dolan's skull faster than the troopers were able to process what was happening. The trooper went limp and slid off his saddle to the ground with a puzzled look on his face and a hole in his forehead from which blood and cerebrospinal fluid gushed copiously until his heart realised that he was dead.

The other police drew their revolvers and yelled at Owen to surrender.

"Surrender be damned!"

Owen fired another shot and galloped at full tilt toward the police. The police fired at him, but their horses flew into a panic at the noise and the bullets missed their target. Owen passed through the group and into the scrub. The police began to chase him. Onward they rode, the police firing at Owen and missing with every shot. He did not look back. He pushed Ruffy as hard as he could.

A bullet struck Owen in the shoulder. He roared with pain but kept riding. Stopping now would be suicide.

Meanwhile, Lilly and Dan were waiting in the bush for some kind of sign that Owen was coming back to join them. When they heard the gunshots and the hooves rushing away from them, they knew something had gone wrong.

"We need to go and find him," said Lilly.

"We can't go on a chase with the wagon," Dan replied.

"Well, we can either leave the wagon here or you can ride ahead and see if you can escort Owen back to me."

"I'll go and see what's happening, you stay here until I get back."

Dan spurred Sancus on, following the road that they had been on when the police arrived. He found a police horse wandering riderless, and a short distance beyond that was the body of Sergeant Dolan with a hole through the head, lying in a pool of blood. *Oh, shit*, Dan thought, *we're in it now*.

He followed the hoof prints into the bush and saw the path of destruction made by so many horses galloping through the undergrowth. He followed the trail of destruction to a clearing. From the edge of the clearing, he could see three men crowding around a prone figure. Ruffy was nowhere to be seen, and closer inspection showed the prone figure to be Owen. Dan was torn. He could rush in there and try to rescue Owen, but if anything went wrong Lilly would be left on her own with no idea what was happening. He watched a while longer and saw the police help Owen to his feet, which showed he was still alive at least. Alive meant there was a chance to rescue him.

Before he could be spotted, Dan rode back to where he had left Lilly. She was hunched over and trembling, her eyes red and watery. She wrung her hands and muttered under her breath.

"Where is he?" Lilly asked with desperation as soon as she saw Dan.

"He's been captured. He's alive, but the troopers got him and no doubt he's to be taken back over the border to be dealt with if they let him live that long."

There was a ringing in Lilly's ears as the world seemed to melt away and the feeling of cold, damp fingers oozed down her spine and limbs. She began to tremble and a sensation like a million tiny sparks crept over the back of her head. Her breathing became quick and shallow. She couldn't seem to fill her lungs, and she began to feel her heart thumping in her chest like it would break free of her ribcage. The baby in her belly became furiously restless. Suddenly she blacked out and fell across the seat. For the next fifteen seconds she was unresponsive and all she could perceive was a yellow and maroon halo in a black void, which she realised was the inside of her eyelids as she regained consciousness from Dan shaking her awake.

"No time for panic, missus. We need to figure out how we are going to get him out of there."

Lilly sat up with a dazed look on her face.

"Where would they be taking him?"

"Well," said Dan, "at a guess I would say that they will need to come back and get the body off the road and then head into the nearest town."

"What body?"

"One of the traps was dead with a shot through his head. I don't want to believe it, but I think Owen was responsible."

Lilly gasped, her heart sank, and tears welled in her eyes. That her sweet, gentle husband could kill a man and leave his body on the road was unthinkable. Now he was destined for the gallows – if the troopers even allowed him to get that far.

"Where's the nearest town?" Lilly asked.

"I don't think there's anything between here and Moama apart from the odd farm. If they don't come back up past us this way, that will be the direction they are heading in."

Lilly took a deep breath and steadied herself. She looked at Dan with a determined gaze.

"Alright. How do we do this?"

Five

The three plainclothes troopers rode eastwards with their prisoner. They had recovered Dolan's horse and body, which they draped over the saddle, and Owen was handcuffed and tied by a rope from the iron darbies to the saddle. The bullet in his shoulder was excruciating and the police had done a number on him, beating him with the butts of their carbines and kicking and stomping on him while he was on the ground. His ears were ringing and his left eye almost swollen shut with bruising. The police had demanded his name, but rather than giving his own he told them that he was, "Jack Cooper."

As he was pulled behind the dead policeman's horse, he found himself growing woozy from his injuries and he collapsed. The police kept going, allowing the horse to drag Owen along the ground. The troopers laughed at Owen's misfortune and one of them, a brawny constable named Thom, struck the horse's flank and sent it bolting forward. Owen was dragged over roots and stones and sent rolling with his arms extended forward, putting great strain on the wounded shoulder. He cried out in pain as he regained consciousness but soon found himself overwhelmed once again by the pain.

"Alright lads, I reckon he's had enough for now. We can't be seen to be bringing two corpses back," said a slim, moustachioed constable named Warner, "unless you want to do extra paperwork."

"Yeah, we wouldn't want to cheat Billy Bamford out of his pay," said Constable Thom miming a hanging.

Constable Anderson, who had been leading Dolan's horse, drew to a halt. Constable Thom then dismounted and helped Owen to his feet. He could not stand unaided and promptly collapsed. His clothes were shredded, and his face was covered in cuts and blood.

"Well, that's inconvenient," said Thom.

"It's getting on. We might as well take luncheon here and let the bastard rest until he can walk," said Constable Warner.

The men rode away from the road and hitched their horses among the trees before sitting down for a picnic. Owen remained insensible on the ground. The horse he was tied to deposited droppings by his head.

As this was unfolding, Dan and Lilly were following the tracks left by the police horses. Lilly was still driving the wagon as the cargo was too precious to leave unattended in an unfamiliar region. They soon saw the trail in the dirt where Owen had collapsed, which Dan pointed out to Lilly.

"Looks like they dropped something, and the horse dragged it along."

"Something or some*one*?"

"Well," said Dan, "one way to find out is to follow the trail."

On they rode until they reached the trees where the police horses were hitched. Lilly tried hard to stop herself from crying out by taking a deep gasp and pointing at the animals. Dan saw the gesture and nodded. He motioned for her to stay put and dismounted. He walked carefully towards the horses and gazed through the trees. He could see three men sitting around a small fire smoking pipes and laughing. *These must be the traps*, he thought.

He moved closer to the horses and could see one with a large canvas bundle tied to the saddle with flies buzzing around it. More careful inspection alerted him to two booted feet sticking out. This was a dead body wrapped in a tent for transportation, but not Owen's. Dan moved his gaze along the saddle and the rope tied to the pommel. At the end of the rope, lying on the ground, was Owen. He was still breathing but the breaths were shallow, and he was almost unrecognisable from the swelling and bleeding about his head.

Dan drew a knife from his boot and rushed to Owen's side. He sawed through the rope and freed Owen's hands, which flopped down, still cuffed. Dan slapped Owen's face to rouse him.

"Hey, wake up, come on!"

Owen groaned as he came around. He could only open one eye.

"Welcome back to the land of the living," said Dan, kissing Owen's forehead tenderly, "Let's get out of here."

With great effort Dan helped him to his feet, grabbed his waist with his good hand and guided him back to the wagon.

Lilly had been looking out for Dan's return and upon seeing him with Owen in such a sorry state felt a sinking feeling in her gut. She climbed down and ran over to help Dan carry Owen.

"Sweetheart, are you alright?"

Owen groaned. He could not speak clearly as he had bitten his tongue while being dragged and his mouth was full of blood.

"Best not to make him talk, missus," said Dan.

They got him up into the back of the wagon and laid him down with a bag under his head as a pillow.

"Now, you and I are going to run like Mercury until we find Jack and Ellen. Don't worry about him right now, we can worry later. We've got him and they don't, that's all that matters. Understood?" said Dan.

Lilly nodded. Dan wiped the tears from her cheeks and hugged her tightly before helping her up onto the wagon. Dan mounted Sancus and spurred him on, Lilly flicked the reins and sent Old Tom racing after.

The sound of the hooves and the creaking of the wagon alerted the police who looked over to the road from their camp, and then over to their horses. It wasn't until they approached their mounts that they realised Owen was gone.

"You have to be fucking joking," said Constable Thom, "someone's stolen the bastard from us!"

"Who did you see?" asked Constable Warner.

"I saw a blackfellow on a horse and a woman in a little wagon behind him," replied Constable Anderson.

"Alright, let's mount up and chase 'em down," said Warner.

"What do we do with Dolan?" asked Anderson.

"He ain't going anywhere," said Thom.

The men got on their horses and charged off, following the wheel tracks. Their horses were nags, but they rode as hard as they could muster.

It did not take long for the rumble of hooves to be heard approaching the wagon. Lilly looked back over her shoulder and could see three horsemen approaching on very tired looking animals.

"Danny, we have trouble," she shouted as she flicked the reigns for Old Tom to go faster. Dan looked back and could see the trouble approaching.

"Fuck!"

The race was on. Despite being attached to a four-wheeler, Old Tom was built for endurance and kept up an admirable pace. The road was rough, and with each bump or pothole Owen was jostled in the back, bringing much pain.

Sancus, being a thoroughbred stallion, took flight with great ease, every muscle and sinew working like a meticulously maintained machine. He soon overtook Old Tom, so Dan pulled him up so that Lilly wasn't left behind.

They could hear the police nags grunting and snorting as their riders dug in the spurs. Constable Thom's horse began to throw his head up and down, straining against the bit, when suddenly his legs gave way and he collapsed, sending his rider rolling away into the scrub. The horse's eyes rolled back in his head as he began to spasm and kick, the poor animal's heart giving out from the strain of the hard ride in the afternoon heat, killing it within moments.

Constable Anderson and Constable Warner kept up the chase.

"Go, you bastard, go," Warner screamed at the horse, jabbing it mercilessly with his spurs until the animal began to bleed freely. It too collapsed, foamy and wild eyed but miraculously alive. On seeing this Constable Anderson called off the chase and returned to his colleagues. Dan and Lilly had succeeded in shaking off their pursuers by the skin of their teeth.

Naturally, the chase had taken a toll on their horses too, but the strain had not been nearly so bad on these much fitter and better kept animals. When they felt like they had gotten clear, the bold fugitives pulled off the road into a clearing just beyond the tree line. Here there was plenty of grass and a lagoon. Dan led Sancus to the water and removed the bit and bridle so he could eat and drink freely.

Props were put up under the shafts of the cart to keep it level as Old Tom was unhitched. The collar and tackle were removed, and he too was allowed to graze near the lagoon. Lilly fetched a pannikin from the cart and filled it with water from the creek. She took it to the cart and climbed up to give some water to Owen. He sipped weakly as the process was painful, and he found it difficult to swallow with his injured tongue.

"I think we might need to get him to a surgeon," said Dan, who joined them once the horses were grazing.

"Where are we going to find a doctor around here?"

"I don't know, but I know he's in a bad way and we can't see even half of the damage."

"Help me get him down so we can get a look at him."

They rolled out a bedroll and with much effort Lilly and Dan lifted Owen safely out of the cart to the ground. Lilly went at once to work on removing his boots and what was left of his clothes. Once he was stripped they cleaned the wounds on Owen's body with damp rags so they could take inventory. There were several long gashes along his back and front caused by sharp rocks in the road. Along his legs, pelvis, buttocks and belly were several smaller lacerations and grazes. The bullet wound in his left shoulder had entered just above the shoulder blade and torn through his trapezius muscle. His wrists were badly bruised inside the handcuffs, which Dan removed with a stolen key he had acquired in his travels and kept for just such an occasion. Luckily, the cuffs were the standard issue for which the cylindrical key was designed, and with a few turns it opened the band.

Having assessed the worst of his injuries on his body and limbs, they wrapped him in a blanket and began treating the injuries on his head. His eye was black and swollen shut, the injury resembling some kind of sickly looking plum. Dan took a penknife and cut the swollen flesh, which allowed the blood to drain and reduced the swelling. There were gashes all over his cheeks and scalp, some of which could not be cleaned properly due to his hair being in the way, but they did their best. His left ear was caked with blood due to heavy bleeding from the spot where the back of it connected to his scalp being torn. Although he had bled heavily from the nose, it was, miraculously, not broken. Inside his mouth, they could see where he had bitten into his tongue, but surprisingly his teeth were unaffected.

"Well, it could be a lot worse," said Dan. Owen was groggy but offered his dear friend an attempted half-smile. He soon fell asleep, exhausted by his misadventure.

Lilly hugged Dan.

"Thank you," she said.

"I would never be able to live with myself if I hadn't at least tried to help him," Dan replied.

They set up a camp on the spot and Dan constructed a small fire close to Owen to keep him warm. As night settled in, Owen was allowed to continue sleeping as long as he could to help him heal. The more severe wounds on his head and body were padded with gauze or rags and bandaged.

Dan and Lilly ate from the rations and chatted quietly.

"You've been through a lot together then?" Lilly asked.

"Owen has always had my back and got me out of a few scrapes."

"How long had you all been on the run together before Ellen and I came along?"

"Jack has been bushranging for about six years, the way he tells it. He picked up Owen about three years ago and I joined them about a year later."

"So, two years on the run for you?"

"We weren't always running. Didn't always have a need to. It's only been the past few months that things have heated up for us," said Dan.

"Why do you suppose that is?"

"Bad decisions. That's all."

Lilly let a little quiet settle over the camp before asking more questions.

"So, what were you doing before you crossed paths with the notorious Jack Cooper?"

"Well, that's a long story. Maybe another time."

"Well, I have time now," said Lilly.

"I'd rather think of happier things. Suffice it to say for now that I was a traveller and good with my fists. Something I can't say anymore," Dan replied, looking down at his maimed left hand. His gaze wandered up to the gap in the canopy where the stars were visible in the night sky. He took a deep breath and held it for a second before releasing it slowly.

Gradually, Lilly found herself becoming drowsy and decided to call it a night. She set up her bedroll next to Owen and slept beside him. Dan remained awake, both as a guard to allow the others to rest, and also because he wanted to be alone with his thoughts for a while.

+++

Dan Thatcher had only been on Australian soil for a few weeks. He had been employed on a cargo ship but decided he was finished with life on the seas and disembarked at Hobson's Bay. He had no money when he arrived on shore so managed to earn a small amount by engaging in prize fights outside sleazy pubs. When he had a reasonable amount saved, he sought his fortune in Williamstown. He had noticed a row of ships anchored just off the beach, all painted bright yellow. He discovered through conversations with the few locals that would speak to him that these were prison hulks, and on board were some of the worst of the worst of the convicts from the colony of Victoria. This had led him to the decision that perhaps Williamstown was not a great place for him to seek his fortune after all.

He had heard that there was still gold to be found and asked anyone he could find about the goldfields. The replies did not fill him with confidence, but a few names had popped up: Bendigo, Ballarat, and Beechworth.

He used his savings to purchase a few things to help him on the road and he made his way north-east on foot. He was surprised at the fact that so few people he encountered along the way had treated him as poorly as those who he had grown up around in the slums of London. It was not unusual for black men to have come seeking fortunes in Australia at the end of a pickaxe, so he didn't look altogether too out of place, although he wasn't exactly greeted with open arms either.

When his money dwindled, as is the case when one has more expenses than regular income, he visited pubs where he could put himself forward as a bare-knuckle boxer for the entertainment of the locals as he had done previously. When it didn't snag him some cash, it at least got him a free meal or a drink of something from the top shelf. However, it was while stopping in at a pub in Whittlesea that he got his first taste of proper trouble.

It was a small but handsome town, with substantial buildings including the post office, two hotels called the Prince of Wales and the Royal Mail, and a recently erected courthouse. There were also many weatherboard houses as timber was plentiful in the area and logging was making the town prosperous.

Dan went into a pub for a drink, having gained a mighty thirst on the road. His first warning was the reluctance of the barman to serve him, prompting Dan to exclaim rather forthrightly, "my silver is as good as any chap's." The resulting death stares he received from men in the bar made him uneasy.

He ordered a mug of ale, and the barman instructed him to leave his money on the counter. When the tankard was placed on the polished wood the barman swept the money off with his cleaning cloth into a container.

After drinking his ale in silence as quickly as he could, Dan made for the door with the intention to get back on the road. As he reached the door two men stood up and began following him. Dan left the building and turned the corner; the two patrons close behind. He dropped his swag and turned to face them.

"What do you want?" he asked, his Cockney accent giving the phrase a little more aggression.

"We don't like your sort coming into our pub and fouling the air," said the taller of the two; a dirty, long-haired, red-faced man with a beer belly and a billycock hat worn at a jaunty angle.

"By the smell of you, the air was foul enough before I got here," Dan quipped.

"Got a lip on him, this little blackfellow," the shorter one said, pushing back his cabbage-tree hat. He was not much taller than five feet and four inches and had a thick beard.

"Teach the nigger some respect, Jonesy."

The shorter man punched Dan in the mouth. It busted his lip and drew blood.

"I already left your fucking watering hole, what else do you want?"

"Bugger still hasn't learned his lesson," said the taller man as he drew close and swung a meaty paw at Dan's head. Dan ducked and the blow missed. The man swung once more and, again, missed. Dan ducked and bobbed to avoid blows from the ruddy behemoth. The little man joined in by grabbing Dan's arms to pinion him for his punishment.

At that moment there was a voice from behind the attackers.

"That's enough."

The big man turned to face the interloper.

"What?"

"Leave him alone or I'll put daylight through you both."

The big man took a step forward and found a pistol aimed at his groin followed by the click of the hammer being cocked.

"I didn't say *where* I would shoot you. I warn you; I'm a good shot – even with small targets like that."

"You can take him, Mick," shouted Jonesy.

"You haven't got a revolver pointed at your balls. Let the black boy go."

Jonesy did as had been requested.

"Good. Now, fuck off," said the stranger.

The attackers left at a brisk pace with their tails between their legs.

"Thank you," said Dan touching his bleeding lip.

"No worries. My name's Owen," said the stranger extending his hand, "Owen Brady."

"Dan Thatcher."

"I'm pleased to meet your acquaintance, Dan Thatcher. You took quite a beating there. Are you okay?"

"Yeah, I've gotten worse from weaker men."

"You on the hump?"

"Hey?" Dan responded with a raised eyebrow as he picked up his swag.

"I see you have a swag. Are you travelling?"

"Yeah. Thought I would try the goldfields in Beechworth."

Owen laughed despite seeking to be quite shaken by the confrontation with the bullies.

"I don't like your chances. Tell you what – come and meet my mate. I reckon we have a better proposition for you."

Owen placed his arm around Dan and guided him to the stables.

+++

Just before sunrise Dan awoke the others. The fire had died down to glowing embers and he began to fuss about packing up the camp.

Lilly was awoken by the noise as she was a light sleeper.

"Wotsdoin'?" she asked, rubbing sleep out of her eyes.

"Best get moving before they catch up to us," Dan replied.

"We need to get Owen dressed," said Lilly.

"Already thought of that. I fetched some fresh bandages and garb from the cart. They're there next to you. Get that shoulder bandaged up again and I'll help you with the rest."

Dan busied himself with gearing up the horses while Lilly helped Owen into a sitting position. The wound in his shoulder had been bleeding heavily and the bandage was soaked through. With some effort she wound a gauze bandage around Owen's shoulder and made a sling for it. She grabbed a spare Crimean shirt from the wagon, which she carefully helped him put on. His left arm remained in the sling under the smock-like shirt. She threw the bloodied bandages into the campfire.

"It would be a lot easier if your shirts unbuttoned all the way down," Lilly complained.

With Dan's assistance she managed to get trousers on him and then loaded him onto the cart. By the time sunrise painted the horizon with lashings of blue and gold they were already gone.

***

Ellen and Jack had found a small inn on the edge of town as their accommodation. The sign above the door simply stated that it was called "Donnelly's Inn". They deemed that staying in the heart of town would be tempting fate too much, so they opted for the least ostentatious place they could find as far away as was reasonable. It was a place that was barely clinging onto life; a small building of bark slabs that had obviously been patched up numerous times as the town had grown along with the industry moving up and down the river. There was only one room available to travellers looking for a place to lay their head. In it was a single bed that was designed to accommodate one person, a rickety wash stand, and the luxury of a small fireplace.

After settling in, Ellen lay on the lone bed, uncomfortable as it was, staring at the ceiling and thinking to herself. Despite giving in to her lust in the euphoric rush that accompanied their successful flight over the river, Ellen was still not prepared to move on from Jack's otherwise reproachable behaviour. Every time she had felt herself wanting to forgive him, she reminded herself of the consequences of his bloody rampage and what he had done to her under the influence of drink.

"Anything interesting up there?" asked Jack.

"I'm thinking."

"About what?"

"About you."

"Is that so?"

"Yes. I haven't forgiven you yet."

"Forgive me for *what?*"

"For abandoning us. For allowing yourself to give in to paranoid delusions. For maiming and murdering, and forcing us to flee even though Lilly and I needed to rest due to our conditions. For *hitting* me. Should I go on?"

Jack lay silent and fuming.

"How many times do I have to apologise?" he asked, exasperated.

"You could start with once," Ellen snapped.

"I'm sorry," Jack snapped.

"I can tell from the tone in your voice that you're not."

"You can't be serious!"

"I'm as serious as can be. 'Sorry' is not some magic word that fixes problems by speaking it aloud. Being apologetic means you understand what you did wrong and want to make amends."

"I'm not a child," Jack said with a scowl.

"So, stop acting like one," replied Ellen.

After a few minutes of heated silence Jack caved in. He sat on the edge of the bed and placed his hand over Ellen's.

"Ellen, I am sorry for what I did to you. It was unacceptable and it was weak of me to have allowed myself to do such a devilish thing."

Ellen cocked her eyebrow.

"I am sorry for my drunken foolishness. I have caused much pain through my selfishness and my carelessness. Can you forgive me?"

Ellen was quiet as she sat up.

"Jack," she said, "you can't bring that man you shot back to life with guilt, nor can you wipe clean the memory of betrayal with soothing words, but we will find a way to make peace with it all somehow. It may take some time. Do you understand?"

"I understand," Jack said.

"Right, well,

"Right, well, let's get cleaned up at least."

Ellen got up and tested the temperature of the water in the basin on the wash stand. It wasn't exactly warm, but it also wasn't cold, so it would do the job well enough. She unbuttoned her dress, slid it off and did the same with her shirt, skirt, boots, chemise, drawers, and stockings. She had not missed all the excessive layers while dressed for bush life. Having stripped down she took a washcloth and soaked it in the basin, rubbed soap into the fibres and began to wash her throat, underarms, under her breasts and around her groin. It was good to have a bath with clean water and scrub away the accumulated sweat and grime, even if she would have preferred a dip in a creek.

Jack sat on a wooden chair in the corner. He loaded his pipe with tobacco and lit it with a match. As he reclined and puffed, he watched Ellen washing. It was not erotic in the slightest, but it was stimulating to him all the same.

"Getting a good view, are you?" said Ellen bluntly.

"Good enough, I suppose."

"Well, you can go next. You need it even more than I do."

Ellen dabbed herself with a dry cloth and moved away from the basin and slid her chemise back on before returning to the bed.

Jack tugged his boots off and then stood to remove his trousers. He whisked off his shirt and long underwear and sidled up to the basin with his pipe hanging out of his mouth lazily. He dunked the washcloth in the water and got a decent lather on it. He dabbed the cloth against his hairy throat, scrubbed under his arms and across his muscular chest.

Ellen reclined on the bed, which creaked under her weight despite her being far from heavy. Jack glanced over his shoulder with a devilish glint in his eye and turned to face her as he ran the washcloth around his privates. He jiggled his testicles in her direction and Ellen rolled her eyes.

"Are you quite right there?"

"You tell me," Jack said grabbing his flaccid penis and wagging it at her.

"Have you been drinking?"

"Just enough to warm my belly."

Ellen glared at him.

"Do you recall what happened the last time you had been into the liquor?"

"Oh, yes, but that was then. This is now."

Jack climbed onto the bed and lifted Ellen's chemise. She pushed it back down again and slapped Jack's hand.

"No. If you're just going to keep doing the same stupid things over again, I don't want you anywhere near me."

"Is this a joke?"

"I am as serious as death. You put that little sausage anywhere near me when you've had a drink, and I'll cut it off and feed it to you. Do you understand?"

Jack sat up with a look of utter confusion.

"Steady on..."

"I am steady enough. I don't want anything to do with a man who can't keep control of himself."

Jack crossed his arms. There was a brief standoff as both parties stared each other down. Jack smirked.

"You are a boss and no mistake, Mrs. McReady. You have my word that I will not touch another drop."

"Swear it?"

"I swear it."

Ellen scrutinised Jack for a moment then nodded.

"Alright, I'm glad we straightened that out."

Jack grinned and moved to lift Ellen's chemise up again, but she slapped his hand away again.

"What do you think you're doing?"

"I thought..." Jack began.

"You *thought* incorrectly. Not a finger on me until you're sobered up."

"But I'm all ready to go," Jack said, gesturing to his newly-formed erection.

"Then you will 'go' somewhere else."

Jack snorted in disbelief but backed off and stood up. To drive home that she was serious, Ellen crossed her legs and folded her arms across her chest. Jack looked crestfallen and didn't know what to do with himself.

"Well?"

"Well, what?" asked Jack.

"Aren't you going to take care of that?" Ellen said, gesturing to the erection.

Jack grinned at her as he began to stroke his member In a manner he thought would be considered erotic. Ellen continued to watch as Jack pleasured himself to completion with a grunt. She smirked as he came. She liked being lusted after, but she liked being in control even more.

"Right, now you can clean that up and we can turn in," Ellen said, pointing to the puddle of spunk that Jack had left on the floor. "I am taking the bed," she said as she got under the bed covers.

"Where am I sleeping?"

"The rug in front of the fireplace looks comfortable enough."

"Fine," Jack grumbled as he used the washcloth to clean up the sticky mess he had made.

He felt degraded, but did his best to conceal the fact. His instinct was to lash out, but he wanted to demonstrate his self-control. The more assertive Ellen behaved, the harder it was for him to walk away. He had an overwhelming desire to regain dominance in the relationship, but he could not ignore the fact that because of his genuine affection for her the thought of their relationship collapsing distressed him more than the thought of her being in control.

Once he was done cleaning up, he grabbed a blanket and rolled up his poncho to use as a pillow then lay on the rug to go to sleep.

Six

Ellen was awake to greet the dawn as azure hues leached through the filthy west-facing window. She saw Jack curled up on the floor in front of the fireplace, where the fire had reduced to smouldering ashes. She got out of bed, dressed in her usual masculine attire and went outside. She saddled up Diana and took off.

For the next hour, she did laps of the town, going down streets and laneways looking for signs of her friends. She was out of luck. Once she was satisfied that she had not missed them, she headed back to the inn. A niggling voice at the back of her mind increasingly filled her with concern for the safety of the others.

"Where have you been?" Jack asked as Ellen returned to the room.

"I've been looking for the others. They aren't here. Something's happened, I know it. I feel it in my bones."

"Alright, we'll go and see if we can meet up with them out of town. Let's get everything together and get moving."

***

Elsewhere Dan and Lilly rode in the direction of Moama with Owen barely conscious in the back of the wagon. They followed the flow of the Murray, knowing that it was the easiest way to get to their destination. When they reached a good spot at Benarca to rest the horses, there were only a handful of hours left to go before they reached their target.

Lilly took the opportunity to climb into the back of the wagon with Dan to check on Owen's wounds, then apply fresh dressings. The bullet wound in his shoulder continued to bleed as the movement of the wagon had reopened it. Lilly cut up a flour sack they had been using to hold loot, and used the scraps of cloth to pad the wound. Dan made sure to wrap the bandage tightly to secure the padding. Owen's belt was repurposed as a sling in order to immobilise his arm.

An hour later, as they were taking in the beauty of the surrounding red gum forest, they became aware of the sound of hooves approaching from the east. As Owen was still in the back of the wagon, propped up against their supplies, he simply drew a blanket over his head to disguise his presence. Both Dan and Lilly climbed down from the wagon and armed themselves with revolvers.

They watched from behind the cover of the trees as the two riders came into view. Both breathed a sigh of relief as they recognised Jack and Ellen.

"Thank God," said Lilly as she moved out from cover.

"Well, there's a surprise," said Jack as Dan also made himself known, "what were you doing back there?"

"We weren't sure who was coming. If you were traps, we'd have probably shot you," said Dan.

"Where's Owen?" Ellen asked.

"In the wagon."

Jack and Ellen dismounted and led their horses into the clearing.

"How have things been for you three since we split?" asked Ellen.

"We had a run in with some peelers," Dan replied, "Owen shot one. They got their own back, but I managed to pry him from their grasp. He's not in a good way."

Hearing the friendly voices, Owen removed the blanket.

"There he is," said Lilly.

"So, I suppose that means there's only two of us without blood on their hands now," said Jack.

Ellen was not amused. "With some luck it will stay that way. What happened?"

"We were making good time but then a party of plainclothes troopers came upon us. Owen tried to create a distraction so we could get off the road without being spotted. We don't know precisely what happened because Owen can't talk," said Lilly.

"He should be alright until we can find a place to go and fetch a doctor," said Dan.

"Do you know if they were New South Wales police or Victorian?" asked Ellen.

"They were in plainclothes," Dan repeated.

"Would the police on this side of the border even know that we've crossed?" asked Lilly.

"It's unlikely that they would be sending out search parties along the river if they did. They don't tend to give a damn unless crimes have happened on their side of the border," said Jack. "My guess is it was Victorian troopers operating outside their jurisdiction."

"In that case," said Ellen, "it seems the Victorian troopers haven't much regard for the rule of law."

"And don't you forget it," said Jack.

The conversation shifted to discussing their next movements. The crux of the matter was finding a town where they weren't likely to be spotted and reported to police, and where they could also obtain medical assistance for Owen. In the end, it would be easier said than done.

They agreed to set their sights for Deniliquin. It was somewhere north of their current location, but even though Jack had been there before, he was not sure of how long it would take. He estimated it should not take them more than a couple of days to reach it if they went at a reasonable pace. They decided they would follow the stock route as that seemed to usually be the quickest road anywhere.

***

As evening set in the gang had set up a camp and ate and chatted by the fire, although Owen was unable to participate much in either activity owing to his injured tongue. Ellen and Lilly peeled away from the rest of the group to have their own conversation.

"How are you holding up?" Ellen asked.

"If I'm being honest," Lilly replied, "I'm struggling. I'm exhausted, everything aches, my emotions are all over the place and seeing Owen like this is breaking my heart. If it wasn't for you all distracting me, I think I would collapse."

"Have you felt him kicking?" said Ellen gesturing at Lilly's belly.

"Oh, yes," said Lilly with a smile, "whenever I'm happy it feels like little bubbles in my belly. It happens when I'm upset too. It's like he's reacting to what I'm feeling."

"Good," replied Ellen, "the next few months are going to be tough. All you can do is rest whenever the opportunity presents itself."

"Owen said he wanted to try setting up a farm at Deniliquin. He thinks there's a chance we could find somewhere to get ourselves settled. Do you think we could stay when we reach there?"

Ellen looked troubled and she gazed at the ground.

"I suppose anything is possible, but let's not get ahead of ourselves."

"I just want to start a new life where people don't know who we are. I want to have my own place where I can live like a normal person," said Lilly with a sigh.

Ellen glanced back at the fire where Jack and Dan were in deep conversation. Owen was asleep, but his expression indicated much discomfort despite him being out like a lamp. *What a mess*, she thought.

***

The next morning everyone was up early to head off. Autumn was arriving and the weather was starting to become windier and somewhat cooler compared to the dry heat of the preceding months. Thus, it was no surprise that there came dark clouds rolling in from the north-east, and with them wafted a strong petrichor that forewarned the outlaws of the oncoming downpour.

The gang all pulled on their coats and hats, except for Owen who covered himself with the oiled tarpaulin that usually kept his bedroll dry when laid on the ground or rolled up to put on his saddle. The wind kicked up and made the treetops sway violently. This was soon followed by the rain falling down in sheets. It was refreshing after days of hot wind and dust, despite everyone getting drenched. They hoped the rain would also deter any search party from looking for them.

The inconvenience of being sopping wet was compounded by the horses and wagon now leaving much clearer tracks in the mud. There was no way to prevent this. One mercy, however, was that in addition to the journey being on mostly flat ground, there were abundant trees to obscure Jack, Dan and Ellen as they rode off-road parallel to the wagon. This limited the visible tracks a search party could follow, and wagon tracks on the road alone were not necessarily worthy of suspicion.

By the evening, they had reached a township called Mathoura. It was a small logging town surrounded by River red gums. These trees were smooth and elegant with leaves of a vibrant green and bark coloured grey and white along the length of the trunk but red and brown at the base and around the knot holes. These beautiful trees were the lifeblood of the town and their ability to handle drought as well as flood was analogous with the town itself. A careful gaze by Dan at some of the trees revealed elliptical scars in the trunks created by Yorta Yorta people cutting the bark for canoes, shields and coola-mon dishes.

The gang headed to the Redbank Inn, an elegant brick building with several chimneys that were all wafting plumes of smoke. The building was surrounded by a vineyard and orchard, in addition to a small market garden. This was an ideal place to dry off and gather information. Jack and Dan helped Owen down from the back of the wagon while Ellen and Lilly went inside. The horses were spelled in a paddock at the rear.

Owen did his best not to appear too poorly, but his stiff move-ments and hobbling as much as the sling around his left arm and the cuts and bruises on his face gave him away.

"He's looking rough," said the barmaid, who was a curvy Lancas-trian woman of forty-something with an impressive head of flaxen curls that were worn loose in rather an unseemly manner for the time.

"Nothing a hot toddy couldn't stave off," Jack said with a smile.

"Anything for the rest of you?" asked the barmaid.

"Scotch all around. We got caught in the rain and could use some belly warming," said Ellen.

The wet coats were hung on pegs by the door to drip dry, and they all took turns standing by the fire. Outside the rain still pelted down on the iron roof and left huge puddles on the road. The sound of the tempest threshing the canopy was like the rush of waves as they crashed onto rocks along the shoreline. The rain hitting the iron roof was loud and perforated the otherwise cosy atmosphere.

"Is it far from here to Deniliquin?" Ellen asked.

"Well, it'd be no more than a half a day's ride that way," said the barmaid gesturing northward, "but it'll feel a damn sight longer in the rain. I think we might have a couple of rooms free if you were intend-ing to stay."

Jack wandered to a small table near the door. On it were several newspapers with different mastheads, but all of them were the most recent editions. He picked up the one on the top and flipped through it. His eyes focused on an article on the third page:

The Peacock Gang – Further Outrages

News has come to hand that the murderers who have held the central and northern towns of the colony of Victoria in such a state of terror have made their way into New South Wales. The *Echuca Bulletin* reports that a party of police were set upon near Swan Hill on Monday, resulting in the hideous murder of Sergeant Dolan. The miscreant, John Cooper, whose previous depredations need no repetition here as readers will already be familiar enough with them, was pursued and captured by the fallen trooper's courageous colleagues. Alas, Cooper effected his escape and provoked a chase that killed Constable Thom's horse and left the redoubtable man himself in a very low condition. It is with much regret we must state that Cooper and his gang remain at large, and it is suspected that they will be making their way towards Wagga Wagga.

Jack frowned. He was not keen on being credited with more bloodshed than he had committed, although he took some ironic pride in his notoriety. Regardless, it was useful for him to know that the search parties would be looking in the east while they headed north.

The gang warmed themselves and had some food and alcohol while waiting for a break in the rain. When it came, they donned their damp, heavy coats and returned to their horses. Soon they were on their way with the smell of rain, damp earth and eucalyptus wafting around them.

Seven

It was dusk when they arrived in Deniliquin, and the gloom was made more profound by the heavy clouds still looming overhead. The lights from the businesses and houses were reflected in the puddles that were scattered along the road and helped the gang see where they were going in the failing light. The rain had reduced to a fine drizzle. Nearby the Edward River gushed and gurgled with the sudden influx of water.

This was a substantial town, with large brick buildings littered throughout. The Anglican church and a post and telegraph office were standard edifices, complemented by a courthouse, gaol, hospital, the Riverine Brewery and the Royal Hotel. One of the buildings that was still lit up was the police barracks. The police in town were on high alert, as bushranging was a problem in the area even beyond the "Peacock Gang", and the town was still buzzing over the recent sentence of death being passed on the bushrangers Bill Duce and William Brookman in the local courthouse. Both had been members of the notorious Blue Cap's gang, but while Duce had given himself the nickname "White Chief", Brookman was better known throughout the colony as the "boy bushranger" as he was only eighteen years old. As far as most locals were concerned, this was just another young life tragically wasted in the pursuit of bushranging.

The gang headed to the Royal Hotel. It was a much grander building than the hotels they had visited recently and was fairly heavily populated. As soon as they entered, they began to realise their mistake. Jack noticed a policeman in uniform drinking at the bar and eyeing him suspiciously. The locals turned to examine these bedraggled arrivals as they walked to the bar. They looked like vagrants and the mood in the room grew sour.

Jack walked up to the counter and motioned for the publican.

"Do you have any rooms?"

The publican looked Jack up and down and then looked over at Dan, Ellen, Lilly and Owen.

"Not for you."

"That's not very Christian of you," Jack replied.

"Christ don't come into it, mate. Bugger off."

Dan felt increasingly uncomfortable, and his gut feeling proved right when a stout man with stained clothes and a puffy face jabbed a sausage-like finger in his direction and yelled out, "No blacks in the bar!"

Another man, thin and elderly with a dirty white beard that grew to his navel, pointed at Ellen and Lilly with a finger that was all knuckle and sinew.

"No women in the bar!"

The crowd began to shout and jeer. Jack turned to the others and gestured for them to head outside. He walked to the porcine man who had singled Dan out. He was tall and wide with long, matted hair and a long beard full of ale dregs. He sneered at Jack.

"What's your problem?" Jack said.

"Don't want no piccaninny in here sullying up the place. You should stick him out in the yard with the other animals before coming in here."

Jack gave the man an intense, unnerving stare down.

"That man happens to be my friend, and he's twice the man of any of you – although in your case maybe not girth-wise."

"Get out of my face," the man snapped, shoving Jack backwards.

Jack responded by standing almost nose-to-nose with him and grinned.

"Are you sure you want to keep going?"

By now the man, who had been deep into his fifth pint, was growing furious. He could feel the blood rushing to his head and balled his meaty paw into a fist. He swung at Jack's head; the blow connected with his cheek and there was a moment of stunned silence as everyone waited for Jack's response. The world was blurry in Jack's eyes at that moment, and a sharp pain washed over his face before giving way to a dull numbness. A sound like steel pinging reverberated around the inside of his skull. If anything was broken, he couldn't tell. His demeanour immediately switched to aggression. There was no thinking anymore, only reaction.

Jack grabbed the man by the collar and slammed him against the wall. He could hear his pulse pounding in his ears and there was almost a feeling of weightlessness in his limbs as he was fuelled by instant rage. The world seemed to slow down as he glared at his opponent with the fury of the burning heart of the sun. The sozzled patron, his back still against the wall, retaliated by grabbing Jack's throat and squeezing hard, his rough hand, honed by years of manual labour, was like a vice. Jack grabbed his opponent by the face and slammed his head back against the wall with great ferocity, growling like a predator ready for the kill. The grip on Jack's throat was reinforced with a second hand. He found breathing becoming harder and he grew lightheaded, but he was not willing to yield.

He grabbed his opponent's wrists and stomped on his foot but without effect. He punched him in the gut but only achieved a grunt. He was now turning red in the face and growing desperate. He could see shooting stars in front of his eyes. He grabbed his opponent's skull and pressed his thumbs into the eye sockets. The large man roared but would not let go. Jack pushed his nails into the thin flesh over the eyes and soon blood began to stream from the punctures.

At this moment another patron decided to intervene and grabbed a ceramic bottle, with which he clouted Jack over the head, knocking him unconscious. Both brawlers fell to the floor as the deadweight of Jack's comatose body slumping dragged his opponent down.

"Get him out," the publican said, irritated. The bottle-wielding patron and one of his drinking companions hauled Jack to the door and let him flop to the ground.

"Get your mate out of here," the publican yelled out to the rest of the gang. With haste, Dan and Ellen grabbed Jack, propped him against the wall and tried to rouse him. Dan went into the bar, grabbed a tankard from the nearest patron, an old drunk who had slumped unconscious on the table, and tipped out the drink. He strode to a barrel of water on the veranda and filled the tankard, then threw the water into Jack's face. The cold splash helped revive him, but it was clear he was badly hurt. Jack's eyes searched wildly, unfocused, and his head wobbled as if at any moment he would fall unconscious again.

With some effort, they bundled him into the back of the wagon. Dan got onto Sancus' back but led Tombstone by the reins. Owen sat beside Lilly on the cart. He took some morbid delight in seeing Jack in a more helpless position than himself.

"Where do we go now?" Dan asked.

Owen frowned.

"Let's see if we can find somewhere in town. There has to be someone out there who will take us in," said Lilly.

"It's too late now to be going through the town looking for a bed," said Ellen as she mounted Diana. "Let's set up a camp just outside of town. In the morning, we can come back and do whatever we need to but now is not a good time to be gallivanting around looking for accommodation," said Ellen.

The others agreed and after riding a quarter of an hour out of town they set up their tents by lantern light near the confluence of the Edward and the Wakool rivers and huddled inside. There was no dry wood to start a fire, and everyone was too tired to go looking. The air was cold and damp, and their bedrolls were soggy from the downpour. Everybody turned in and left no sentry as sleeping on soggy bedrolls was still a better option than sitting in the pitch blackness with a gun all night.

Ellen shared her tent with Jack. She began to worry about how badly he had been injured in the fight. Before they got him into the tent he had vomited and struggled to stay upright. He lay on his bedroll moaning and moving very little. That he was still moving and making noise at all was not a bad sign, but Ellen got very little sleep regardless.

Meanwhile, Dan kept an ear out in case anything happened to Owen or Lilly. There was not enough room in the tent for three people, so Dan and Lilly cuddled like spoons to allow Owen space to lie more comfortably.

"I hope this isn't awkward for you, missus," said Dan.

"It's fine," Lilly replied.

Her thoughts turned to how much her relationship with Dan had changed since she had first joined the gang. Initially she had been intimidated by him, perhaps even a little perturbed, but now she could see him for who he was: loyal, brave and reliable. She realised that her initial dislike of Dan had come from her own prejudices. As much as she didn't like to acknowledge it, chief among them was the colour of his skin. Having been brought up by a family of English persuasion who aspired to be middle-class, distrust of the "other" was hammered into her from as early as she could remember. Of all the those she was told to hate and fear, the poor and anyone who had dark skin were foremost. It was only when she began to experience life outside the nest that her beliefs were challenged. Dan represented almost everything her family hated, yet he had treated her far better than any of them. She felt embarrassed at how she had behaved.

She reached behind herself and drew Dan's arm up over her side and locked her fingers in his. Neither said a word.

***

Morning came and with it a substantial fog. Dan and Ellen collected enough dry wood to build a small fire. They piled more wood next to the flames to help it dry out before they used it as fuel. Lilly made damper, which was smothered with jam and eaten eagerly by all.

Jack complained of a severe headache, slurring and mumbling as he spoke, and a quick examination revealed a large lump on the back of the skull near the right temple.

"I can't say I'm surprised you've a headache. If the blow had struck in a slightly different spot, it might have killed you," said Ellen.

"So, are we going back into town?" Lilly asked.

"I don't expect we'll be getting a warm welcome if we do. After last night, I wouldn't be surprised if the peelers in town were looking to arrest us as vagrants," said Dan.

"I'm surprised the trap that was drinking there last night didn't intervene," said Lilly.

"If he had we'd be in much bigger trouble," said Ellen.

The others nodded. Jack making a scene hadn't helped them, but it could have been worse if their identities had been exposed. They agreed that the best thing to do would be to find somewhere not too far away where they could set up, at least for a while, and keep a low profile. However, this was all alien territory for them, and they would be just as well heading east as west for there was no knowing what lay in any direction without some kind of map.

"I think we're overlooking something important," said Dan.

"What's that?" asked Ellen.

"If we had people protecting us, we wouldn't need to run."

"What are you suggesting?"

"I say we look for a farm where we can convince the people there to shield us from the police. It may require us to pay them."

"Buying support?" Lilly asked.

"Unfortunately, people are more likely to give you help if there's something in it for them," said Ellen.

"That's how we all met isn't it, missus?" said Dan.

Ellen nodded.

"Money or goods in exchange for shelter is our best option for now. Let's see if we can find a candidate."

"Well," said Lilly, "if we're going to bribe people to harbour us, we'll need regular income and goods. Given our situation, we won't be able to get these things honestly."

Dan was the first to respond.

"I say we cross the rivers and head north. We bail up any large farms we encounter along the way. Perhaps the odd highway robbery. If we have no harbourers here, it doesn't really matter who we rob, does it?"

Even though they had come to New South Wales for a start fresh, it had taken less than a week to fall back on crime to survive long enough to escape capture. The realisation weighed heavily on Lilly as her hopes of staying in Deniliquin and starting a small farm with Owen evaporated.

They tore down the camp and started on their journey. They soon realised that the Wakool and Edward rivers were not safe to get across and elected to follow the Wakool, which they simply identified as the "smaller" river, around to the southwest in the hope of finding an easy

spot to cross at. They quickly realised it was not such a small river after all and abandoned hope of finding a way across.

The day's journey had been pleasant enough with clear skies and
plenty of bush to shield the gang from prying eyes. By the time they
set up that night's camp they had covered much territory but there
was a fear creeping in that perhaps they were heading into parts of the
country too sparsely populated to be of benefit to them.

"What do we do if we can't find any farms out this way?" Dan asked
as he rode alongside Ellen and Jack.

"We will have to head back the other way," Ellen replied.

"I hope our supplies last us long enough to double-back," Dan muttered.

A short while later the decision was made to stop for the day
and establish a camp. The cart was propped up, the horses hobbled,
and the firewood was collected. Once the fire was lit the tents were
pitched and the gang gathered to eat as had become routine. It was the
only sort of stability they had anymore. For the meal they had the last
of the salt beef and damper. The supplies were getting low so it was
starting to look like they would have to do some hunting soon if they
wanted meat.

"If we had a bit more lead and powder, we could try hunting
boomahs for our meat," Jack said with a mouthful of food.

"Urgh, no thank you," said Lilly, "unless you put the meat into a
stew it's awful. Tough and gamey."

"Ah, you've just never had it cooked right. Brady's a dab hand at
cooking kangaroo over a naked flame," said Dan.

Owen shifted uncomfortably. He tried to speak but it was still too
painful. He had been eating oats instead of the meat and bread because
solid food was too difficult to eat with his damaged tongue, especially
anything salty. He found that unless he kept his tongue as immobile as

possible the wound would infrequently reopen, and his mouth would fill with blood.

"Let's give it another day before we start thinking like that. We have enough supplies to last a few days if we are sparing," said Ellen.

As they ate, the gang became aware of the sound of footfalls crunching through the undergrowth. They remained quiet and listened intently. They all exchanged glances, barely breathing. Jack reached for his revolver. A moment passed in silence and then they were greeted by the sight of a tall man with a mighty salt and pepper beard that cascaded from his chin to his chest. He wore a threadbare sack coat, and a cabbage-tree hat full of holes. Over his shoulder he carried a gunny sack and poking through the gap in his coat was the walnut grip of a revolver he had tucked into his belt.

"Hulloa, mates," the jolly bushman hollered to announce his arrival, "have you got a spot at the fire for a traveller, by chance?"

"That depends," said Jack, "Who is the traveller?"

The man chuckled and planted himself on the log next to Lilly.

"I wonder if you have heard of Jack Power?"

"The bushranger?" said Lilly.

"Aye," said the man tapping his chest, "now you've a face to the name."

The others were uncertain of what to make of this intrusive arrival and what possible motives he had in imposing himself on their camp.

"What brings you to our fire, Mr. Power?" asked Ellen.

"I been follering you all most of the day and couldn't help but wonder at what you were doing here. This ain't what you'd call a pop'lar place."

Jack Cooper folded his arms.

"We do a bit in your line of work," he said.

"Is that so?" said Power incredulously.

"We've just come from over the border in Victoria," said Jack, "but we're looking to find somewhere to lie low for a while."

A sly grin spread across Power's face.

"My darling feller," he said with a drawl, "if you're looking for farms you're going the wrong way. You'll be best to head back east. The bush is too thick the other way and beyond that it's dry as a week-old carcass in the sun."

Ellen eyed him suspiciously.

"If you're such a seasoned bushranger, why are you out in these parts?" she asked.

Power gave her a hard stare then abruptly broke out with a peal of laughter.

"Because I'm bloody well lost! I was deprived of my horse and my swag because I ran into some bloody bluebottles at my camp and had it on my toes rather than be caught. I've been wanderin' around out this way for a few days waiting for someone to show up in the hope I might get a spot of tucker. I used up the last of my bullets trying to catch a wallaby for my dinner. So here I am, no wallaby and no bullets."

Ellen eased up but remained cautious.

"Well, Mr. Power, we don't have a lot to share but we can arrange something," she said.

"Ah, you're a good woman. No need to call me mister, I might add. Power on its own will suffice," Power replied.

Ellen set about scrounging up some of the leftovers from their meal to give to their guest. She presented the damper and salt beef to him on a buckled old pewter plate. He accepted the offering, meagre as it was, with much grace.

"My sincerest thanks, ma'am. Here, let me tell you all of some of my adventures," he said preparing his pipe before he ate. "Now, you may recall a few years ago that the scoundrel Gardiner made short work of the gold escort up at Eugowra. A lot of people don't realise that not every man in that gang was accounted for. To be sure there was the dashing young rogue Johnny Gilbert, that rascal Jack O'Meally, and there was Dan Charters and his chum Benjamin Hall. We all know what became of Bow and Fordyce and Manns," he said crossing himself, "and of course that dandy Sir Fred Pottinger and his men claimed they recovered all of the booty because it would not do for them to reveal that the forces of the law were less than effective."

He took a stick and poked the end into the campfire to light it, then used the flame to ignite the tobacco in his pipe with a series of small puffs.

"At any rate, I was one of those gunmen up on the rocks that day. I didn't have a lot of experience with robbery – not yet – but I did my level best and got a decent pot from the takings."

"What was Darky Gardiner like?" asked Jack.

"Hmm. Charming cove at first. Well-dressed. Temper on him like you wouldn't believe. Demanded absolute loyalty and submission. I couldn't pretend to know why young Mrs. Brown wanted to leave her husband to skive off with him, but I suppose he was a pretty-looking feller in her eyes and that was enough. I was glad to part ways with him so soon after the score. I can't say I shed a tear when I read that he'd been sent to Darlinghurst for thirty years or more. He was lucky he didn't get a short drop and a sudden stop like poor Harry Manns," he said, crossing himself again.

As Power sat by the fire reeling off one story after another, as if needing to offload his memories before an encroaching deadline reached him, his mood bounded from one extreme to another. Ellen scrutinised him as he spoke. He was a man of middle age, careworn in appearance but strong as a Mallee bull and over six feet tall. His dark brown hair was greying and worn long and carefully brushed, as was his beard. His eyes were as green as gum leaves and in his lighter moments they squinted delightfully to give him a jovial countenance, but when he became serious, they were like chunks of obsidian beneath his furrowed brow.

"Here, do you mind if I make my way with you lads and ladies for a time? A feller might do fine on his own, but it's the want of company that brings him undone at the seams like a cheap pair of breeches."

"I suppose so," said Ellen, "that is, if there are no objections."

He looked at the others who all indicated through nods that they had no qualm with allowing this newcomer into their ranks.

"Ah, God bless and keep you all," Power said with a wide grin.

Eight

Elliot McKenzie sat impatiently in the parlour of Wilhelmina Churchley's homestead, waiting for the hostess to greet him. One of her maids had been very accommodating, plying him with whiskey while he sat by the fire in what had once been Jim Churchley's chair. The floor had been carpeted to hide where stubborn bloodstains from his gruesome demise were visible on the floorboards.

He had heard Mrs. Churchley moaning upstairs and making exclamations in German. Soon after, the lady herself emerged from her bedroom looking flushed, accompanied by her young maid, Anna, who tried to straighten herself out before giving her employer a respectful nod and returning to work. The mistress gave the girl a smile and returned the nod before walking confidently to the parlour. With her diminutive height, dark hair, icy blue eyes and plump build, she reminded McKenzie of Queen Victoria, although her features were much softer than the monarch's.

As she entered the room, McKenzie rose to greet her. He extended his right hand as he was accustomed to do but was very quickly reminded of the inappropriateness of the gesture when he looked down to see a wooden prosthetic where Wilhelmina's right hand should have been.

"Mrs. Churchley..."

"Please, we are friends. You can call me Mina if that would suit your purpose better. Be seated, Elliot," she said tersely in her native German accent as she sat in her armchair.

"Ye know why I'm here," said McKenzie.

"You wish to discuss the bandits."

"I will be direct. The police are not capable of bringing them to heel. Just look at what happened lately. They were over the border without the appropriate permits, trying to capture them outside of their jurisdiction while mounted on nags and without a means of conveying them back if they were successful. It's no surprise to me that one of them had his brains blown out and the bastards got away, if ye'll pardon my language."

"You are a man of passion," Mina said, "I agree that these men are not able to complete the task of capturing such bloodthirsty criminals. They are poorly equipped and poorly trained. It is only by divine providence that there has not been more bloodshed. What is your proposal?"

McKenzie sat up and leaned in towards his hostess.

"I want to form our own force to hunt them down. Our best men, best horses, best guns. We don't need permission to go after them, and we will do it a damn sight better than the police."

"Have the others in the league agreed?"

"Frank Barnard has. The others were not so ready to throw their resources into such a pursuit."

"Well," said Mina, "who could blame them? To send their best men out with their best horses and tools when there's business on the farms to attend to would be a very risky thing to do. What makes you think I would agree?"

McKenzie's gaze wandered to the wooden prosthetic that hid the mangled stump left behind when Lilly had unloaded a shotgun into her hand. All that had remained to salvage was her thumb and the lower part of the palm, so the prosthetic was designed to slide on in such a fashion that she could still use her thumb. It was more cosmetic than practical.

"I never thought highly of James Churchley. I found him to be unimaginative, a poor conversationalist and he thought with his cock.

We worked well together at times, yet I was unsurprised by the nature of his demise, and I think he probably deserved it. But what happened to ye, on the other hand, was wrong – if ye'll pardon the expression."

"I inherited a large estate and money from my husband."

"But ye suffered. Don't ye ever dream of seeing that little whore strung up and dancing on air for what she did?"

Mina shifted uncomfortably. She raised her prosthetic limb and stared at it.

"I will admit that this has been hard. You have good insight, Elliot. I will join you in your pursuit, but I will not be subordinate to you. We are equals or nothing, is that clear?"

"Like crystal," McKenzie replied.

"*Wunderbar*. Now, I hope you will forgive me, but I am feeling rather 'under the weather'. I must call this meeting to a close. Would this time next week be suitable so that we may discuss strategy?"

McKenzie accepted the invitation and left with a feeling of accomplishment. Mina watched him leave and when the door was closed and locked, she ordered one of her maids, a young Irish woman named Marie Ronan, to come to her.

"Yes, Ma'am?"

"My girl," Mina replied as she hitched her skirts up to reveal her naked lower half, "I require kisses."

She parted her thighs and reclined in her chair as the maid got on her knees and leaned in to press her lips against her employer's most intimate parts. Mina sighed with a relaxed smile.

"Perhaps you will become my favourite, yes? More, more my lovely..."

The gentle kisses gave way to licking and Mina clutched at Marie's scalp, grabbing a clump of crow-black hair. It took very little time for Wilhelmina to orgasm, her breathing became shallow and rapid, and she writhed with blissful agony, howling and cackling with pleasure.

"*Hör auf, mein süßes mädchen,*" said Mina, instructing her servant to stop now that she was too sensitive to enjoy further cunnilingus.

Marie did not understand the words, but the meaning was clear enough — her mistress was finished. She rose, curtseyed and excused herself, wiping her mouth as she left. Being used in such a manner made her feel dirty, but it was still preferable to what she was made to endure when her old master, the departed Jim Churchley, was still alive.

Mina sat back with her thighs parted and sighed. Her dead husband had made it a habit to abuse his power over the maids in their employ to satiate his carnal urges. Now that she was the head of the estate, Mina was utilising the perks of her power in the same manner. She believed that for a woman to thrive in a man's world they must be like the men they were competing with. If she desired, she could seduce any of the men in her employ, but in her view the men were vulgar, filthy, unintelligent, and lacked the desirable gentleness of her maids. But she was discovering the hard way that it all left her feeling empty. The physical pleasure alone brought her no satisfaction, nor did the incredible control she could exert over her staff. Mina Churchley was learning the hard way that sex without love was an anaemic and unsatisfactory experience. Every time she engaged one of her maids in alleviating the ache in her loins, she suffered the guilt that one will only feel after an act of infidelity, and it was down to her feelings for one person in particular.

Her personal attendant was Anna Johansson, a fair-haired daughter of Swedish immigrants, aged nineteen. Her eyes were blue like glaciers and always sparkling, and she smiled often and genuinely, which were qualifications enough for Mina to desire her for the role. She had quickly proven to be diligent and eager in seeing to all of her mistress's needs. In fact, Anna's attentiveness was beyond that of a mere subordinate, it was affectionate, and this often confused Mina. *After all*, she often thought, *who could love a crippled widow?* But Mina had soon found herself reciprocating Anna's affections in private.

Despite the impropriety of such a union between employer and servant, let alone between two women, Anna was unashamed in her love for Mina. Her position had granted her access to her in unguarded moments, and she would gaze wistfully at her in a moment of contemplation or introspection. She admired her intelligence and resilience and sensed that the cruel and severe façade was merely the armour to shield her warm heart. Many times, she would lie in bed at night imagining being able to wake up beside her mistress and spend the whole day in her embrace. Other times she would write love poems but hide them under her pillow. She was angry at how Lilly Brook had so horribly maimed her beloved Mina and often wished she could enact a revenge on her behalf. She lived in hope that one day Mina would come to her senses and allow herself to be loved by her and return the affection in kind.

So, in the dim afterglow of her impulsive intercourse with Marie, the emptiness quickly overtook the pleasure and opened the door once again to that feeling of guilt. At that moment Mina Churchley decided to make changes. She could be as bold, sly, and determined as her husband without being cruel and further abusing the women in her employ. It was time she allowed herself to accept her feelings for Anna and exercise the restraint Jim Churchley had been incapable of. She would not simply emulate her male rivals; she would be better than them.

***

After a fortnight of planning, the posse was ready to go in pursuit of the bushrangers, with Elliot McKenzie and Wilhelmina Churchley leading them. Aware that life in the bush would have its hardships, Mina had brought along Anna to accompany her for company as much as service. They were both riding in a covered wagon that not only carried the rations and equipment but would be used as their shelter in the bush. Most importantly, however, it was intended to be the means of transporting the captured outlaws back to Victoria, regardless of if they were alive or dead.

Each of the men in the party had a copy of the reward notice on them. It had been updated since the £2000 reward was offered for the capture of "John Cooper, Ellen McReady, Lillian Brook and two men whose names are unknown" nearly two months earlier. Back then, they were only wanted for murdering Jim Churchley, maiming his wife, stealing Diana and Sancus from Barnard's stud, robbing a gold escort, as well as a myriad of home invasions and highway robberies. Now added to the list were the recent murder of Sergeant Dolan, the murder of Constable Bowen and the wounding with intent to kill of Harold Henley, J.P. – both of the latter being whom Jack had shot in his drunken rampage near Rochester. In light of these events the reward had been quickly bumped up to £4000, which was an eye-watering amount. The bulk of the men had no real interest in crossing paths with the gang, but the reward was a massive motivator to bring them in as even a portion of the total would set them up for a long time.

The entire party consisted of McKenzie, Churchley, Anna, and seven men sourced from various farms belonging to members of the Upstanding Citizens League. From McKenzie's staff was Tom Kaplan and John Draper, both of whom were known as crack shots. From Churchley's farm was Brian Knapp and Nigel Brown. From Francis Barnard's staff was Peter Wisher and Stuart Steel, both of whom were horse breakers, Barnard himself had pulled out at the last minute claiming an attack of gout prevented his attendance. Last was Jack Lee, who was from Mick Cornell's station.

The group headed towards the border at Echuca as their plan was to head into New South Wales and find the trail of the gang from there. They stuck to the roads on the way to the border, which made travel easier. They stayed at inns on the way up and upon reaching Echuca found that the volunteer army had already departed. Clearly, they were of the opinion that the gang was New South Wales's problem now.

Over the bridge they went, then into Moama, where they realised that without any reliable news reports to go on that they would need to do some investigation to find clues about their whereabouts. However, it was fortuitous that Jack Lee found an article in a two-day-old newspaper left on a table in the pub that gave them an important update.

Bushranging:— Reports indicate that the notorious Peacock Gang were spotted in the vicinity of Walla Walla. A group matching the descriptions of the wanted offenders was seen heading towards Culcairn, and they have a new companion who is said to match in every detail the description of the outlaw Jack Power, who has been unaccounted for in the past month, leading to speculation that he had escaped the colony into South Australia. What these dangerous brigands have in store is unknown, and authorities are on high alert.

Lee showed the article to Elliot McKenzie and Mina Churchley. There was a brief discussion, and the pair agreed on a new destination – Culcairn.

Nine

Following Power's impromptu membership into the gang, the bushrangers had begun heading east. They knew that the closer they got towards Sydney, the more likely it was that they would find farms where they could foster some support or at least perform some decent robberies.

As they travelled, Ellen began to think about her daughter Susie and her family. There was a possibility that she might be able to convince the whole gang to escort her all the way to the city. At the least, Jack would accompany her if he kept his word. She knew that it was not a journey she could safely make on her own. Beyond that it would be the first time she had been able to see her daughter since her wedding, and her first time seeing her grandchildren. The notion of a family reunion filled her with a sense of optimism, but also nervousness as she contemplated the danger of being found by authorities in such a densely populated area. It was a risk worth taking to reunite with her flesh and blood.

When they arrived at the outskirts of Walla Walla, Jack Power excitedly pitched an idea to the rest of the group.

"Here," he said, "I know a good spot around here where we can camp. It's a lovely rocky outcrop that gives you views all around for miles."

"Do you know how to get there?" Ellen asked.

"Well, I've never come at it from this direction before, but I'd say if we keep heading nor'-nor'-east we'd be on the right track."

After a few hours, during which Power regaled the gang with more of his tall tales, they finally saw their object in a clearing. It was a collection of enormous boulders bunched together as if collected by some giant and dumped in a pile on a hilltop. As they got nearer, they saw the nooks and crannies, but especially a narrow channel that seemed to cut right through to the centre of the mound.

They hobbled the horses close to the mound and propped up the wagon. The men immediately went exploring to check out what features this new hideout offered. With some effort, the Cooper and Power scrambled to the highest point and looked out. They could indeed see for miles around them in any direction. The land around the outcrop was quite flat and mostly cleared for farmland, allowing a greater range of visibility.

The others explored closer to the ground and located some good spots to set up beds and a fire. It was soon apparent that firewood was in short supply close to the hideout, so Dan and Owen rode out to the nearest copse of trees in Lilly's cart to fetch what they could.

Now on her own, Lilly had a chance to sit and collect her thoughts. She clutched her belly and slunk into a nook where she was suddenly overcome with a profound misery. Everything ached, every step was an enormous effort, and it was only now in the safety of this granite fortress that she was able to begin the unpleasant task of processing it all. She sat nestled between the boulders and as the physical pain met her psychological pain she sobbed bitterly. Upon hearing the sound of Lilly in distress, Ellen investigated.

"What's the matter?" Ellen asked as she slid into the nook beside Lilly.

"I can't do this anymore," Lilly said, "I'm in so much pain. Everything feels like it's burning. I'm starving all the time and I'm tired of having to shit into a hole in the ground like an animal. I can barely walk or stand anymore, and I just want this bloody baby out of me! On top of all that I can't stop thinking about all the horrible things that

have happened. When I close my eyes, I hear Mrs. Churchley screaming and all I see in my mind is blood everywhere."

"I understand," replied Ellen, "but it won't be this way forever. We
can stay here for a while. It's safe and you can rest. Getting some good
sleep will make all the difference. Trust me, rest gives you time to heal
and a new perspective on things."

Lilly enveloped Ellen in a hug, desperate for comfort. Ellen knew
that it would take more than some sleep to fix all of Lilly's problems
but being well-rested would give her the brainpower to handle the
situation better. She wondered what toll this lifestyle was having on
the baby. They were exhausted, eating poorly and often exposed to the
ravages of the weather. For any person this could be enough to break
their spirit or their body, but with the added stress of pregnancy it was
almost a miracle that mother and baby still seemed to be healthy. Her
thoughts turned to the potential risk posed to the ongoing survival of
the gang by Lilly's condition growing more delicate. She suppressed
the thoughts and focused on the moment. For now, they were all safe
as houses.

***

Night draped over the hideout peacefully. On top of the outcrop
Dan sat nursing a bottle with a dwindling supply of Scotch in it. It
was the first time since Rochester that he had touched alcohol, but he
wasn't drinking it, merely holding the bottle. He was trying hard to
suppress the urge to break his streak of sobriety.

Power clambered up and sat next to him. He pulled out his pipe
and kit and began to prepare a smoke.

"D'you smoke?" Power asked.

"Sometimes. Not really in the mood for it."

"Mind if I do?"

"No."

Power took out a cake of compacted tobacco and used a knife to shave off a small amount. He rolled the off-cuts with his fingers to loosen them into flaky, twisted pieces of dried out and shredded tobacco leaf. With his rough fingertips his pinched the tobacco and pushed it into the bowl of his pipe. He lit a Lucifer match and sucked the flame into the bowl, toasting the contents until they glowed a deep orange and puffs of smoke began to arise.

"Ah, nothing like a good smoke. This is the Navy style tobacco. It's a bit rougher than what I like, but it lasts a lot longer."

"Goes well with rum and hard tack," Dan replied.

"Can't say I'm much of one for hard tack."

"If you did enjoy it then you should be in Bedlam. You do occasionally miss it, though, in a strange way."

Power puffed thoughtfully.

"So, you was a sailor?"

"Yeah," said Dan, "I jumped ship when we got to port. I'm in no rush to get back into that life."

"Can't blame you. It's a hard life, and not a very rewarding one. Give me a forest or sprawling plains and I will show you heaven on earth."

Dan gazed at the light reflecting off his bottle and remained quiet.

"Not much for talking, are you?" said Power.

"Not lately, no."

Power ran his gaze over Dan. He examined his handsome face, prematurely worn by hardship, and his sad expression. He was a man deeply troubled but seemingly unable to relieve his burden. Power, on the other hand, could speak fluently on most anything that came to mind, especially if the topic was himself, and rarely could he suppress the urge to vocalise any thought that entered his head. He felt like he was faced with a challenge in trying to pry at Dan's secrets and began to consider how to get him to open up.

"You were a seafaring man, then?"

"Yes," said Dan, annoyed at Power repeating what they had already established.

"What made you give it up?"

Dan paused, gazed out at the horizon.

"It's a long story."

"I have plenty of time for stories."

"Hmm," Dan grunted.

"Go on then."

"I was mistreated. I feared for my life. As soon as I saw an out, I took it."

Power furrowed his brow.

"Who mistreated you?"

Dan's words caught in his throat. He struggled to speak as his mind spiralled back to the darkest time in his life.

+++

The cargo hold was a safe place for Dan to go away from prying eyes. When others retired to their hammocks he would sneak down with a candle and occupy himself with one of his hobbies. Some days he would be knitting, others he would be carving something out of a lump of wood he had picked up in port. This was the only way he could avoid the ill-treatment the rest of the crew targeted at him.

It was during the year he spent as a mate on the ship known as the *Pugilist* that he met Christian Holter, a rigger on the same crew. He was slender, of average height, and boyish. It was the playful twinkle in his sea-green eyes that had caught Dan's attention to begin with. As the voyage continued, he found himself taking stock of the smooth, fresh face; the red lips that always seemed to be peeled back over strong teeth in a pleasant smile; the chestnut brown hair that he wore long and tied with a ribbon into a ponytail; and the long-fingered hands that were strengthened and callused by his duties on the ropes. Eventually he plucked up the courage to engage Christian in conversation on the deck and to his great delight the apple of his eye expressed a reciprocal feeling.

When the ship hit the doldrums, the crew had nothing to do but wait for a favourable wind. While waiting, they gambled and indulged in rum – against the captain's wishes – and brawling usually ensued. Dan and Christian, on the other hand, would sit for hours chatting like old friends and soon began to open up their deepest secrets to each other.

Dan told Christian many stories about his misadventures as a child in London, messing around with kids like Davey Davis — who his mother, in her typically insensitive way, always referred to as "the Jew boy" — and Katie Chapman whose father was Romani. All three of the children had been brought together by a shared experience of prejudice and vilification.

"One day, the three of us decided we would try and nick a loaf of bread from Old Tim, the baker," Dan told his companion, "We didn't need the bread, we just wanted to see if we could do it. So, Katie went up and started asking the poor blighter questions about his bread — how he made it, how much it cost — and Davey and I waited until he had his back turned then we snuck up to the back of the stall and snatched a loaf. Davey shoved it in his coat. I gave Katie the nod and we all took off home. Old Tim was none the wiser and we thought we were now master thieves. Davey took the bread home and when his mother found out where it had come from, she beat him so hard across the backside that he couldn't sit down for a few days. She ate the bread all the same though."

Christian laughed musically at the tale and Dan's spritely recounting. He reached out and held Dan's hand tenderly. The pair of them could feel their hearts beating like they were about to burst out of their chests and Dan trembled. They said no more for a while. Instead, they sat, holding hands and looking out at the water.

As time went on, they craved more intimacy and one night they made their way to a spot near the stern where, under the cool moonlight, they kissed. It was a chaste affair, and afterwards they sat against the mast holding hands, knowing the whole time that if they were found they would be in deep trouble. Dan was terrified, but Christian seemed to delight in the risk.

Soon the weather was once again favourable, and the duties of sailing consumed most of their time. Christian was employed on the rigging, while Dan went around doing checks for the boatswain, and both were good at their jobs. In the evenings they would dine with the rest of the crew and after lights out they would sneak out for some time together. When they were almost caught by the first mate, they agreed that they needed to find a safer location. Dan decided it was time to introduce Christian to the small, secluded spot in the cargo hold where he would hide to get away from the rest of the crew.

"It's a lucky thing that you knew this little nook," said Christian.

"My duties give me access to all parts of the ship, so I know where all the private places are," Dan replied, "but I wish we didn't have to hide down here with the rats. Next port we arrive at I'm getting off this blasted ship and never getting back on. Would you join me?"

Christian held Dan's hand and kissed his knuckles. "Sure. Now, if you don't mind, I have something else I'd prefer to do now than talk."

Christian kissed Dan tenderly and stroked his thigh. Dan's heart was beating so hard he could hear his pulse in his ears. Christian unbuttoned Dan's trousers and worked his hand into its cloth confines.

"Do you want me to keep going?" Christian whispered.

Dan nodded.

With some awkward shuffling about, Christian slid Dan's pants down and took the engorged member in his mouth. Dan reclined against a crate with a look of shock but allowed himself to enjoy the sensations until he came with a tiny exclamation that he tried to stifle by clamping his hand over his mouth. The whole experience had been no more than a couple of minutes, but it immediately seared itself into Dan's brain. He gazed lovingly down at Christian, who was using his neckerchief to wipe his chin and lips.

Suddenly they heard the hatch open and footsteps near the stair. They blew out the candle they had taken down with them. Dan pulled a sheet over them, and they waited as they heard the sound of one of the crew entering the hold, pacing around, clearing his throat and leaving with a bottle of rum. When the coast was clear they relaxed with a giggle.

Not every night afforded them a chance to escape to their hideaway, and not every opportunity was taken. They could not afford to raise the suspicion of the crew, who they knew would leap at the chance to do something to them if they discovered the true nature of their relationship.

Eventually, their luck ran out when some of the crew noticed the pair going down to their secret spot and followed them. They discovered Dan and Christian in their nook, pants down and frigging each other passionately. This led to both men being dragged onto the deck and stripped nude before being bound to the mast with heavy hemp ropes. The captors called out as many people as they could muster and pointed to the humiliated pair while calling them any derogatory epithet they could think of. Their manliness was mocked, their bodies were mocked, and they were left there overnight unable to free themselves and exposed to the bitter cold of a night on the ocean while the coarse ropes bit into their skin. Christian wept like a child, but Dan would not allow the others see him broken.

The next morning the men returned and continued to mock Dan and Christian.

"Careful around the black boy. He'll bend you over and stick that big black truncheon of his right up your arse," said a sailor of early middle age, pointing to Dan's exposed penis. He was a scullion by the name of Rupert Britton and had a reputation of getting too drunk to do his job properly. This had led to several instances of gastrointestinal distress in the crew over the course of the voyage, and one death.

"What's the matter, Cookey?" Dan said, "never seen a real man's cock before? I always heard you liked the taste of black pudding, how about you get a mouthful of this one?"

"Still got some fight in you, blackie?" Rupert retorted.

"Get these ropes off and I'll show you!"

The challenge was accepted, and hasty preparations were made for a fight on the deck. The crew stood in a circle before pushing Dan and Rupert into the middle and cheering.

Dan sized up his opponent who had stripped down to his waist and still wore his apron. The cook was flabby and mostly hairless. He was balding and missing most of his front teeth due to past bouts of scurvy and the odd losing fist fight. His penchant for rotgut had taken a noticeable toll on his health and general appearance. Dan was still naked as a newborn as he prepared his fists and readied himself for combat. He had no shame anymore; his deepest secret had already been exposed and in his mind there was nothing left to lose but his life. He was determined to claw back some dignity by showing the others how formidable a fighter he was.

Rupert lunged at him, but Dan simply stood aside and let his opponent's momentum work in his favour. Rupert steadied himself and swung at Dan but could not land a blow. Dan dodged and ducked, landing blows with precision in between.

The fight went on in this manner for only a few more minutes before Rupert decided to fight dirty. He doubled over, ploughed headfirst into Dan's gut and grabbed him by the testicles. He squeezed them hard, and Dan bellowed with pain. He brought his elbow down on Rupert's neck and he let go. Now fuelled by adrenaline and rage, Dan knocked Rupert down and stomped on his head until he lay still. The crew fell silent. Rupert was still alive, but unconscious and bleeding from the nose and mouth.

"Is that what you wanted?" Dan screamed at the onlookers.

The captain finally appeared, and he strode into the makeshift ring. He was irritated by the behaviour of his men and had long ago given up attempting to discipline their misbehaviour with the cat-o-nine-tails.

"Take these men to the brig. I will sort them out later," the captain said dismissively.

Dan and Christian were kept in a cage below deck while Rupert was conveyed to the sick bay where the ship surgeon could monitor him. Dan tried to hold Christian to comfort him but was rebuffed.

When the captain interrogated them, Christian was quick to defend himself.

"He seduced me, Captain. You saw what he did to Rupert. He told me that if I didn't allow him to have his way with me, he would kill me."

Dan felt incredible pain in his chest. It was as if it was collapsing in on itself and being ripped apart at the same time. He could not figure out if he was about to slide into despair, explode with rage, or die.

The captain asked no further questions. The white man's unsubstantiated claim was apparently sufficient to condemn the black man. Christian was allowed to go free. Dan, however, was kept locked up.

"Listen here," said the captain, "we shall be arriving at our destination in a few days. This afternoon you will be flogged for your crime and allowed to rest in the sick bay until we weigh anchor. When we reach land, I will hand you over to the authorities. Then you can see where sodomy gets you."

That afternoon as the sun began to sink into the horizon Dan was tied to the mast with his back exposed and given fifty lashes with a cat-o-nine-tails. His back was a mess of lacerations, welts and blood as he was dragged to the sick bay.

For the remainder of the trip Dan did not speak or eat. He allowed himself to drink water, but nothing else. He lay on his belly and waited for the wounds to scab, all the time thinking about how he had been betrayed. His heart was broken, and he swore he would never allow himself to fall in love again if he survived this trip, and he would never trust a white man.

When the ship weighed anchor, Dan was loaded onto a boat with some of the cargo and rowed towards the mainland. When they were a short distance from the shore he rolled into the water. His hands had not been bound and he swam freely. The salt water stung his wounds such that he almost passed out, but despite the pain he persisted, knowing that it was the only way to avoid what Hell awaited him.

+++

"Who mistreated me?" Dan said, repeating Power's question, "perhaps the more appropriate question is who didn't?"

"Seems like it must have left quite the mark on you if you don't want to speak of it. Still, you're here today and that's not so bad compared to the alternative," said Power as he took a big mouthful of smoke and slowly released it in a swirling cloud in front of his face.

Dan unplugged the Scotch bottle and took a mouthful. The burn distracted him slightly from the pain of his memories. He silently cursed the fact that it was never enough to stop them completely. There was only one person he had ever felt safe enough to share those memories with – the man who had nearly died trying to protect him and Lilly from the police only a matter of days earlier.

Ten

It had been almost a week since the gang had taken up residence in the formation of boulders that they began to refer to as the "Rock Fort". Power had told the others over the campfire that he knew the place because it had once been the stronghold of the notorious bushranger Daniel Morgan. In fact, during an absent-minded wander one morning, Lilly had poked around in a little crack and discovered a something bundled in cheesecloth and covered with dirt. The parcel contained a revolver, bullets, firing caps and a gunpowder flask. She wondered if Morgan the murderer had concealed these items when hiding here from the troopers. She took the items and showed them to Owen but kept them to herself. She wanted the treasure to be their little secret.

That afternoon, Owen took a stroll around the fort to clear his head. His mood recently had been quite low, partly due to the slow and painful recovery from his injuries but mostly due to losing Ruffy. The bond between him and his horse was strong. He hoped she had was living free and happy with a pack of brumbies, but she had been shot during the pursuit, and he didn't like her odds.

When he first encountered her, it was soon after burning his police uniform and fleeing to the bush in protest of the abominable conduct he was made to be party to as a constable. He had spotted her in a field making short work of a haystack and decided he was done with getting around on foot. He stole Ruffy that very same hour and rode her bareback all the way to his camp. He was astounded at how calmly she had responded to him taking her away. There was no sign that she had been wary or uncomfortable with him, in fact it was almost like he had been riding her for years. Beyond that, it was a miracle that nobody had followed the tracks to find him. Ever after, Ruffy was his constant companion and had been the only stable thing in his world until now.

Lillian found Owen thinking to himself and staring at the expanse that surrounded the hideaway. She came up behind him and gently placed her hand on his shoulder. She felt moisture and realised it was blood.

"Stay here," she said as she rushed to find their medical supplies, "the bloody wound has opened up again."

A few moments later, as Owen sat undressed while Lilly stitched the bullet wound shut, he sighed.

"What's the matter?" she asked.

"I was thinking about Ruffy."

"We will find you another horse."

"I know that, but a horse is not just a horse," Owen said with some difficulty due to his injured tongue. He found talking to be less difficult now that it had mostly healed, but still uncomfortable and his words were somewhat malformed and slurred.

He continued, "When you and your horse are bonded you know they will take you wherever you need to go. You're like a centaur, a whole being, as if you shared one mind and one body. You can't get that from just any old horse."

Lilly nodded. She had a lot of experience with horses herself. Although she had never had her own horse before they got Diana from the stud farm, she had been taught to ride by the stockmen on the Churchley farm when she was employed there as a maid. This gave her an insight into the kinship riders have with their mounts. She was a fast learner and in a surprisingly brief time she was able to not only race the men but outpace them, but control over an animal was not the same as a bond. The loss of Ruffy had upset her as well. It was as if a member of the gang was gone. Ruffy's position may be filled, but *she* was irreplaceable.

Lilly completed tying the final stitch and snipped the extra thread off.

"There. I could have been a seamstress, you know. I would suggest we leave these garments off for a while so it can get some air and heal."

Owen felt cold as the dusk seeped in.

"What if I just draped my coat over my shoulders?"

"No, nothing. It needs to breathe. Besides, I like looking at you with your shirt off."

"Oh, well that makes it alright then when I catch a chill."

"Don't fret. I'll warm you up," said Lilly with a smile.

***

It was rapidly becoming apparent that they needed more resources if they were to continue hiding out at the Rock Fort. They needed ammunition and gunpowder, food and medical supplies. None of this was available close by.

Dan and Owen headed out early in the morning with the intention of finding what they needed. Not knowing the district meant needing to employ the expertise of locals to find what they needed. They waited on the side of the road and when a traveller came past, they flagged him down. He was a tall, thin man mounted on a sad-looking nag.

"Excuse me, but could you tell me where the nearest town is?" Owen asked.

"What do you need?"

"We need supplies."

"Well," said the traveller, "a few farms around here might give you some goods. They're still afraid to turn away a traveller even though Dan Morgan is long gone by now. But if you keep heading east, you'll eventually hit Morven, go north-east and you'll reach Doodal Cooma. Not many places around there to give you relief, though. The drought is keeping food out of all of our mouths. Keep going in that direction and you'll reach Wagga Wagga in about a day. Not much else I can recommend."

They thanked the man and allowed him to pass.

"Nought around here for miles by the sound of it. If there's no towns nearby where we can buy what we need? Perhaps we should help ourselves to supplies at the nearest station?" Dan said.

Owen's injuries still ached, and his shoulder had not come good yet, leaving his left arm very weak. The idea of sneaking onto a farm and stealing supplies was not hugely appealing, but he did not see any other option presenting itself and agreed with Dan's position.

The pair rode, Dan on Sancus and Owen on Diana, until they found a station. There were fences all around and huge paddocks that were dry and devoid of crops despite the furrows in the dirt. From the road the homestead was only just visible.

"They must have something worth taking in there," said Dan. Owen nodded.

They jumped the fence and quietly rode to the homestead. There were no other horses around, so the pair assumed either the residents were absent or the horses were in a stable somewhere. Hitching their horses to the veranda out of view from the road, they cautiously approached the door and listened carefully. They looked at each other with apprehension as there was no human activity to be detected.

Owen tested the doorknob, and it turned. The door swung open gently with only a slight creak. They went inside and crept from room to room as quietly as possible in case there was someone there. Both had their hands on the grip of their revolver ready for action. The house was elegant and airy with large windows that let lots of light into various rooms including the dining room, parlour and drawing room. There were many paintings hung proudly on the walls as well as decorative ceramic vases, figurines and crockery on shelves and pedestals, and a large piano for entertaining guests. Whoever lived here was flush.

Upstairs were the bedrooms, which Dan decided to check out. He nervously ascended the staircase, which creaked with each step. With each footfall he expected someone to come out and try to tackle him or riddle him with lead, but nobody came. He discovered there were four bedrooms: a master bedroom, a nursery, a nanny's room and a room for the older children, which had three iron framed beds in it. Everything looked as if the occupants had just gone out for a breath of fresh air and were due back any moment. Dan went into the master bedroom and grabbed some clothes, including some new boots and a cabbage-tree hat with a blue ribbon around it for himself. He picked up a lace shawl he thought would be ideal for Lilly. He moved on to the nursery, hoping to find things that would be useful for Lilly when the baby came. The cot looked as if it had not been used in some time, but everything around the room was arranged as if the family had just popped out for the afternoon. Dan felt an eerie sensation seeping in. A gust of wind outside rattled the window and blew a cloud of dust high above the ground.

Downstairs, Owen stuffed some paper and a writing kit into his satchel from an elegant writing desk. He then went looking for the kitchen. Gazing through the dining room window he could see the kitchen was a detached building clad in whitewashed weatherboards. When Dan came back downstairs, he called Owen over.

"This place is like a tomb. Not a living soul to be seen."

"We should head out to the kitchen for supplies. It's not far, but it's exposed," said Owen.

Dan laid his clothing haul out on the floor.

"First things first. See anything you like?"

Owen sifted through the menswear until he found something useful.

"The white shirt looks good. The tweed waistcoat too. Help me get these off so I can try them on."

With some effort Owen shed his satchel, coat and shirt. Dan examined the unbandaged wound in his shoulder, tenderly poking the red area around where the bullet had torn into the flesh. It had been hastily stitched after the gang had settled into their new hideout.

"Still hurts?'

"Yeah. Makes it hard to move my arm. At least it doesn't bleed all the time now."

"You were bloody lucky not to get infected."

Dan helped Owen pull on the formal shirt, which buttoned all the way down unlike the Crimean shirts they were accustomed to.

"That is a lot of buttons," said Dan.

As Owen set about doing up the shirt, Dan gently tied a green silk cravat around his collar, which he smoothed out with his good hand. Despite the missing fingers on his left hand he was still very able when it came to tying knots.

"Green is a good colour on you," he said.

"Well, you'd know better than me."

They layered the grey tweed waistcoat over the top before putting Owen's coat and satchel back on. He adjusted himself and tested his range of motion then gave Dan a nod of approval.

They went outside and Dan stowed the remainder of the clothes in a bundle on his saddle before he joined Owen walking to the detached kitchen. Both felt very uncomfortable. There was something unnerving about the lack of people on the farm. The strange stillness that was everywhere made them feel claustrophobic even though they were outdoors. It was like the place had been bewitched.

From the homestead they looked out and saw clouds of dust swirling around all of the huge empty fields that were bone dry. A farmer would be lucky to get the plough to dig through such hard-baked soil, much less grow anything.

Entering the kitchen, they were again greeted with another room that looked like the occupants had just ducked out the back. There were utensils on the bench, even crockery that had relatively recently been eaten off of. They wasted no time in grabbing sacks and shoving as many provisions in as possible. They grabbed potatoes, cured meat, preserves, flour and tea, even a can of treacle. Even though the spuds were sprouting they figured they would be good to eat for the time being.

As they left the kitchen they heard movement in a detached shed behind the kitchen. Dan walked around to look at the noise that sounded like it may have been an animal that had been chained up growing restless. If there was a guard dog they needed to know how to keep it quiet. He saw a door with a window beside it and peered through the filthy glass. It was hard to see but he made out the shape of a small person in a grey smock seated in a corner, chained to the wall. Their hair was long and knotted where it hadn't been pulled out in clumps, and the smock was covered in filth.

"Oh, God..." Dan muttered. He turned to Owen and gestured for him to come and look. "There's someone in there."

But when Owen looked through the window, he saw nobody. There was a chain on the floor but certainly not a person chained up like a dog sitting in their own filth.

"The room is empty," Owen said.

"What do you mean? There's a person chained up," Dan said with urgency. He looked through the window again and Owen was correct;

there was nobody in there. He felt a shiver run down his spine and the hairs on his arms pricked up.

"I'm getting a really bad feeling, Owen."

"I want to check out the barn," said Owen, skating past Dan's comment.

Both men stowed the loot on their horses and rode down to where a large wooden barn was situated. Outside was a wagon big enough to haul a reasonably large family on their trips to church or into town. Owen tried to push the doors of the barn open but there was some resistance. Dan could feel a lump in his throat and his muscles tensing. He noticed what appeared to be water damage or some kind of stain on the lower portion of the door.

"Give me a hand," said Owen.

Dan walked over and the pair threw their weight against the door. It gave way and opened just enough to give them room to enter. The first thing they noted was a stench of rot.

It was a split second for them to comprehend the terrible scene that lay before them. From an overhead beam a body hung from a hemp rope, lifeless. The body was that of a man of middle age. At his feet was a milking stool that had been knocked over, evidently what they had been standing on before going to meet their maker, and a greasy puddle where various fluids had drained out of the corpse and dripped down. The flesh was putrid and black where it was most rotten, but red with a waxy texture where it hadn't been eaten away by maggots.

Turning around, the obstruction that prevented the door opening became apparent. A row of bodies was slumped against it. A woman roughly the same age as the man holding an infant, two boys no older than twelve, and a girl somewhere in her teens dressed in a filthy nightshirt. Evidence immediately observable indicated that they had been shot then dragged against the door, presumably by the man hanging in the middle of the barn, to prevent anyone coming in. All of the bodies were in an advanced state of decomposition, which was not surprising given the prolonged heat, and presented a grisly spectacle. They were far more decayed than the hanging corpse. They had been maggot infested, leaving very little soft tissue. The eyeballs were gone and what skin was left was dried out and full of holes through which bone was visible. The mother's body had slumped forward when the door was forced open and behind where she had been resting was a patch where bodily fluids and liquid flesh had seeped into the wood and caused it to start rotting. The murder weapon rested against the wall next to a cartridge bag as if it had been set down ready to be used again.

To describe the situation as repulsive was an understatement. The men were so shocked they could not help but soak in every detail with horror. Owen reflexively doubled over and emptied the contents of his stomach out onto the floor.

"I guess times got too tough. He killed them then did himself in," said Dan.

"But there was plenty of food," said Owen.

"Yes, but how long would that last if they had no crops to sell? They must have sacked the staff then the old man did the deed in here."

"Should we do something? Do we bury them?"

"I don't know. There's nothing we really *can* do. If we notify anyone, they'll be asking questions we don't want to answer, and the ground is too hard to dig into."

After regaining their composure, they found a tarpaulin to drape over the mother and children as the bodies were too decomposed to move, but they could not get high enough to cut the man down. Dan took the gun and cartridge bag. These poor souls would not need them anymore. They went back to their horses, mounted and galloped away. They were glad to be out of such a place haunted by misery and pain.

***

That evening the gang ate well. Dan relayed the information the traveller had given them.

"Seems like Wagga Wagga will be the best place to head to," said Lilly.

"We need to get moving again," said Ellen, "the horses are running out of grass to eat, and the longer we stay in one place the more likely it is that we'll get caught."

"I know the way from here," said Power, "we'll get there in no time at all."

After the meal, Lilly and Owen stood looking out at the stars. Both were in a contemplative mood. The air was warm around them but cooling down quickly, and cicadas filled the air with their droning chirp. Owen could not get the image of the dead family out of his head, so tried to refocus on something else. He turned his thoughts to a more present matter.

"I suppose it won't be long before the babe is with us," said Owen.

"The way I've been feeling, the speed my belly has been growing, I expect it will be very soon," Lilly replied. "It's hard to comprehend. I'm only just eighteen. I feel like I'm no more than a child myself."

Though she hadn't had a calendar to mark the days, Lillian knew that with the period of time that had elapsed since joining the gang her birthday must have passed by now. Celebrating birthdays was something her parents did because they wanted to emulate the upper class, but she had never felt the need to make a point of marking the anniversary of her birth with festivities. She had fortified that mind-set while working for the Churchleys, as days seemed to bleed into each other with the monotony of a servant's life. As a servant, her life was not her own, so years meant nothing. Her youth had frittered away, and she had barely seen it go.

"Well, the way the lawmakers see it, when you reach your eighth year you know right from wrong and that makes you an adult," said Owen. "Can you imagine an eight-year-old on the gallows for committing a crime? My father was sent here as a convict when he was ten years old. A constable back in Ireland got him done for stealing a pair of shoes for his younger brother. He met my mother at the female factory in Ross. He was a constable himself by then. She had been sent from England for slipping silverware into her apron when she was working as a maid."

"Your mum was a maid?"

"Yeah. Started working when she was twelve doing odd jobs around the kitchen for one of those landed gentry types."

"Are your parents still around?"

"Nah, they got cholera back in the '50s and it killed them. That's why I ended up on the goldfields. I had been looking after them, but once they were gone I had no reason to stay there."

Lilly frowned.

"I would have liked to have met them."

"They taught me a lot about the nature of the world. They didn't talk often of their childhoods, but I knew enough to understand that they didn't get to have one," said Owen glumly.

"Childhood means nothing if you're not born into wealth. Even then, it's only ever the boys who get to enjoy it. Imagine being a girl who has barely begun to grow into a woman, and you already have men twice your age or older trying to court you. I mean, my God, men won't even *court* you if they think you're below their station, they'll just use you for their own pleasure and discard you like a plaything. After all, who would you complain to? The police? They'd lock you up for defaming the bastard."

Owen reached out his hand and tried to clasp Lilly's. She yanked her hand away.

"I'm sorry," said Owen.

"I've tried to be alright. I've tried to accept what happened and get on with things. I can't do it anymore, Owen. Do you know how many times I've wished I could have this thing plucked out of me? Can you even contemplate what it's like to have no control over your own body? To know that whether you put the baby out for adoption, have it killed or raise it without the father you'll still be treated like scum – and it wasn't even your choice to have it to begin with!"

Owen listened in silence while Lillian got her feelings out into the open.

"I didn't choose this. I didn't want Jim Churchley's bastard child in me. He told me that he would leave Wilhelmina and marry me so that I could rise above my station and raise a family with him in luxury. He made so many promises and none of them were sincere. I was just his little whore, nothing more. Something to shoot his slime into and be discarded when his reputation was at stake. I feel like such an idiot for believing him. A stupid girl with her head in the stars hoping a prince would whisk her away to his castle."

Lilly held her head in her hands

"What would you do if I gave the baby away?" she asked.

"Well," said Owen, "I don't know. I would like you to keep him so we could raise him together and make him a better man than his father ever was. But if you really wanted to give him away... Well, I would stand by you. It's not for me to say what you should or should not do. I've done far worse and suffered less. Whatever the outcome we'll face it together."

Lilly nodded.

"Well," she said, "thank you." She paused. "I should make myself clear, though, I'm not giving him away."

Owen sighed.

"Testing me?"

"Yeah, I just wanted to see what you'd say."

"Tell you what," he said, "after all that, it sure makes me feel like a foolish jackass."

"Oh, you're definitely a jackass," said Lilly, giving Owen a little kick in the shin, "but you're *my* jackass."

She leaned against him and rested her head on his shoulder.

Owen's mind drifted back to the dead family on the farm. He thought about how desperation turns some people to crime, but some are too proud to struggle and instead let their desperation destroy them and the people that love and trust them. How often had he placed the barrel of a gun between his own teeth and threatened to pull the trigger? Yet, he would never turn the gun on Lilly. It didn't make sense that others should pay the ultimate price when they were blameless.

"Life is hard," said Owen.

"Yeah," Lilly replied stroking his back. They kissed and returned their gaze to the night sky.

Eleven

Morning came peacefully and Ellen was up at dawn to freshen up and put the billycan over the fire to boil. Every morning someone was allocated to trek to Billabong Creek, only a few minutes' walk from the fort, and collect water. Ellen returned with enough water to prepare tea throughout the morning, as well as enough for everyone to have a wash.

With the fire stoked, and the billycan hanging over it to heat up, Ellen filled a pan with water and stripped down to her waist. With a wet cloth she scrubbed at her armpits and throat, under her breasts and in her navel. She splashed water onto her face and rubbed as much dust and soot off her skin as possible before using the cloth to scrub her hands. She hoped that wherever they stopped in Wagga Wagga had a bathtub and soap.

She was met by Lilly, who had gotten up to relieve herself and decided to wash while she was up and about.

"Fresh this morning," Ellen said as she dressed.

"Fresh enough," Lilly replied as she disrobed. It gave Ellen an opportunity to observe the progress of the baby belly.

"Looks like the bun is almost ready to come out of the oven."

"I'll be glad when it does," Lillian sighed.

"You know, I missed out on all of these things with my Susie. All the way up in Campbelltown while my boy and I tried to keep the farm going down in Myers Flat."

"That must have been hard," said Lilly, trying to pretend she hadn't heard all of this before.

"Well, I've been thinking," said Ellen as she pulled a card out of a small pouch on the leather belt she had been wearing. It was the *carte de visite* Susie had mailed her of her twins. "Now we're over the border, I want to head to Campbelltown to see my daughter and my grandchildren. Jack has already agreed to accompany me as a way of proving himself."

Lilly continued washing her neck and chest as she looked over at Ellen with a mix of curiosity and scepticism. It sounded bonkers to suggest going so close to the largest city in the country when you're wanted by the law.

"I know you think I must be mad. If we keep a low profile, we can reasonably find our way there without getting into trouble. I think it would be good for you too," said Ellen.

"Good for me?"

"To have someone else who has gone through all of this that you can talk to that isn't as old as I am. I'm sure Susie would help you out if you needed advice. We women been having babies since time began, but you can forget some things when you haven't done it in a while."

Lilly washed under her breasts, which were heavy and tender. As she moved the cloth around her nipple, she noticed a droplet of a milky yellow substance leaking from the tip. Her initial reaction was to panic silently while she tried to figure out what was going on. She pressed the area around her nipple and more of the colostrum came dribbling out.

"Ellen..." Lilly said with a pinch in her voice.

"What's wrong?"

"I don't know what's happening," Lilly said presenting the leaking nipple towards Ellen so she could look at it.

"Oh, it's nothing to worry about. It's just your body telling you it's just about ready to be feeding the little one."

"What do I do?" Lilly asked, frantic.

"You can just clean it up and put a little bit of cloth down your shirt to stop it soaking through."

"So, I'm safe? I'm not sick?"

"Better than safe."

"Okay," said Lilly, dabbing at the leakage with her washcloth. She began to think that perhaps she did need that help more than she realised.

***

After everyone had eaten and packed up the camp, they set off for Wagga Wagga. Jack, Ellen and Dan were mounted on their horses, while Lilly, Owen and Power rode on the wagon. They made their way to the road and followed it down through Walla Walla and Gerogery, then began heading north. All the time Lilly and Owen were regaled with more of Power's anecdotes about his adventures, although by now they had begun to cotton on that most of it was bullshit.

"Do you know, I knew a woman in Gerogery many years ago whose husband was a notorious cattle thief? He was said to have once stolen fifty cattle from a squatter's station and herded them overnight to an auction where he sold them all."

"Wasn't he required to show some sort of paperwork as proof of ownership?" Lilly asked.

"He was a clever cove. He forged the papers. He made a small fortune and then took off for Sydney."

"What about his wife?"

"He left her behind. Or at least that's what she told me when I was six inches deep with her ankles around my ears," Power boomed with a throaty cackle.

"You're a pig," said Lilly with a scowl.

"Call me bacon, then!"

Lilly looked to Owen and rolled her eyes.

"Where should we stop?" Owen asked Power.

"Before long we'll reach where the swamp is. I reckon that's the place to pause."

For the next hour and a half, they rode until they drew close to Doodal Cooma. The area was lush with various box trees, grass and reeds. Slate-grey Herons stalked through the water and pecked at invisible things beneath the surface with pointed beaks. Nearby, maned ducks bobbed along the surface of the water and ibises took flight with bright, white wings and long, hooked beaks like a plague doctor's mask. Marsupials and bats nested in the tree hollows, waiting until dark to emerge for food.

On an open patch of grassy area, the gang decided to rest the horses and relax for a while before making the last leg of the journey to Wagga Wagga.

"Here's a spot where Dan Morgan did a bit of work," said Power, "in fact, around here there was a party of troopers who were out looking for him, and in the middle of the night Morgan and his mates found the camp and riddled it with bullets."

"What happened?" asked Dan.

"Well, most of the traps got away without even a scratch, but their boss got a bullet in the chest. He died a little while later."

"Awful," said Ellen.

"Well," replied Power, "that was Morgan for you. Ruthless. He was like a wild animal backed into a corner. It didn't take much to get him biting."

"Why do you suppose it is that he was so violent?" Lilly asked Power.

"It was the prisons that made him mad. They broke him. You should pray you never end up in those places. They treat you worse than beasts."

"There's no fear of that for us," said Jack.

"So long as we keep our heads, then I agree," said Ellen giving Jack a pointed stare.

***

In the evening, they reached Wagga Wagga. It was much larger and more modern than they had anticipated, with the exception of Power who was well equated with the town. The roads were lined with a number of shops and pubs, some of which were large buildings of brick and stone. As they rode through the streets looking for an ideal place to seek accommodation for the night, they passed a rough-looking weatherboard butcher's shop on Gurwood Street with a thatched roof and a sign that read "T. Castro". It was here that the Tichborne claimant had run his business only a few years earlier before going bankrupt and unsuccessfully attempting to establish himself as a long-lost baronet in order to change his fortunes.

They made their way to a huge, multi-storey building with signs declaring it to be the Australian Hotel. A glance at the upper level indicated there were at least a dozen rooms and there were three chimneys protruding from the shingle roof. It was one of the grandest buildings they had yet come across. Ellen dismounted and hitched Diana to a post outside before going inside to ask for rooms.

"Who do I talk to about accommodation?" Ellen asked a barmaid.

"Hang on, I'll get Petey for you," the barmaid replied.

Ellen was soon greeted by a stout, middle-aged man with an impressively bushy moustache and stern eyebrows that arched above narrowed, yet twinkling eyes.

"Looking for a room?"

"Actually, there's six of us looking for a place to sleep tonight."

The licensee peered through the window and saw the others waiting on the street.

"Got money?"

"Of course.

"You're lucky, I have some rooms available. Ten shillings each for the night."

Ellen reached into the pocket of her coat and produced a valise. After fingering the notes inside she withdrew £3 and laid the money on the counter.

"How many horses?" the licensee asked.

"Four horses and a wagon."

"Eight shillings for full livery for the night."

"For each of them?"

"Yes, for each of them. I'm not a bloody charity."

Ellen produced a further three pounds and placed them on the counter.

"Don't worry about the change," she said.

Across the road from the hotel was the post and telegraph office. It was here that the town was fed information from across the colony, and evidently where the news of the reward for the gang would have been received as on the notice board outside was a copy of the reward poster. While waiting for Ellen, Jack had noticed it and was reading it over. Making sure nobody was around to see, he ripped the poster down, rolled it up and stuffed it into his trousers. He ventured inside where the postmaster was preparing to lock up.

"We're closed."

"I apologise for arriving so late, but I've been on the road all day and have been terribly lost. I was hoping you might have a map that I could purchase to help me find my way as I am expected in Doodal Cooma tomorrow and I need to know the way."

The postmaster sighed and pointed to a shelf where there was a stack of folded maps of the colony. Jack collected one and pressed two shillings into the man's hand with polite thanks before leaving to join the others.

Once the horses were stabled and the cart safely stowed, the bushrangers went to their rooms to freshen up. Ellen and Lilly were to share a room, Dan and Owen shared another, and the last was left to the two Jacks.

Everyone freshened up with a quick wash in the porcelain basins that were provided, then they changed into their freshest clothing. The final flourish was the women spritzing themselves with lavender perfume and the men oiling their hair to keep it neat. They all felt much more comfortable to be out of the dirty, smelly outfits that were caked with dirt, soiled with soot from the campfires, and infused with the sweat.

Over dinner as they all discussed the plans, Ellen took the opportunity to announce her intentions.

"I intend to see my daughter and my grandchildren. I have nothing left for me back in Victoria, but in New South Wales I have family and I need to connect with them."

The others were quiet but the looks on their faces betrayed their discomfort.

"Do you know whereabouts she is?" Dan asked.

Ellen hesitated. She was still wearing her belt with the pouch on it, so she reached in and produced the portrait of Susie and her husband. She flipped the card over and read a handwritten note directing anyone who found the picture lost to return it to an address in Campbelltown. She showed it to the others.

"Ah," said Power, "Campbelltown, is it? I know the place well. There was a lass I was visiting at nights there some time ago. She was a laundress and living in a boarding house with another woman who spoke very little that wasn't in Gaelic. The landlady was a sour old biddy, but she softened up when I worked my charm on her. One night I even managed to persuade all three to join in an evening of decadence, the like of which has rarely been seen since the fall of Rome."

Ellen interrupted Power.

"I'm far more interested in getting to this address than hearing any of your bawdy stories."

"Of course. Well, from here it's about a week's journey north-east. You'll be going through some varied terrain – plains, mountains, forests. Plenty of towns along the way, though."

"Do you think your son-in-law would allow us all to stay there?" Jack asked.

"I have no doubt they will accommodate us. I am told they have rather a large house. Thomas has been in poor health, and Susie has twins keeping her on her toes – they'll be glad to have extra hands to help around the place," Ellen replied.

Jack produced the map he had purchased earlier and unfolded it, laying it flat against the table.

"Let's plot this thing out," he said.

After much discussion, Power suggested a route that would take them east to Goulburn, then north to Campbelltown. He used his knowledge of the areas to forewarn the gang about what they would encounter.

"I won't be coming with you all the way," he said, "I don't want to tempt fate by getting too close to the city. Too many people would recognise me, y'see. I can get you halfway and then I will take my leave. You'll be fine after that."

The others nodded. Though Power had proved useful in helping them navigate the foreign territory, they were glad there would be fewer mouths to feed with their already scarce supplies, and both Ellen and Lilly were relieved at the prospect of never having to hear another of his tawdry tales of crime and sexual deviancy. Finally, after months on the run there was a feeling that there was finally a goal, and it was only a matter of days for them to reach it.

***

The next morning arrived without fanfare. The dry heat of the previous day had given way to a sharp frost overnight. When Ellen looked out of her window on the second level of the Australian Hotel everything was coated in sparkling white. Luckily, the hotel was well heated from the multiple fireplaces and the overnight chill had not seeped in.

"What's Susie like?" Lilly asked Ellen as she prepared her things for the road.

"Well, she is quite a cheerful girl, very optimistic. A lover of animals and has a mischievous streak. I would say she is a lot like me, but she's not. She's more like her father. Always quick to laughter, always wanting to help others. I'm very proud of her."

"I hope she doesn't mind the five of us coming to invade her home."

"It's only for a short spell. I had entertained the possibility of looking to purchase a house nearby with some of the money left over from the escort robbery. I know the others have been very hesitant to use their share of the money for fear of raising attention, but what good is it at the bottom of a sack? It would be ideal to use it for something important."

"How much do you think a house in the city costs?" Lilly asked.

"Well," said Ellen hesitantly, "I don't actually know, but we can find out once we get there. It couldn't be that much more than what it cost to get my place back in Myers Flat."

The entire gang gathered downstairs and made their way to the stables where they prepared their horses and the wagon.

"Say, why don't you have a horse of your own?" Lilly asked Power as they bundled their things into the back of the cart.

"Not much of a rider and I fear it would make it harder to stay a step ahead of the troopers. Horses leave trails in the dirt, they crush vegetation, and they need a lot of food. You've seen how this lifestyle has knocked the horses up. Look at the one Ellen is on. Beautiful thoroughbred but she's all skin and bones now. Last night was probably the best feed she's had in months, wouldn't you say?"

Lilly looked at the sad condition Diana was in and realised how hard they had been working her and how poor her diet had been. The whole area around the Rock Fort had been little else but scrub, tussocks and dry grass, which was barely proper food for a goat, let alone a thoroughbred like Diana.

"That's interesting," said Lilly, "because you told us that you abandoned your horse when the traps almost caught you."

"I thought you meant why didn't I get a new horse of my own," said Power, "Ah, tricky things words."

"Well, it won't be long now until we get to Campbelltown and then we won't need to be doing these long days of travel. They can finally rest," Lilly said.

"Ah," said Power, "but how can you afford to keep a horse in the town? No paddocks there."

"I hadn't really considered that."

"Of course not. I've been doing this a long time, girl, and I've had plenty of time to consider it. No, I don't think I'll get my own horse so long as my own legs can carry me."

The gang headed out from the premises in a calm and orderly manner, not thinking there could be any issues. After all, Jack had taken down the reward poster and he presumed nobody would have remembered their descriptions. However, as the postmaster was opening up for the day across the road, he directed his gaze towards the Australian Hotel and got a decent look at the group leaving the livery. He took special note of the pregnant woman and the black man who were with them. It jogged his memory, and he glanced over at the notice board where he had put the reward poster up a few days earlier — it was gone. He went inside and looked through his papers and found a dispatch from the police that described the Peacock Gang. Apart from the old man in the back of the wagon, the descriptions were spot on. Not wasting a moment, he ran to the police station, which was only a few blocks away.

Oblivious to the man running at top speed to notify the authorities, the gang proceeded towards the bridge that crossed the Murrumbidgee River. It was a vast wood and iron structure that had been built by a private group who were now recouping their money with hefty tolls. Locals frequently complained that the tolls were too expensive, but as it was the only way across the mighty river that separated Wagga Wagga's businesses from their residences there was no alternative but to pay. Luckily, the gang had plenty of coin so that they could pay their way and avoid suspicion.

Power was busy describing all of this to the others when he noticed the sound of hooves galloping towards them. Looking back down the road he saw a constable in full uniform on a bay horse charging in their direction and a second was gradually gaining ground behind him.

"We've company," Power announced.

Lilly glanced over her shoulder and saw the men, Constable Creek and Senior-Constable Abbott, for herself. She flicked the reins and took off, the others following closer behind. Onwards they galloped down the street until they reached the bridge. The toll collector waited by the approach, but rather than receive payment, he was bowled over as three mounted bushrangers raced past him, followed by a wagon and two mounted troopers. The sound of the hooves and wheels on the wooden bridge was cacophonous. The wagon created a barrier between the police and Jack, Ellen and Dan. Power, seeing the

forces of law and order coming too close for comfort, drew his pepperbox revolver and aimed it at the policemen.

"Keep back, you damned bluebottles! Keep back or I'll pepper you!"

The troopers either ignored the threat or didn't hear it; Power
couldn't tell which. Without a hesitation, he fired just past the head
of the foremost trooper. The shot scared the horse, which shied and
whinnied. This forced the second trooper to pull up as the terrified
animal was blocking the way. It was only a few seconds of relief for
the gang, but it gave them some breathing room while they rode
across the river.

They did not stop once they reached the north of the town. On
they raced, their mounts foaming and panting with the strain of the
chase, hoping to put as much distance between themselves and the
troopers as humanly possible.

"We should split up," said Jack as he turned to Dan and Ellen.

"Why?" Dan hollered back.

"There's only two of them. We split up and they won't know who
to follow."

With a nod, Jack and Dan peeled away from the rest of the gang
and took off down the side streets. Ellen fell back and rode alongside
the wagon.

"The others have split to try and confuse the traps. I'm going to
do the same. Don't stop moving until you're out of the town. We will
find you."

Without hesitation, she turned Diana around and blocked the
bridge, waiting for the pursuers to catch up. It was not long before
they did. She blocked the road and stared them down.

"Get off your horse and surrender in the name of the Queen,"
said Senior-Constable Abbott, the senior of the two troopers. He
couldn't have been older than twenty by Ellen's estimation, and he was
growing a moustache in an attempt to look older. The younger was

Constable Creek, an awkward-looking man with a lisp who echoed Abbott's words.

"If the Queen wants me to surrender, she can get off her fat arse and arrest me herself," quipped Ellen.

"Last chance," the trooper replied.

"What's your name," Ellen asked.

"I am Senior-Constable Abbott. Dismount and surrender."

"No, I don't think I will. If you want me, you'll have to catch me."

Ellen winked, turned and galloped away.

"I'll get after her, you find the others," Abbott ordered Creek. The junior policeman nodded and took off after the rest of the gang.

Down between domiciles Ellen galloped, trooper Abbott close on her heels. He managed to find a spot wide enough to get beside her.

"Pull that horse up, you're under arrest," Abbott shouted.

"Hardly a compelling argument," Ellen replied.

"Get off, God damn it!"

Abbott got neck and neck and reached over, grabbing Ellen by the arm. After a brief tug of war both were unseated and landed on the road, the horses not stopping. Senior-Constable Abbott reeled. The fall knocked the wind out of him as he hit his head hard on the road. He lay there wheezing to try and get his lungs working again as he tried to get his eyes to focus. Everything looked blurry and there was a ringing in his ears. The pain in his head was excruciating.

Ellen's head was spinning as her brain redirected all energy into survival. Adrenaline rushed through her bloodstream and her heart began beating with great force. Her skin tingled as it became flushed, and her breathing became shallower. She got up and crawled on all fours until she was over the trooper who had just about gotten his breath back, straddling him.

He was smooth-cheeked and had deep brown eyes like a calf. His red lips quivered behind his curled moustache. Ellen could feel herself losing control just like she had when she and Jack had made it over the bridge into New South Wales. She knew she had to stop him from getting up and pursuing the others, but the adrenaline was messing with her mind. She could not tell whether she wanted to fight the young man or copulate with him as both impulses vied for dominance in her brain.

"Well, trooper," said Ellen, "you've got balls, I'll grant you that."

She began breathing heavily as the world around her began to seem hazy and all she could think about were sensations – touch, smell, taste. She leaned in and kissed Abbott passionately, her dry lips pressing into his, her tongue forcing its way into his mouth and exploring it. Abbott fought to throw her off, but he was still woozy from the fall, and she overpowered him easily. She moved her hand to his crotch.

"There they are," she said in a breathy voice. Abbott brushed her hand away and rolled her off, but as he attempted to crawl away Ellen clung onto his back. She used her weight to roll him over then curled her legs around his while locking her left arm around him in something like a sleeper hold. With her free hand she reached for his groin.

"Get off me," Abbott said, as he tried to get loose. His head was pounding, and he could taste rust. He felt like he was about to pass out.

Ellen was no longer thinking, all she could do was act on impulse and her body was heaving with lust. It made her feel powerful to have control over this young man and to feel him squirm against her. It felt good. When she felt the already significant bulge in his pants growing under her hand, quite independent of his own impulses, it aroused her further.

"Don't fight. I know you want this," she growled in Abbott's ear.

"Please..." he whimpered. He had never felt so impotent. His brain was screaming at him to fight her off, but his body refused to act the way he wanted it to. He was confused and frustrated and scared all at once.

Ellen held him in place as she moved her hand up to unbuckle his pistol belt. Abbott closed his eyes. Resistance was getting him nowhere and he was feeling faint from the knock to his head.

Having been roused by the commotion, a woman approaching her senior years peered out of the window to see what was happening behind her house. When she spotted Ellen McReady dressed like a man enthusiastically groping Senior-Constable Abbott in broad daylight she was flabbergasted. Not flabbergasted enough to look away, though.

With the trooper defeated, Ellen took the opportunity to remove the darbies off the unbuckled belt, then slid out from under him.

"What are you doing?" Abbott said weakly, almost in a sob. He lay helpless on the ground as a rivulet of blood began rolling down his cheek from his nostril. He wanted to vomit. As he rolled onto his back Ellen handcuffed him. It was at that moment, as the adrenaline eased off slightly, that Ellen had a second of clarity. She saw the blood running from Abbott's nose and tears in his eyes and was struck with a pang of guilt.

"I'm sorry," she mumbled as she got to her feet. She convinced herself it had been necessary to ensure escape for her and the others.

Leaving Abbott handcuffed, Ellen took off on foot to track down Diana. She found her only a short walk away slurping at a public trough. She mounted the horse and with some gentle persuasion got her going in the direction the others were heading.

Elsewhere, the second policeman had caught up with Dan, who had been turning around to look for Ellen. The pair raced down the street taking sharp turns and looping around in a game of cat and mouse that Dan hoped would kill time and give the others a better chance of escape. Finally, Sancus decided he had had enough, and he came to a halt. Constable Creek did likewise.

"You gonna arrest me?" Dan asked.

"I have to. You're wanted for robbery and aiding and abetting murder. Will you come quietly?"

"For you, I might," Dan said with a teasing smirk.

Constable Creek dismounted and approached Dan, holding his darbies in his trembling right hand. He had never made an arrest before.

"I am arresting you in the name of Her Majesty, Queen Victoria," said Creek, "Uh, can you get off the horse please?"

At that exact moment, Ellen came galloping down the road, creating enough of a distraction for Dan to take off and follow her. As he watched the pair ride away, Constable Creek felt a small sense of relief, but knew he was almost certainly out of a job now. He never wanted to be a trooper anyhow; he wanted to run a lolly shop. He supposed this would be his opportunity.

✳✳✳

Around three quarters of an hour later, the gang found each other on the outskirts of town. Ellen had already filled Dan in on her stalling tactics on the ride there, and he had promised not to tell anyone. Ellen herself was feeling overwhelmed by the experience. The thrill of the chase, the feeling of control she had experienced in overpowering the trooper. Never before had she used her sexuality as a tool in such a way. Never before had she acted so impulsively yet remained so levelheaded. Part of her couldn't wait to try it again. Yet this was countered by the feeling of guilt from injuring a young man and forcing herself upon him in such a way that it clearly left him demoralised. The look on his face when she had handcuffed him was heart rending and reminded her of her son. That in itself had stirred up some complex feelings in light of her behaviour. Furthermore, she realised that she had not simply prevented him from pursuing her and her friends, she had more than likely cost him his job and very probably impacted the way he was viewed and treated in the community. She suspected it would have an impact on how he viewed himself as well. She was beginning to understand the way that her own reckless acts could have a ripple effect.

It was now clear that there was a need to stay away from towns, if possible, at least until they reached Campbelltown. It was courting danger to ride brazenly into heavily populated areas where news of their depredations would have preceded them.

"So," said Ellen to Power, who was now smoking a pipe and dangling his legs off the back of the wagon, "you're the geography expert here. Where are we off to next?"

"Ah, well," Power replied, adjusting his crotch, "nearest town to here is Junee. I say we head in that direction."

"Why would we head into another town after what just happened?" Owen asked.

"It ain't much of a town," said Power, "there couldn't be more'n a couple dozen people there. Mostly crop farms and gold prospectors hoping to get fellatio from Lady Luck. We shouldn't need to stop there long. Just long enough to rest the horses and get our bearings."

The gang, having rested, proceeded towards Junee, only stopping twice to rest the horses as the area was so dry and dusty and vegetation was remarkably sparse.

Only a couple of years earlier the place had been little more than a smattering of farms. In the past few months, however, the discovery of a sizeable quartz reef and the potential for good gold yields had boosted its appeal and it was slowly starting to become something remarkable. There were businesses, including a reasonably sized pub, that somehow had managed to pop up and survive despite the lack of a sustainable water supply and frequent drought conditions that baked the soil rock hard.

The weather was warm and windy when they arrived, kicking up wispy dust clouds. The town was quiet as a tomb with only a couple of wandering locals moving around the place. The gang drew to a halt and exchanged looks.

"Dead as anything," Jack muttered.

They found a secluded spot on the edge of town where they could rest in the shade of a tree and the horses could attempt to graze on the scant grass.

Power occupied himself with preparing his pipe. Although he had supposedly tried to conserve his tobacco, he always seemed to be puffing away whenever anyone saw him.

"Where to next?" Ellen asked him.

"Oh, from here we strike out further east to Yass I reckon."

"Will it take long?"

"A couple of days. Depending on which way we go, we could stop near Gundagai to stay the night then on to Yass. After that, we make for Goulburn, which is about another day or two of travel. That's where I leave you."

"How long from Goulburn to Campbelltown?"

"Two days at most, I reckon. You shouldn't have any problems getting there," Power said, puffing his pipe.

Ellen slumped down next to Power under the tree. The sun was unrelenting, and it was even hot in the shade.

"So, why are you leaving us at Goulburn?"

Power stroked his beard.

"I don't care for civilisation. There's something so unnatural about it that I can't tolerate. Besides, I know the country far better away from the towns."

Ellen chuckled to herself.

"I would believe that if you hadn't joined us because you got lost."

"Nothing gets past you, Ellen. I suppose the real reason is that the closer to the big city we get the bigger the chance of getting caught. You lot can handle yourselves alright, but I'm an old man. I don't want to hold you lot back or spend what precious few years I might have left wasting away in a dungeon. I want the story of Jack Power to end on my terms. Not as a prisoner, but a free man. The trees will be my tombstone."

Ellen nodded.

"Alright. I can't blame you for that. Where will you go?"

"Not sure. Maybe I'll head back to Young and see if Darkie Gardiner left any of his treasure behind."

"Do bushrangers really bury their treasure?"

Power laughed and shook his head.

"What's the point in stealing it if you're going to bury it? No, I have some old friends out that way and I will try and reconnect with them before I figure out what way the last chapter of this grand story will end."

The conversation continued on for a few minutes, but never lingering on anything too deep. Soon the gang were on the move yet again, albeit slowly as the horses were becoming quite worn out in the heat. As they travelled, the scenery was mostly comprised of flat land, orange dust and yellow grass. Occasionally, the bleakness was punctuated by sheep bones scattered around a dead paddock with scraps of woolly skin clinging to them. Once lush gum trees stood bare, their leafless limbs jagged and twisted like lightning bolts locked in time and fossilised. The drought had ravaged this land and even though it was autumn, the heat and dryness were as excruciating as the height of summer. Not a single member of the gang could wait to be away from such a miserable, bone-dry wasteland.

The next stop was Gundagai.

Twelve

As the bushrangers were making their way through Wagga Wagga, the posse led by Mina Churchley and Elliot McKenzie was continuing towards the township of Jerilderie, a small sheep town along Billabong Creek.

The area leading up to the town was scrubby and dry, and there was a certain tang in the air that came from breathing in the dust that seemed to fill every gust of wind. The town was not busy. The odd person could be seen on the streets here and there going about their errands, but it was hardly a thriving hub of activity.

The posse split up upon arriving at the main drag and assessing their options. Mina Churchley and her staff headed to the Traveller's Rest Hotel, a small establishment that doubled as a general store. As for McKenzie and the rest of the men, they headed to the Cape Hotel, which seemed to have more vacancies.

Once safely ensconced in her room, Mina took stock of her surroundings. Tiny room; tiny bed; peeling wallpaper; bare and dusty floorboards; no wardrobe; single wooden chair; wobbly vanity table with a chipped hand basin. She sighed. Anna stood close behind her.

"Mrs. Churchley, shall I ask the men to bring your trunk in now?"

"I suppose so. As much as I am loathe to stay in this derelict place, it will suffice, and I must have my things."

"Very good, mistress."

As Anna turned to leave the room, Mina grabbed her hand.

"As I reconsider, I realise that there is no urgency. I think perhaps there is another way we can make this room more accommodating."

Anna nodded and came close to her mistress, stroking her cheek tenderly before kissing her in the French manner. She began to undress Mina, unbuttoning and peeling away each layer carefully and laying it out on the bed.

"I am glad I have you with me," said Mina.

"I am glad to be with you, mistress."

"You know that there is no need for formalities in the safety of the *schlafzimmer*. We are intimate enough, no?"

"It is not my place to say, mistress."

"It is mine, however, and I say behind that door you may address me in familiar terms."

"As you wish... Wilhelmina."

"Mina, *bitte*."

"Mina," Anna repeated.

Mina now stood as nude as an artist's muse, except for her prosthetic hand. She caught a glimpse of herself in the dingy mirror on the vanity stand. She ran her eyes over the milky-white curves and folds then stopped at her deformity and frowned.

"Ugh! How could anyone feel love for such a broken creature?"

"It is not a challenge to feel love for you," Anna said, disrupting Mina's self-pity.

"What do you see when you look upon me?" Mina asked.

"I see a woman. A woman of great inner strength and resilience. A woman who does not wait for men to offer her a seat at the table, she takes it by force if necessary. A woman whose passions make her a terrible force to be reckoned with. A woman who is firm but can be tender as a lamb when it is warranted."

"You do not see a woman of great beauty?"

"What is more beautiful than a woman of strength and character?"

"You know my meaning, Anna. Does not my appearance repulse you?"

Anna locked eyes with Mina and caressed her face.

"Never."

The women embraced each other and kissed passionately. Mina kept her maimed hand by her side, but Anna reached down and raised it up to her face. She gently removed the prosthetic hand to reveal what remained underneath – little more than a thumb. She kissed the scars on the mangled stump where Mina's surgeon had hastily sewn together as much flesh as could be salvaged, then took the lonely thumb into her mouth, slowly and sensually. Mina watched the action with deep lust in her eyes and sighed.

"Mein mädchen..."

"Mina, I would die for you."

Anna dropped to her knees and swept her hands over Mina's body, worshipping every bulge, nook and imperfection. Mina closed her eyes and allowed herself to feel the sensation.

"Anna, child, you must remember our love is an abomination."

"How could love ever be an abomination?"

"It does not matter how. All that matters is that it must remain hidden."

Anna wrapped her arms around Mina's hips and hugged her, burying her face in her soft belly.

"Why must we hide who we are, always? Where did God declare our bond to be a crime?"

Mina stroked Anna's hair, comforting her.

"It was not God. It was men."

"Then let us declare a war on men until we can live our lives in truth and peace."

Mina smiled and gazed wistfully into middle distance.

"A pretty fantasy."

At that moment there was a knock at the door.

"Oi, Anna," said Brian Knapp on the other side of the portal, "d'you want us to bring the old girl's trunk in now?"

Anna giggled and stood up. She opened the door a crack and peered out at the grubby stockman.

"She can hear you, you know?"

"Do you want the bloody trunk or not?"

"Yes. Be quick about it and hold your tongue."

Knapp turned and went outside, grumbling under his breath. Anna returned to Mina and gently kissed her shoulder.

"We should put your clothes back on."

Mina sighed.

"Why can't these outlaws go somewhere pleasant? Why must they haunt these awful places of poverty?"

"Perhaps you can ask them yourself when we capture them?"

***

The following morning, Elliot McKenzie was up early to explore the town and look for leads. When the post and telegraph office opened, he was quick to go in and ask about any updates on the bushrangers. The postmaster sifted through the telegraphic communications and found a fresh one from up the line at Wagga Wagga.

"This sounds like what you're looking for. It says some bandits were pursued through Wagga Wagga by troopers Creek and Abbott but managed to shake them off and escape."

"Is there any more information?" McKenzie asked impatiently.

"I'm afraid not. As today is Wednesday, our newspaper should be available. There could be something in there."

"Where can I get one?"

"You might get one from the Powells down the road."

McKenzie grunted and left. After a short walk he reached the Traveller's Rest. He went inside and saw Mina Churchley in a red dress at a counter reading a newspaper intently.

"Anything in the paper about the bastards?" McKenzie asked without further greeting.

"*Gut Morgan*, Mr. McKenzie. I trust you slept well. I have read a small piece that described the outlaws being chased through the streets of Wagga Wagga. There is something here about a policeman having been injured and restrained by Mrs. McReady, who is being called the 'Lady Outlaw'. There is an expectation that he will be dismissed from the police force for his failure to apprehend the woman or her colleagues, but the support of his neighbours may be his saviour. I suspect that the best chance we have of picking up their trail is to go there and learn what we can about their movements."

"Aye," grunted McKenzie, "Wagga Wagga it is. I'll get my men."

McKenzie took his leave and stomped back to Davidson's hotel. When he arrived, the men were in the bar drinking.

"What are ye about?" McKenzie barked, "it's near enough to eight o'clock and you're drinking already? I need ye sober as judges."

It was Jack Lee, the man from Mick Cornell's station, that piped up first.

"Lay off, you grouchy Scotch bugger. We've been riding for days in this drought looking for these bushrangers. Least you can afford us is some liquid refreshments before we take off again."

McKenzie's eyes grew intense, and he loomed over the younger man. Without a word of warning, he struck Lee across the face with the back of his hand. It took Lee a few seconds to process what had just happened. The rest of the men could only muster a chorus of "whoa" and "steady on" while trying to create a barrier between the two men.

"Remember where ye stand, boy," McKenzie growled, "ye won't always have these bonnie lads to protect ye. The rest of ye wastrels, get packing. We're for Wagga Wagga and I want to be there before we lose the trail."

The men glared at McKenzie as they finished their drinks and made their way back to their lodgings as slowly as they could muster as a silent protest.

"What were you doing giving them alcohol at this hour?" McKenzie asked the barmaid.

"Money's money, sir."

McKenzie grunted and plonked his hat on the bar.

"Would you like a drink, sir?"

"Aye. Scotch. Neat."

Thirteen

Having had their fill of Junee, the outlaws continued on towards Gundagai. Travel was hard, not because of precarious terrain but because of the tedium and the relentless dry weather that made them all feel as if they would turn to dust themselves. Gradually, the terrain became more forested as they drew closer to the Murrumbidgee River, dark green bleeding into the rust-coloured earth and the yellowed grass.

To lighten the mood Jack decided to strike up a tune. His voice now was hoarser than when he had sung to ease the nerves brought in by the intense storm back at the miner's hut all those months ago, but it remained tuneful. His choice of song was a half-remembered version of *The Cyprus Brig*.

> The hardships we'd to undergo, are matters of record,
> But who believes the convict, or who regards his word?
> For starv'd and flogg'd and punish'd, deprived of all re-
> dress,
> The bush our only refuge, with death to end distress.

> Hundreds of us were shot down, for daring to be
> free,
> Numbers caught and banished, to life-long slavery.
> Brave Swallow, Watt and Davis, were in our noble band
> Determin'd at the first slant, to quit Van Dieman's Land.

March'd down in chains and guarded, on the Cyprus
Brig convey'd
The topsails being hoisted, the anchor being weighed.
The wind it blew Sou'Sou'West and on we went
straightaway,
Till we found ourselves wind-bound, in gloomy
Recherche Bay.

'Twas August eighteen twenty-nine, with thirty-one
on board,
Lieutenant Carew left the Brig, and soon we passed the
word
The doctor too was absent, the soldiers off their guard,
A better opportunity could never have occur'd.

Confin'd within a dismal hole, we soon contriv'd a
plan,
To capture now the Cyprus, or perish every man.
But thirteen turn'd faint-hearted and begg'd to go
ashore,
So, eighteen boys rush'd daring, and took the brig and
store.

We first address'd the soldiers "for liberty we crave,
Give up your arms this instant, or the sea will be your
grave,
By tyranny we've been oppress'd, by your colonial laws,
But we'll bid adieu to slavery or die in freedom's cause."

Though his memory of the words faded out at that point, what he
recalled seemed to mean a lot to him as he put great emphasis on them

when the emotion struck him. Power looked back at him with a wry grin.

Power had come across many young men like Jack in his day. He had fought and robbed alongside them, and rarely had they shown much pluck when the pinch came. He did not rate Jack highly on his list. He viewed him as someone trying to emulate their idea of a real outlaw like Gardiner, Hall or Gilbert and failing. Power had become friendly with everyone in the gang, or at least he believed he had, but Jack Cooper just didn't see eye-to-eye with him. His idea of what he stood for was hollow, the words were correct but there was no genuine feeling in them. He was a pretender hoping nobody would tear aside his mask.

As they reached Gundagai the sun was beginning to set. The town was far bigger than they had expected and was actually in a different location than the town had originally been in, which Jack Power made a point of informing the others about.

"About a decade ago the original town here, which was on the opposite bank of the river, was washed off the map by a huge flood," said Power authoritatively, "it killed around a third of the town's population. It was like something Biblical. They had been warned by the blacks for years that it was bound to happen, but the whites figured they knew better. Well, as it turns out, a group of Aboriginal men headed out in bark canoes to rescue the white people from their own hubris. They pulled about a third of the townsfolk out of the drink. A year later there was another flood, and they finally got the message and moved the whole town up here."

"You sure do know a lot about every place we go to, Power," said Dan.

"You learn a few things if you listen when people talk."

The gang made their way to a hotel known locally as Riley's but was actually named The Milton's Head Hotel. Inside the bar room was a remarkably small space for such a facility, with a laughably under-sized counter that resembled a ticket-taker's desk from a playhouse. It was at this tiny counter that Lilly approached Riley, the publican, and arranged for three rooms for the night.

Power headed straight to the bar and began drinking. After depositing their swags in the rooms, the others joined him, although Dan and Lilly opted to drink lemonade instead of alcohol. Within an hour Power was roaring with drink and recounting his stories to everyone in earshot. If the others had not also been inebriated by this time the obnoxious bushranger might have driven them to some desperate act.

They ordered meals and were served what they assumed was lamb's fry and boiled potatoes, but they weren't convinced. However, as they were buzzing from the drink, they barely noticed the taste, which was fortunate. They purchased more drinks and took up a spot at a round table in the corner just outside the bar room.

Owen was now fairly intoxicated, and he leaned in and whispered in Lilly's ear. The words, slurred as they were, provoked a giggle and Lilly stood up and took Owen by the hand. They bade the others good night and took their leave. Owen attempted to fondle Lilly's backside through her skirts as they made their way to their room.

"Do you know," said Power, "I never would have picked that boy as the sort that would have an interest in the fairer sex!"

"Well, he's got his end wet plenty since that girl joined our ranks," said Jack with a hint of disdain in his voice.

"So have you," said Dan.

Ellen slumped forward and planted her elbows on the table. Her eyes were lazy and unfocused.

"Now, listen here, Dan – don't you be kicking a wasp's nest!"

"Say it ain't so," said Power, "you can't have had this rogue plundering your maidenhood?"

"My maidenhood is long gone, and even if it wasn't it's none of your business, Power," Ellen replied, jabbing her finger at Power's reddened face.

"Jack, my boy," Power said, turning to Jack, "what was it like?"

"Don't..." Ellen said threateningly.

"Exquisite, if not adventurous," Jack replied defiantly.

"Ah! I knew it. You can't beat a woman with experience. They know what they're doing," said Power, leering and beating the table like a drum. "The best I ever had was a woman who was about sixty years old. The sun, so relentless in this country, had shrivelled her face like a beggar's scrotum and bleached her hair to the colour of ashes, but from the hips down she was like a woman half her age."

"I don't want to hear this," Ellen grumbled as she drained her tankard with a look of disgust on her face.

"She was so excited to be with the famous bushranger Power that her quim was dripping!"

The others cringed.

"Good Lord, man," Dan said, "that's enough."

Power did not, in fact, stop. Despite the loud protests he proceeded to describe multiple lurid and occasionally improbable sex acts he had supposedly engaged in with this woman, who he only referred to as Mrs. Carroll. Ellen finally reached the point at which she ceased to tolerate the obnoxious vulgarity of the man, so stood and emptied the remaining contents of her tankard over Power's head. The others cheered, except for Power whose face was a mix of shock and outrage.

"Wha–Huh? Why'd you do that you madwoman?" Power spluttered as he wiped ale away from his face.

"Go to bed. You're done for the night."

With a "harrumph" Power stood up and wandered back to the bar and asked for a cloth to dry himself off with.

"Have you about had enough of our illustrious company, then?" asked Jack.

"That man may not have been a hindrance to us, but he gets on my nerves with those awful stories. How did he expect me to respond?"

"Only a couple more days and then he's off on his own adventures," muttered Dan, "I will keep an eye on him tonight."

***

At three in the morning, Dan knocked on the door to the room Ellen and Jack were sharing. Ellen, bleary-eyed and dressed in a shift, answered the door.

"What's the matter?"

"I can't do it," Dan replied. He was dressed in his Long Johns and appeared frazzled.

"Do what?"

"Bloody Power... He came up to our room about a half hour after I did, with a woman in tow. He spent twenty minutes doing... things to her on the bed right next to me."

"You just lay there while he did that?"

"Well, I thought he'd be done after a few minutes like a normal man, so I pretended to be asleep, but after twenty minutes I got up and left. I waited until I couldn't hear the bed squeaking anymore then went back in."

"So, why are you here now?" Ellen asked, rubbing her eye.

"Well, he got really... morbid. He was just sitting there on the bed weeping and saying he had wasted his life. He kept going on about how he wished he had never gone to the bush, how he wished he had found a proper job. He said something about his mother, but he was sobbing too hard to understand. Keep in mind, the whole time he's got this naked woman on the bed next to him trying to comfort him. I tried not to look at her but I couldn't help it..."

"Is he still doing it?"

"Come," said Dan, gesturing for Ellen to follow him. She gently closed the door and followed Dan to his room. She pushed the door open and peered in through the crack. In the room she could see Power and the woman, who she assumed must have been a prostitute, laying on the floor in a stupor next to a small lamp where they had been smoking opium from a bamboo pipe. Both were naked as newborns.

"Well?" said Dan.

"Grab your things. You can stay with Jack and I."

Dan entered the room and tiptoed around the stupefied pair and grabbed his belongings from his bedside. He could not help but get a good look at Power who lay spread-eagle on the floor, his hairy belly rising and falling in an almost hypnotic fashion, his limp penis flopped lazily to one side, the opium pipe resting in his outstretched palm. His gaze drifted to the woman, more out of curiosity than anything else. To his mind the female body was so strange, but he had never really seen a nude woman in person before. It raised a lot of questions that he would never be bold enough to ask. He was snapped to attention by Ellen hissing at him and gesturing for him to hurry up.

When they got back to the room, Dan realised that Jack was in a separate bed to Ellen and there was no other furniture apart from a wooden chair.

"I'll sleep on the floor," said Dan.

"Don't be silly, you can share the bed with me. There's enough room for two and it's already late so I'd rather not delay my sleep any further by fussing around."

Ellen got under the covers and wriggled across for Dan to snuggle next to her. They lay in the bed close together and Ellen drew the covers up.

"Do you think Power is a liability, missus?" Dan asked.

"I thought we'd gotten past that 'missus' talk? After tonight's display, I think he might be. Let's see how he goes in the morning. So long as he can get us to Goulburn there's nothing to worry about. If he keeps up this nonsense he could be putting us in danger."

"I agree. I like him, but he's not a good fit. We can't afford any other unpredictable behaviour. He likes you. I wonder if dumping your drink on him had more of an effect than we realised."

"I'm glad you came and fetched me," Ellen said, swiftly changing the topic, "There's something else I've been meaning to say," said Ellen.

"What's that?"

"I'm proud of you. I've noticed you staying away from liquor. I know it must be hard for you."

Dan sighed.

"It's the hardest thing I've had to do in a long time. It used to be the only way I could drown out the bad memories."

"What changed?"

"Responsibility. I realised I'm no good to you drunk."

"What about the bad memories?" Ellen asked.

"Well, they're for me to worry about."

Ellen put her arm around Dan and hugged him close.

"Once we get to Campbelltown and we're all safe, then we can have a good talk about it all, I promise. Just hold on for a few more days. Right now, it's time for sleep."

***

The stopover in Gundagai had been brief and eventful, but now, thankfully, they were on the move again. Power was his usual chipper, annoying self as he helped load everything into the wagon.

"Off to Yass now. Lovely little place."

"Yes, I'm sure it is," sighed Owen as he took a seat next to Lilly at the front of the cart. He held her hand and smiled at her. She beamed back at him.

The way to Yass was heavily forested. Finally, it felt like they were getting away from the bleak, sun-blasted landscape and heading towards somewhere that people could survive. They rode close to the flow of the Murrumbidgee River, travelling frequently through thick tracts of bushland, but stopping only very occasionally. The un-tamed nature of the path was torture on the wagon, which would get snagged on a tree here, stuck in a rut there and slowed the journey considerably despite their haste. By the afternoon they had just passed Mount Wee Jasper and were pleased to find a picturesque spot to rest and let their horses have a drink. The location was serene and smelled faintly of eucalyptus, which was soothing after so many days breath-ing in dust.

"Good place to range, here," said Power.

"Is that so?" said Jack unenthusiastically.

"My word, yes. Caves all around here, you know. I used to spend a lot of time here after I had knocked over enough coaches and trav-ellers to keep me supplied. Nothing like it, I should think."

"I'd rather not go back to dwelling in a cave," said Dan as he looked out at the sea of trees.

Feeling the need to press on and reach Yass by nightfall, they were soon back on the road. As it turned out, Power's directions had not been as precise as he had made out and the gang found themselves go-ing off course. They were still attempting to cut through the bush as night enveloped them. Seeing no alternative, they reached a clear spot on the banks of the river and camped. Power was allocated to stay on guard duty during the night as a punishment for getting them lost.

Although he did as he was directed to, Power was not happy about the arrangement and grumbled under his breath as he sat with a shot-gun near the fire. The chill of the night air seemed to seep into his bones, and he frequently wandered around the camp to keep his muscles from seizing. By the early hours of morning, he had curled up by the fire and fallen asleep.

It was Jack who arose first, stiffly emerging from his tent to stagger over to the tree line and empty his bladder. As he stood in the dawn chill and coated the bark of a gum tree with urine, which steamed in the cold air, he looked around for Power. He shook the last golden drops off the tip of his member and tucked it away, then headed to the fire to warm his hands. There he saw Power in blissful slumber. He gave the old bushranger a sharp kick to wake him up.

"Eh," Power snapped as he rolled over and opened his eyes a crack.

"Get up you lazy bastard."

"Who are you calling... uh... lazy..." Power growled as he awkwardly rose to his feet.

"You stupid old fool. You were on guard. You don't sleep when you're on guard — you guard the bloody camp!"

"We're all fine, nothing happened, what's your problem, boy?"

"And what if something *had* happened? It's the guard's responsibility to look out for danger and you can't do that with your bloody eyes closed!"

"Don't you talk to me like that. I could flog you within an inch of your miserable life!"

"I'll talk to you as I damned well see fit."

"I demand respect," shouted Power, flecks of spittle flinging outwards from his mouth at Jack.

"You'll get it when you've earned it!"

By now the two men were screaming full volume and had woken the others. The rest of the gang got up just in time to see the two Jacks grappling with each other like territorial kangaroos. Jack got Power in a headlock and tried to throw him on the ground. Power managed to thrust an elbow into the younger man's gut. They both fell and continued to wrestle, grabbing each other by the throat. Power managed to roll Jack on his back and, with one hand on his windpipe, he grabbed Jack's testicles. It was a fair handful of organs and Power squeezed them with his powerful mitt, attempting to give them a bit of a twist through the trousers. Jack bellowed with pain and indignation then swung his fist into Power's face. Power released his squirrel grip and clutched his eye while cursing. Jack slipped out of Power's grasp and grabbed him by the beard. First, he yanked Power's head down to throw him off balance, then yanked it up to expose his throat, to which he delivered a chop with the side of his hand. Power let out a strangled cough and doubled over.

"What in Hell's blazes are you doing?" Ellen shouted at the men.

Jack, still in agony from his testicular trauma, was bent over and struggling to breathe through the pain.

"This stupid bastard was asleep on guard duty."

"Is this true Power?"

Power had a hand to his throat. Instead of speaking, he nodded.

"What is wrong with you?" Ellen said.

"Sorry..." Power replied with a croak.

"Sorry won't do, but we have more pressing things to worry about. Let's tear down this camp and get moving."

Despite not having a clear idea of how to reach Yass from their location, the gang followed the flow of the river until they saw the first signs of settlement. By the afternoon they had reached Yass and the first thing they did was locate accommodation while avoiding attention as much as possible. The township was well-established, and the streets were lined with stone buildings made in the Georgian style. A sturdy bridge spanned the Yass River, and the telegraph line was draped along a row of wooden poles that ran the length of the main drag. On opposing slopes looking down on the town were the churches, their tall spires piercing upwards to remind the locals to be pious. In stark contrast to the places that they had been through on their way there, Yass was alive with activity. People moved about the streets in lines like worker ants gathering crumbs to carry back to their queen.

They soon found their way to Hart's Royal Hotel. It was a large structure with two levels. Windows studded the walls, and a deck allowed those accommodated on the upper level to step out and look over the street like lords and ladies.

After putting their horses in the paddock at the rear of the hotel, the gang procured rooms. This time they made sure there was no alcohol consumed, and they turned in early. There were no repeat performances by Power.

Fourteen

The following morning the gang rose early and met up outside the hotel, thankful for a quiet night. The topic of conversation immediately turned to the most pressing and recurring of issues: the lack of supplies.

"I don't think we have enough food to get us through the next couple of days," said Lilly. She had taken inventory of their stock they had as they loaded it into the wagon. It had now dwindled to a small amount of flour, some tea and a can of corned beef.

"How much do you think we have?" asked Dan.

"If we ration it maybe you could get a single small meal out of what we have left," Lilly replied.

"Have we got money for more supplies?" Owen asked.

Ellen frowned.

"Only if we chip away at what we had put aside from the escort robbery."

"Well, I lost most of what was left of my share when I lost Ruffy. I kept it in my saddlebags along with my flute," said Owen.

"I've been using mine to cover the cost of these hotels, but I have a bit left," said Ellen. She had more money than she let on, but wanted it kept secret so that she could use it towards setting herself up once they had reached Susie.

Jack and Dan admitted that they still had money, but they would need potentially need it to cover expenses if the gang needed to flee the colony. There was a moment of anxiety as they all shared the same thoughts, but nobody wanted to be the first to say them out loud.

"Chrissakes, let's do a robbery," Power growled.

"We will be fine," said Ellen, "you will be taking your leave when we get to Goulburn."

"Bugger that. I'm gunna prove to you that I'm not useless. Once we're out of town we'll pick a station and bail it up. Grab money, grab supplies, head to Goulburn. That's the plan."

The others looked at each other to see if the others thought it seemed like a good idea. Ellen raised her eyebrows at Owen. Owen nodded.

"Alright, that's our plan then. One last robbery and then we go to Goulburn and on to Campbelltown where we will keep a low profile until we can figure out our next move."

***

When the gang's pursuers reached Wagga Wagga, Elliot McKenzie wasted no time in getting to the business of acquiring information. He interrogated the postmaster and the local police. Neither were pleased with the grilling.

"Where were ye when the bushrangers were riding through the town?" he asked Senior-Constable Abbott.

"As soon as the news reached us, we rode out. After some pursuit the gang split up and Constable Creek and I separated to follow them. I concussed after coming off my horse when I was in close pursuit of Ellen McReady. Creek lost the others around that time as they had all begun riding in different directions through the streets between houses. If we had more men, there would have been no problem."

"Where did they go after ye let them slip through your fingers?"

"From what we could gather they were seen riding eastwards, presumably towards Jugiong or Gundagai. We haven't been able to get an update, nor have we caught up with them on our patrols, despite our fervent desire to meet up with them again and put things right."

McKenzie grumbled and left without a goodbye. He returned to where the others were waiting for an update.

"Useless bastard in there says he thinks they're heading east. If we ride to the next town in that direction, we might find what we're looking for."

Despite the frustration of having so little to go on, the group set their course for Jugiong.

***

The house the gang had isolated as the target of their next robbery was a large homestead that appeared to have been built decades earlier and slowly expanded in line with the owner's wealth. The architecture was rougher than more recent buildings but very English, and the outside was painted bright white as many of the houses favoured by squatters were. Outside the house were numerous fruit trees and garden beds full of ornate flowers. The outlaws reasoned a house like that would be perfect to strike as the occupants clearly had plenty to spare.

On the veranda, John Memphis, the superintendent, smoked a pipe with the station owner, Hugh Bradford. Memphis exhaled slowly into the breeze. It had been a busy day of tending to the cattle and his men had knocked off early to go into town for a dance. He was too old for that sort of thing now, in his mind at least, and had decided to stay back with his boss.

Memphis and Bradford had been friends for a long time, the former coming into the employ of the latter when he was just starting to hit his stride with the farm. He had been a witness to Hugh's wedding to Aoife O'Donnell and was the godfather of their children. Meanwhile, Memphis himself had never married or started a family. In fact, the whole idea of romance was strange to him and sex held no appeal. He was happiest when working with his cattle.

"Who the devil is that down there?" said Bradford, peering into the gloom.

At that moment Ellen, Power and Jack were approaching them on horseback. The pounding of hooves on the dry earth rumbled towards the homestead. Ellen was wearing her bone-white *Bauta* mask, Jack Cooper followed suit with his grotesque *Il Capitano* mask with its phallic nose and wild moustache. Unlike the others, Jack Power did not conceal his face, believing he had nothing to fear by exposing his identity.

As the horses came into view, Memphis and Bradford stood out from the shelter of the awning to see what the commotion was.

"Who's there?" Memphis called out.

In response, Ellen pulled up to the veranda, her green eyes gleaming in the light from the homestead through the mask's eyeholes. She drew a pepperbox revolver from her belt and pointed it at the men. The two Jacks drew revolvers as well.

"We're here to relieve you of your excess wealth," said Power. "If you would be so kind as to make your way inside..."

The bushrangers and their victims entered the house and headed to the parlour, where a beautiful grand piano took pride of place under a framed portrait of Victoria and Albert. In the commotion, Bradford knocked over a pedestal and smashed a vase.

"Watch yourself," said Power.

"Who else is here with you?" Jack asked.

"It's just us and my wife; the stockmen are in town for a dance."

He repositioned himself near the door that led to the bedrooms, keeping his hands up.

"Don't hurt us! My wife is in bed and poorly," he said loudly.

"Shut up. Have you got any money about the place?" Jack snapped.

"No, I keep it all in the bank in town. I can write you a cheque..."

"A bloody cheque?" Power said with a derisive guffaw.

"We're just honest farming folk," said Memphis, placing himself between Bradford and Jack's firearm, "please leave us be."

"Well, if there's no money, I'm sure there's plenty else for us to take that will fulfil our needs," said Ellen. She knew Bradford was lying but grew tired of the delay. She shot Jack a glance and left to search the rooms. She found the master bedroom, but the bed was empty. She looked around and under the bed, where she found a stocking stuffed full of banknotes, but nobody was in the room.

"Come out!"

There was no reply. Bradford had lied about the money. *What else was he hiding?*

Ellen proceeded to search the room for cash and valuables. Apart from the secreted banknotes, there was surprisingly little of note, and none of it they could exchange for goods. Having had so little success in the master bedroom, she decided to check the other rooms.

Her booted feet made a din as she stomped down the passageway towards another closed room. She pushed the door open and burst inside with her revolver drawn.

"Bail up!"

A cursory glance around the space indicated this was a child's bedroom as there were books and toys over the floor and three tiny brass-framed beds. There would be nothing of value in there, she figured. She turned and left. Had she inspected the room more thoroughly, she would have found three young children cowering under the beds with tears rolling down their cheeks, trying with all they could muster to stay still and quiet.

Meanwhile, Power had taken it upon himself to locate the larder and grab provisions. Unusually, the kitchen was not detached from the house. Rather it was in the basement and accessible by stairs. Power walked down the stairs slowly, trying to minimise the noise as the steps creaked under his weight, and he found himself looking at a long stone room with a wooden door on his immediate left that led to the larder. In the middle of the room was a bench where food was prepared and nearby was a large cast iron oven where bread was baked daily. He turned to the larder and grabbed the doorknob, giving it a firm tug. The wooden door swung open quietly to reveal a terrified woman, Aoife Bradford, hiding amongst jars of jam and preserved vegetables, trembling and curled up on the floor. She was dressed in a slip and her wild, straw-coloured hair reached to her buttocks. In her hands was a shotgun.

"Ah," Power said under his breath just as the shaking woman turned the gun on him and squeezed the triggers. The blast was deafening as both barrels were emptied. A load of high-powered shot hit Power in the face, pulverising flesh and bone. He died instantly as brains, blood and chunks of bone hit the wall. The nearly headless corpse flopped to the ground with a heavy thud.

The captors and captives, ran to the noise and saw Power's dead body on the floor, blood gushing out from the pulped mess where the top of his head ought to have been. Ellen reeled. Jack cocked his revolver and levelled it at Aoife.

"Out of there!"

Aoife stood out from the larder and levelled the shotgun at Jack, shaking violently. Jack stood firm.

"Drop it and I won't put a bloody ball through your head," he ordered.

The woman stood wordlessly, too terrified to move. Jack aimed at the ceiling above her head and fired, repeating his order. Aoife screamed and reflexively squeezed the trigger of the shotgun, but the weapon was empty. A look of panic flashed across her face as Jack stormed up to her, snatched the gun and smacked her across the face with the butt of his pistol. Aoife fell to her knees and clutched her cheek, which stung and began puff up.

"You mongrel," Hugh Bradford roared as he tried to rush forward, but Ellen grabbed him and used her entire weight to hold him back.

Jack threw the shotgun away and grabbed Aoife by the hair. She screamed as he yanked her head back. He bashed the back of her knees to make her crumple then dragged her along the floor to bring her face to mangled face with Jack Power.

"Look what you've done! Look at it!"

Jack almost rubbed her face in the gore. Everything from the tip of the nose up was pulverised, a glossy red mass of mincemeat and gristle. The single intact eyeball bulged from where the socket once was. Aoife's hands and knees were slick from the blood on the stone floor, and she slipped slightly. Ellen approached Jack and grabbed him by the shoulder.

"Jack, that's enough!"

Jack looked up at Ellen, his own eyes full of fear and anger behind the mask. He hated Power, but it could have just as easily been himself who had suffered the fate, and that had brought the demon out of him. He released Aoife and went into the larder, emerging a moment later with a calico bag that had once held a ham. He slid it over the remains of Power's head. He ordered the men to help him pick up the body and take it outside.

Ellen sat Aoife at the kitchen table. The terrified woman sobbed bitterly clutching at her injured face, smearing Power's blood on her cheek. This was meant to be a simple operation but suddenly it was complicated and that filled Ellen with rage. She gripped Aoife's chin tightly and turned her face towards her own. They would not leave here empty-handed.

"You know what we want. Where is it?"

Aoife whimpered as she looked up at the inhuman mask Ellen wore, beaked like some strange bird but smooth and white as bleached bone.

"I don't..."

"Don't try and fuck me in the arse, I want money – *where is it?*"

Aoife's eyes flicked to the larder. Ellen levelled her pepperbox revolver at her.

"Get it."

Aoife stumbled back to the larder, trying not to look at the gruesome mess she had made, put a wooden form in front of the shelves and stood on it to reach a bread tin that was perched up high. She fetched it down and showed it to Ellen.

"Do you talk? What's in there?"

Aoife sniffed and tried to speak through sobs.

"It's... our... savings."

Ellen yanked the lid off and inside was a roll of banknotes. She examined the roll and estimated it to be roughly two hundred pounds. Ellen stared at the money and thought about the plastered walls, the beautiful flower beds outside, the full larder stacked with jams and preserves. She thought back to her selection back in Victoria, dry and dusty, barely able to produce enough food in her kitchen garden to keep her fed, her house little more than a crumbling hut devoid of comfort. She looked behind her and saw the blood and gore spattered on the wall and pooled in the grooves between the stones on the floor. She pocketed the money and motioned for Aoife to make a move upstairs. As the sobbing woman left, Ellen pulled out a flour sack that was tucked into her belt and filled it with food from the larder.

When Jack and the men returned from draping Power's body on Tombstone, the captives were all taken to the parlour and ordered to get on their knees.

"You murdered our mate. Give me a reason I shouldn't do the same to you," Jack said in a low voice to Aoife. She bawled, begging to be let go. Ellen found the woman's cries irritating. She turned to the men.

"Who is the husband?"

Bradford raised his hand. Ellen gestured for him to stand up. He did as he was told. He was not an overly tall man and thin. Ellen did not see any threat in him.

"You have children?"

"Yes, three."

"What are their names?"

"Uh, James, Mary and Elijah."

"Do you love your children?"

Bradford began to panic. He worried that this madwoman would find where the children were hiding and harm them.

"Of course I do," he answered.

"Woman," Ellen snapped at Aoife, "I will allow your husband to live. That is far more generous than what you did to our mate."

Aoife clasped her hands and thanked Ellen.

"Quiet! I won't be letting you off without exacting some recompense."

"You took our money, what more do you want?" Aoife asked. Ellen looked her in the eye.

"Blood for blood."

Ellen levelled her pistol at Aoife and fired without hesitation. She collapsed and screamed at the burning pain caused by the ball passing through her shoulder. John Memphis jumped up and tried to wrestle Ellen to the ground. Jack intervened, putting a bullet through his knee. Ellen gathered herself up and turned to Bradford.

"Don't think about making a move or I'll shoot your cock off."

Ellen and Jack left the building and mounted. Ellen looked mournfully at Power's corpse, draped over Dan's horse. They rode off, never looking back.

Inside the house, John Memphis cradled Aoife and Hugh Bradford ran to the children's bedroom.

"Mary, Mary come out!"

A small girl of seven years emerged from under the bed. Hugh crouched and rested a hand on her shoulder.

"Mary, you must run to the neighbours. Tell Mr. Winter that there were bushrangers, and your mother and Mr. Memphis have been shot. We need the police and the doctor. Do you understand?"

Mary nodded and ran out the back door as fast as her feet could move. She did not stop until she reached the next farm, whereupon she rushed to the homestead and knocked rapidly upon the door.

"Mr. Winter! Mr. Winter! I need help!"

When the door opened and the warm light from inside washed over the traumatised girl it was no small relief.

***

When Jack and Ellen returned to the meeting place, the others had lit a fire and were waiting patiently. They had not expected the others to come back with such grim cargo.

"What the hell happened?" Dan asked.

"Power got his brains blown out because he scared a woman with a shotgun. We got some money and a few things out of the larder, but that's all," said Jack.

"How much?" asked Lilly.

"About £300," said Ellen.

There was a moment of silence as Ellen and Jack dismounted.

"I'll get something to dig with," said Owen as he stood and walked to the cart.

As the men buried Power, Ellen and Lilly remained at the fire to debrief.

"Something awful came out in me," said Ellen, "I was so angry, I terrified that poor woman, and I put a bullet through her arm. I've never done anything like that."

"You've shot at police," replied Lilly.

"To defend myself, yes. This time was different. I can't justify it. It was ugly, it was dangerous, and it was stupid. I am so ashamed of myself. I feel like I'm becoming a monster."

Lilly did not try to offer Ellen comfort or fluff her up. She merely sat with her and allowed her to feel the torrent of emotions that her actions had brought up. After all, she had plenty of experience with the same thing and knew that there was no comfort words could bring.

Power's grave was in a small clearing in the bush. It was not marked with a cross or a headstone. Instead, Dan took his penknife and carved into the trunk of the nearest tree:

Here lies Jack Power
Bushranger

He felt sorry for Power that this was how his story ended. He had hoped he might have been killed in a dramatic shoot-out with police, or that his heart might have given out during a passionate liaison with a beautiful woman – something befitting the notorious outlaw and Lothario. Alas, not every story ends poetically.

Fifteen

Jugiong had been fruitless for the pursuers. Gundagai, however, had proven to be more of a success and they were now catching up to the gang's movements. Enquiries around town had led them to the hotel where the bushrangers had stayed. More significantly, they found the young barmaid that had spent the evening with Power. She identified herself as Peggy, and was much more respectable looking now that she was fully dressed, her blonde hair bundled up neatly under a cap. However respectable she appeared to the observer, engaging her in conversation immediately shattered the illusion.

It was Johnny Draper, from McKenzie's crew, who found her and pumped her for information while drinking at the bar.

"You see any bushrangers around here lately, sweetheart?"

"Yeah, I seen some. There was a big fella named Jack Power. Had some fun with him."

"Fun, eh? What kind of fun?"

"Well, he was in the bar for ages getting drunk and he offered me a tenner to go up to his room. He was sharing the room with some black fella who was pretending to be asleep."

"What then?"

"He fucked my brains out."

Draper choked on his drink.

"Sorry, go on."

"He was good at it too. If I had've known how good he was, I would have done it for free. His tackle wasn't that impressive, but by Jove he knew what to do with it." She grinned. "Well, after he had gushed, he started to get really upset, like crying and all. I tried to cheer him up best I knew how."

"How's that?"

"I gamahuched him. Once they blow in my mouth that usually cheers them right up. But not this chap. He just sighed and stroked my hair while he told me nice things about myself. A proper gentleman."

Draper rubbed his temple. He was repulsed by the crude language as much as the apparent moral bankruptcy this woman displayed, but he knew there was a good lead there.

"Well, what was he crying about?"

"He kept saying he wasted his life. He said something about a woman who I think must have been a wife or something. Sounded like she died, and he thought it was his fault I couldn't really understand him. The weird thing is that almost as soon as it came over him it went away, and his truncheon was ready for action again. Anyway, after the black fella left the room, he told me he had this magical smoke he got from a Chinese. He got on the floor and lit this little lamp and pulled out this big pipe. It wasn't like the tobacco pipes. Well, I don't know what it was he had in there, but I've never felt more relaxed. I swear to God; it was the best night's sleep I ever had."

"So, where did they go to?"

"Well, I did remember him saying they were heading off to Goulburn."

"Goulburn?"

"Yeah. God knows why. I wish I could have him back here for another night like that. My notch could use another good pounding."

Draper finished his drink and thanked the barmaid for her information before returning to his boss and announcing their target was Goulburn.

✳✳✳

The morning after Power was buried, the gang finally reached their last stop before Campbelltown. Goulburn was a thriving town with the usual amenities as well as a modern hospital, a courthouse and an impressive gaol with outer walls of brick that culminated in an imposing gate that looked like the entrance to a medieval keep. This level of development was the sign the gang needed that they were coming close to their goal.

"Listen here," said Ellen, "there's a good chance that there's going to be people looking out for us here, so we're not staying in town overnight. Owen, Lilly, get us stocked up with whatever we're missing at the store. Jack, you head to the post office and see if you can get any news. Dan, you come with me."

The gang split and went their ways. Ellen and Dan, knowing that they would be the most conspicuous due to their appearance, headed to the edge of town to keep a lookout. Owen and Lilly took the cart to the far end of town to find a store where they could equip themselves with the necessary supplies.

On his way to the post office, Jack passed the cemetery and the flour mill, as well as the courthouse, which was temporarily operating as the telegraph office. He tipped the brim of his hat low over his eyes, dismounted carefully, and hitched Tombstone outside the post office. As he looked around, he noted with some degree of discomfort that the gaol was directly opposite the post office on the other side of the town square. He curled his lip. Outside, beside the door to the post office, was a notice board. Pinned to it were a number of notices, including a reward notice identical to the one that he had torn down in Wagga Wagga. He removed it and went into the building.

There was a desk with stacks of newspapers on it that included some of the local rags and the Sydney-based papers. He picked up the first one he could see and began to flip through the pages. On the second page he stopped, and his eyes settled on an article:

Bushranging Outrage

–*–

Death of Power

–*–

Family terrorised!

A report has been received from Gundagai that Jack Cooper and his gang have struck again. Last night, Cooper, along with his companions the Lady Outlaw McReady and the seasoned brigand Jack Power, held Mr. Hugh Bradford at gunpoint and demanded he turn over his valuables. In the drama that thereafter occurred, Bradford's overseer, Mr. Memphis, and Mrs. Bradford were shot and injured. The situation proved deadly, however, for the notorious Power who was killed by Mrs. Bradford who had valiantly armed herself to protect her children. When the brigand threatened the woman, she shot him dead on the spot. Cooper and McReady, the ringleaders of the notorious band of desperadoes that has lately brought their particular brand of depredation to our fair colony from our sister to the south, were forced to escape with their lives, carrying the body of their fallen comrade away with them, lest they meet the same ignominious fate. It is expected that the government in Sydney will see fit to complement the reward offered by Victoria's leaders with a reward of their own in light of this appalling crime.

Jack screwed his nose up. No word on police reinforcements, but it would be foolish to assume that they could move through the area without the risk of some morally empowered citizen recognising them and making things hot for them. Without a word he grabbed one of each of the papers, threw some money on the counter and left, making sure to keep his head down.

As he returned to his horse, he felt like everyone was staring at him. In fact, there were people staring at him, but not for the reason he assumed. In his effort to remain incognito his behaviour looked strange, and it was this strangeness that drew attention to him. After all, no other people on the street had their hats pushed down over their face or were walking with their chin tucked into their chest so tightly that they could not turn their head. He mounted and turned back toward the flour mill and set off at a trot.

Jack soon found Ellen and Dan waiting by the road to Gundagai. He wasted no time in informing them that their visit to the farm the previous night had made it into print. In fact, he reckoned, it was the quickest their crimes had made it into the papers. The three of them then rode further into town, keeping their faces hidden, until they located the wagon.

As all of this had been unfolding, Owen and Lilly had located a store where they predicted they could find some non-perishable items to stock up on. They pulled up in front of the store and Owen helped Lilly down. By now her pregnant belly was about as big as it was likely to get, and movement was getting difficult. Although Owen was weaker now due to his injuries, he still proved to be strong enough to give her a hand where necessary.

They entered the store and let their eyes adjust to the gloom. It was a pokey little general store with a limited range of items and a solitary figure standing behind the counter. Lilly recognised the figure and froze as the shopkeeper recognised her in kind.

"Oh, my stars! Lillian Brook is that you?" he shouted in an English accent.

"Uh, hulloa Uncle Charlie."

The shopkeeper, a man of about forty, tall and willowy, rushed out from behind the counter and embraced her.

"Oh, my goodness, look at you! It has been a long time."

"A few years..."

"And I can see you've got a bun in the oven – no ring on that finger, though, you little troublemaker."

"No, I am married, we just... a ring is just a thing. We have more important things to spend our money on. That's my husband over there," said Lilly, pointing to Owen as he perused the shelves.

"He looks like a bit of a go-alonger. Don't you be taking advantage too much," Uncle Charlie said with a wink. "What brings you here?"

"We're going to the city and needed some supplies for the journey. We've got friends there who we can stay with when the baby comes."

"Sydney, my word! It's the place to be. Certainly, a lot nicer than out here with all these sheep and cattle everywhere. You know, I'm surprised you got married. A good man is hard to find around here. I should never have left Sydney, honestly."

"You don't have to tell me twice," Lilly replied.

"Still, bad men have their charms too," Charlie said with a waggle of his eyebrows.

Once Lilly and Owen finished their shopping, Charlie helped Owen load up the cart.

"You'll find a little something I slipped in there for the baby," Charlie said quietly to Owen.

"Thank you."

"Such a shame about her parents."

"How do you mean?"

"You don't know?"

Owen furrowed his brow.

"Oh, I shouldn't have said anything," Charlie said, slapping his own wrist in chastisement.

"Lilly told me her folks were strict church-going types."

"Well, the whole family is. That's why I've come out here. I'm not really one for all of that."

"So, what happened with Lilly's parents?"

"They kicked her out of home. One of their neighbours caught her kissing a local boy and told her folks about it. Apparently, that was an egregious sin. They gave her enough time to get a bag of belongings and then they cast her out. It broke my heart when I heard, but I wasn't surprised."

Charlie looked down and sighed.

"Then their house burned down with them inside of it that winter. People think the chimney caught on fire and the house went up with it. Little wooden cottage. There was no hope. Now the poor thing is an orphan. I wish I could do more."

Owen nodded.

"I think it will mean a lot to her to know she still has you on her side. That's the most important thing," he said.

Charlie looked up at Owen with a half-smile.

"There is wisdom in that. I can see why she picked you."

A few minutes later the others passed by on horseback and Owen knew it was time to leave. Lilly gave her uncle a kiss on the cheek and a tight hug then Owen helped her up onto the cart. With a flick of the reins, they were off.

A short ride to the edge of town later, the gang assembled and discussed the news.

"Do you think they will send police reinforcements?" Owen asked.

"Well, all the troopers that were down this way looking for the Clarkes have been sent up north to find Thunderbolt. I don't know if they're going to send them back down again," Jack replied, referring to other notorious bushrangers that were at large. The Clarke brothers, Tommy and John, had been captured alive after a siege near Braidwood, while the highwayman Captain Thunderbolt was rumoured to be around the Queensland border.

"How do you know that?" Lilly asked. In response, Jack waved the newspapers.

"What about the Victorian police? Surely, they've gotten an extradition in place that will allow them to come up here looking for us?" Owen said.

"It's a possibility, but not one I want to dwell on. We need to concentrate on getting to Campbelltown," said Ellen.

"Alright, we'll keep moving, camp out tonight, then finish the journey tomorrow. If we keep quiet, we should be fine," said Owen.

They all agreed to the plan, but every one of them knew that it was only a matter of time until their luck would run out.

***

McKenzie and Churchley, knowing they were close on the heels of their target, pushed their men to go hard and cover as much ground as possible. They had ridden through the night to reach Gundagai by morning, and their horses were exhausted. A quick perusal of the newspapers confirmed that the Peacock Gang had been in the area the previous day. Not wanting to waste time, the posse took flight immediately and although the horses were exhausted and struggling, they soon came upon Goulburn.

The horses were taken to a boarding stable to be fed and watered while enquiries were made around town about the gang. Most people turned away from the visitors, others wanted to help but claimed they had seen nobody matching the descriptions offered.

It was the postmaster who, when questioned by Mina Churchley's men, gave them the confirmation they desired.

"Well," the postmaster began, "there was a man who was here earlier today looking through the newspapers. He seemed quite unhappy about something he was reading. Gave me a pound for three newspapers and left without a word spoken. He looked colonial. Long hair, flash clothes. Had his hat tipped low over his face. There are only two types of people that would do that: people who are trying to avoid being recognised and people who had something horrible happen to their face. From where I stood, he didn't look disfigured, so I reckon it's fair to say it was the other reason."

Further enquires revealed that a group of three horsemen and a couple in an open wagon had been spotted leaving town that morning. They knew then that if they were to have any hope of catching them, they needed to get going.

With haste, the horses were retrieved and geared up. The men took off at top speed along the road with Mina and Anna bringing up the rear on the covered wagon.

"Should we increase our speed, mistress?"

"No. Let the men run headlong into danger and we will arrive when it is safest to do so. After all, is not a man's life to be spent in such pursuits while the women stay safe?"

"Very good, mistress," said Anna with a smirk.

***

The gang found a secluded spot off the road to set up a quick camp and partake of luncheon. A small fire was lit over which the tea was brewed, and the women set about preparing food. Fresh bread with blackberry jam and a dollop of chutney served on a plate made from a chunk of tree bark.

The horses grazed nearby. By now they were severely knocked up and looked it. After so many hard days of endurance riding the gang were finding it harder and harder to keep their mounts moving, and the stops were becoming more frequent.

The gang sat quietly around the fire enjoying the calmness of the day as they ate.

"With the horses in the condition they are in, I think it's going to take us a lot longer to get to Campbelltown than we had planned," said Owen.

"What are your thoughts?" Ellen asked.

"Power reckoned it was only a couple of days from here to there, but it has to be much longer with the horses in this condition. They just aren't cut out for it."

The others nodded.

"We'll take our time. We have supplies to last us a while. Let's go slowly and try to keep the horses in working condition," said Ellen.

There was a lull in conversation and Dan decided to change the subject to take their minds off their predicament.

"You're looking about ready to pop, missus," Dan said to Lilly.

"I just hope he holds on until we get to Campbelltown," Lilly replied.

"It shouldn't be too far now. We'll get there alright. If anything happens, you've got us," said Ellen.

"Any thoughts on a name?" Dan asked.

"Well," said Lilly, "we haven't really discussed it. I think Owen Junior would be a good name. I've always thought a baby's name should be a way of giving them something to live up to."

Owen shifted uncomfortably.

"I always thought Bruce was a good name for a boy," said Dan, "a strong name. You know, like Robert the Bruce."

"Why not Robert, then?" Jack asked, "Bob for short."

"I can't think of any Roberts that I like," Dan replied, "but I know a few I dislike a lot."

"I think Owen is a fine name to live up to," said Ellen.

Owen's ears pricked up.

"What's that?"

"What's what?" asked Jack.

"Hooves. Coming fast..."

Owen got up and moved closer to the road to see the commotion. His eyes landed on the posse. He did not recognise any of the men until he spotted Elliot McKenzie at the back of the pack, and a short way off a wagon with two women driving it.

"Shit."

Owen ran back to the rest of the group with a look of panic.

"McKenzie is here with a bunch of men. Hide!"

"McKenzie? What on God's earth is he doing here?" Jack snapped.

"Take a guess," Owen snapped back.

The sound of the riders halting caused all of the gang to whip their heads to face the road.

"Ellen, get Lilly to cover. Owen, Dan, you know what to do," said Jack.

Ellen went to argue but knew that protecting Lilly was the most important task at that moment and whisked her away deeper into the bush.

The men prepared their firearms. Their hearts were racing. Not a single one of them was in the condition to fight, certainly not against a larger number. They needed to fight clever. They fanned out and sheltered behind trees. They could hear the crunching of the men walking through the scrub.

"Keep those bulldogs ready to hand," they heard McKenzie growl, "their camp must be just through the trees here."

Jack cocked his shotgun and peered around the trunk of the tree he sheltered behind. There were four of them he could see. He had no idea who they were, but he could see they were stockmen. He wondered why any of them would bother putting their neck out for a bastard like Elliot McKenzie. Only two of the men he was looking at were McKenzie's – Tom Kaplan and John Draper who were at the forefront of the group – the rest of the quartet comprised of Brian Knapp and Nigel Brown, from Mina Churchley's staff. Alongside them was a second group comprised of McKenzie, Peter Wisher, Stuart Steel, and Jack Lee. The red wagon carrying the women remained on the road. All men were armed; all were creeping through the scrub hoping to catch the bushrangers off guard.

Owen and Dan stayed as still as possible, hoping the men might decide to turn back and no confrontation would arise. Their hearts were beating so hard that they began to sweat.

"Reckon we should try flushing the buggers out, boss?" asked Kaplan.

"Be my guest," McKenzie replied.

With that, Kaplan raised his Tranter double-action revolver and fired into the tree line. The bullet zipped past Owen's head. Despite the urge to jump out and fight, the outlaws stayed still. Kaplan fired again. This time the bullet struck the trunk as it moved and caused splinters to fly up into Owen's face. He flinched, revealing his hiding spot.

"Jeezuz, I didn't even realise he was there!"

Owen raised his revolver and fired blindly while clutching his eyes. The shot struck Kaplan in the chest, but it was a glancing shot and left only a flesh wound. The other men opened fire on Owen, who dropped to the ground then crawled to cover behind another tree. As enthusiastic as the men were to fill Owen with holes, they were dreadful shots and not a single one hit its target.

Seeing his mate in danger, Dan broke cover and began firing. He managed to wound Wisher and Lee, but nothing too serious: a bullet cut across Wisher's hand, causing him to drop his pistol, and a bullet was embedded in Lee's forearm. Dan's firearm was a clunky Colt revolver that required cocking between shots. The result was only a handful of bullets being launched before it became too unsafe to proceed.

Jack, who was on the far side from the others, emerged from hiding and fired his shotgun into the crowd. The result was Brown and Draper copping a blast of shot each. Neither was killed outright, but they were in bad shape. Without missing a beat, Jack drew his pistol from his belt and shot Kaplan and Knapp, the former copping a bullet to his ear and the latter receiving one in his neck. Knapp was immediately paralysed and fell heavily with a weak scream.

Owen sat with his back to a thick red gum and peeked around it to see the attackers. They were distracted by Jack's assault, and he took the opportunity to take a couple more out of the fight. He took aim at Steel and fired a bullet into his right knee, bringing him crashing down. Jack Lee, who was beside him, tried to catch him but with his injured arm he could not support his comrade's weight. Owen seized his chance and fired again, hitting Lee in the shoulder.

"You fucking mongrel," Lee shouted.

In the mayhem, McKenzie had retreated to the road where Mina and Anna were watching the battle.

"Do you not wish to fight alongside your men, Mr. McKenzie?" Mina said with a cruel sneer.

McKenzie glared at her as he went to his horse and drew a revolving rifle from his saddle.

"Well may ye smirk while ye sit up there on yer fat arse, Wilhelmina Churchley, but don't forget they already got ye once. Think about what they'll blow off your body when they catch up to ye next. With a bit of luck, it'll be yer fat fucking German head!"

McKenzie stormed back to the fracas, a pistol in one hand and his revolving rifle in the other. He saw Owen peeking from cover and fired a shot at him. The bullet struck him across the scalp and the wound bled freely.

Close by, Jack was trying to wrestle Kaplan's revolver away. Kaplan, roaring with frustration, struck Jack repeatedly in the face with the revolver, but the bushranger would not give up, instead grabbing Kaplan by the wrist and wrenching the revolver from his hand. He then head-butted Kaplan in the face, which gave him some room to move. Spotting this opportunity, McKenzie fired at Jack with the revolving rifle, hitting him in the chest. Jack shouted and staggered.

The wound burned, and with blood already running down his face from a nasty gash above his eye, he was both in pain and disoriented.

"Come on ye bleeding cunts. Face me and take yer medicine," McKenzie screamed.

Upon seeing McKenzie, Dan began to panic. His heart raced and his chest felt like it was being crushed. He squeezed his eyes shut and tried to calm himself. He could have killed for a swig of whiskey to steady his nerves. He opened his eyes and glanced over at Owen who had blood running down his face.

The injured bounty hunters tried to evacuate, leaving Kaplan and McKenzie to the fight. Jack was struggling with his wounded pectoral but refused to be caught alive. He shot Kaplan in the shin with his own revolver, bringing the stockman crashing down. Another shot from McKenzie, however, took Jack out of the fight. With a bullet to his thigh, Jack finally collapsed.

It was at that moment that Dan grabbed hold of himself and broke from cover. He aimed at McKenzie and fired. The bullet struck him in the shoulder blade, and he spun. The whites of his eyes were on full display as his face became a portrait of raw animalistic rage. He dropped the rifle and levelled his revolver at Dan, who refused to shrink away or back down. Instead, he stood his ground and stared McKenzie down.

"Come at me you relentless whorepipe. Let's see how you like me when I'm not already strung up," he snarled.

He ducked and leapt at McKenzie, bowling him over. Despite his left hand being severely crippled, there was enough strength in his remaining fingers to restrain McKenzie's weapon while he used the other to throttle him. McKenzie spluttered and squawked.

"I have wanted to do this for quite some time," said Dan as he stared straight into McKenzie's eyes. The squatter went red in the face as Dan tightened his grip. Suddenly, he went limp. Dan paused and lifted his hand from the man's throat. He was still breathing, but unconscious. Dan noticed a tin hanging from a string around McKenzie's neck. He grabbed it and yanked it so that the string broke. He opened the tin to reveal his own severed fingers, mummified, inside. Dan staggered and vomited on the ground.

At that moment, Owen approached with his revolver cocked and ready. He aimed at McKenzie's head.

"Do you want me to finish him?"

"Eh?"

"Do you want me to finish him, Danny?"

Dan hesitated. Of course he wanted to see McKenzie's light snuffed out, but was he willing to take a life in revenge for his traumas? McKenzie was scum, there was no mistaking that, but did he deserve death for it?

"No," said Dan, "He's not worth the bullet it would take to kill him."

Owen nodded and made his weapon safe before withdrawing. As he did so, Kaplan, having grabbed Jack's revolver when he fell, took aim and fired at Owen. The shot hit its target, the bullet punching through the soft tissue of Owen's side and lodging near the base of his rib cage.

Seeing his companion fall, Dan howled with rage and wrenched McKenzie's revolver from his hand and, quick as thought, fired at Kaplan. The shot struck true, puncturing Kaplan's right eyeball and entering his brain. Kaplan barely managed a surprised yelp before he died.

"Owen, are you okay?" Dan asked, panicking as he fussed over Owen's bleeding wounds.

"I'll live. Check on Jack."

Dan raced over to where Jack was groaning and writhing on the ground. The posse members that were still alive were slowly making their exits, helping each other where they could. Dan did not stop to get a look at his handiwork as he stepped over Kaplan's corpse to reach Jack.

"Jack," said Dan, "are you alright?"

"What does it bloody look like? Help me up!"

The trio pressed gingerly deeper into the bush, away from the battlefield.

"How in the name of mercy did we survive that?" Owen said breathlessly.

"Don't jinx it. Let's find the girls," Jack replied.

Meanwhile, Knapp, Draper and Brown were lifted into the back of Mina Churchley's wagon as they were too injured to ride. Brian Knapp's neck injury proved to be little more than a graze and it was bound with his neckerchief to slow the bleeding. Wisher and Lee did their best to help Steel onto his horse due to his shattered knee.

"Where are Mr. McKenzie and Mr. Kaplan?" asked Anna.

"I'll go back and check," said Knapp.

He wandered back to the battlefield and found Kaplan lying dead and McKenzie laying on the ground groaning. He jogged over and helped McKenzie up.

"What happened?" McKenzie asked, groggy.

"The bushrangers have gone, and we need to go back and get to a hospital. Kaplan is dead. What do we do with the body?"

"Kaplan was an idiot. Leave him here for the dingoes."

Embittered by their failure, McKenzie had no patience for silly things like sympathy. He decided instead that he would accompany his men to the hospital for treatment and then devise a plot to catch the bushrangers once they were patched up. When he reached the road, Mina Churchley had a look on her face that could best be described as poorly concealed satisfaction. The corner of her mouth twitched as she tried to suppress laughter.

"What are ye looking at?"

"No success, then, Mr. McKenzie?" said Mina.

"Our suffering is a great amusement to ye, is it?"

Mina's mirth gave way to something dark and intimidating. It was as if shadows had shrouded her face out of nowhere.

"Your suffering is the price of hubris. You raced in with no plan. What is to be expected when you make no effort to conceal your arrival or devise a strategy? Wars are not won with chaos and impulse."

"And ye Germans are the experts on warfare are ye?"

"We have some experience in winning wars, yes."

"We're heading back to Goulburn. We have injured that need tending."

With that, the wounded warriors turned their exhausted mounts around and slowly made their way back from whence they had ridden.

As for the bushrangers, a short wander in the bush reunited the men with Ellen and Lilly. The women had been hiding behind the wagon, which was out of view of the clearing where the fighting took place. Upon seeing Owen bleeding from the head and clutching a nasty wound in his right side, Lilly shrieked and ran to him. Ellen ran to prop up Jack, who was drooping and barely conscious.

"What happened?" Ellen asked Dan.

"Elliot McKenzie had a party out to gun us down. They outnumbered us, but we won the fight."

"This is what winning looks like?"

"If we'd lost, we'd be dead, and you two not much better."

"We need to find a doctor," said Lilly, sobbing.

"Sure," said Owen, "know any that specialise in patching up bullet-riddled outlaws?"

Ellen and Dan laid Jack out on the ground; Lilly laid Owen next to him. Ellen looked Jack over to see where he was injured. There was bleeding on his left thigh just above the knee, and on the right side of his chest. There was also bleeding from his nose and a deep gash above his left eyebrow where he had been struck in the face by Kaplan during their struggle. She next examined Owen's wounded scalp and the bleeding on his side.

"We'll need to cut these clothes off to get a better look," said Ellen.

"We can't hang around here and do that, what if they come back?" Lilly asked.

"They will be off to a hospital by now. Let's get the boys right and then we can go," said Dan.

Lilly's dressmaking scissors were procured from the gang's luggage in the back of the wagon and Ellen cut away the clothing around Jack's wounds. The wound on his chest was relatively minor, as the bullet had cut along the length of the muscle, leaving a long, shallow gouge before being embedded in the shoulder muscle. It was a similar story with his leg. The bullet had cut across the muscles above the left knee, but nothing appeared to be broken. The wounds were promptly bandaged.

Ellen now turned her attention to Owen. She parted the hair around his injured scalp to see where the bullet had grazed his head. It was not a deep wound, but it bled a lot, so a bandage was wound around his head to help stop the flow. Owen's shirt was lifted up and the bullet hole located just at the base of his rib cage. It was located in a spot that was precarious enough to be of real concern, but it didn't seem to be life threatening. At least that was what Ellen tried to convince herself of.

"Will he be alright?" asked Lilly anxiously.

"We'll plug the wound and bandage it. He'll survive," Ellen replied.

The question was now how would they find a doctor to treat the men? They couldn't go back to the town where McKenzie and his men were getting treatment. All they could do was keep moving forward and pray that there was somewhere along the way where they could get the help they needed.

Sixteen

Marulan was a small town on the ridge between the valleys of the Shoalhaven and Wollondilly rivers that had existed since the 1830s. Although it had once flourished it was now slowly fading away. The area was about to become a stop on the Main Southern Railway to Sydney and the finishing touches were being put on the new railway station and stationmaster's house in the newly established township of Mooroowoolen, two miles away from the existing township, where the trains were due to begin operation in only a few months. The placement of the new railway station had been selected after pressure was put on the government by some of the wealthier landholders who stood to profit from increased traffic in their neck of the woods, and it had a clear detrimental effect on the older settlement as the changes to the roads forced traffic to bypass Marulan completely. This meant that the once thriving township was now mostly abandoned as the local businesses gradually shifted to the new one in order to keep their doors open. Thus, many of the old shops, that had kept the place alive for almost two decades, were already falling into disrepair.

This information was not of particular interest to the Peacock Gang as they arrived in town looking for somewhere to obtain urgent medical treatment. They could not have cared less about the sudden withdrawal of multiple businesses from the main road unless one of them was the local surgeon.

Ellen rode ahead of the others. Directly behind her, Dan rode alongside Jack, holding onto the reins of both Sancus and Tombstone as, due to the heavy blows to the head he had received from Tom Kaplan, Jack had been passing out as they rode. Bringing up the rear was Lilly and Owen in the cart.

The ride had been a rough one for Owen. As they went, every bump in the road reminded him that there was a bullet lodged in his rib. He had become quite pale and clammy as shock had begun to grip him, but as they reached the town the colour had begun to return to his face somewhat.

After some searching, they were able to locate a surgeon who was operating from a building next to a defunct clothier's shop. Ellen went in to find the doctor. A bell mounted on a steel coil above the door rang as it swung open. From the back room emerged a burly man with a thick brown beard and spectacles. He was dressed neatly in fashionable clothes, although they were looking slightly worn and frayed from continued wear, and his hair was oiled to keep it smooth and in place.

"Good afternoon," said Doctor Smedley.

"Good afternoon," replied Ellen.

"What is the matter?"

"I have two men who have been shot that require attention," Ellen replied.

"Bring them straight through," Smedley said with great urgency.

Owen was brought through first and whisked away into the doctor's office. An inspection of his wounds was conducted and Doctor Smedley instructed Owen to lie down on a table at the far end of the room. The first thing the doctor attended to was stitching up the injury to Owen's scalp. Next, Owen was stripped to his waist and instructed to sit upright so the bullet wound could be examined. The doctor washed his hands in a small basin and dried them with a white cloth, then made Owen raise his right arm to give him access to the injury. He poked his index finger into the entrance wound, which was puffy, red and inflamed. He felt the path of the bullet go upwards at an angle toward the ribs. Owen winced, tears rolling down his cheeks, but he remained silent. Smedley began to poke the area where the bullet must have gone, noting a slight bump at the base of the ribcage.

"There she is," the doctor said, "must have gotten lodged in the tenth rib. Can't feel any cloth or anything in there. Pretty clean shot. Strange angle. Seems like maybe it bounced off your belt there."

Smedley cleaned the area around the wound and prepared for surgery. He instructed Owen to recline on the table and bite down on a piece of a deer's antler if he felt any pain. A tray of surgical instruments was brought over, and Smedley selected a scalpel.

"I won't lie to you, my darling, this won't feel very nice but if you stay still, it will pass much more quickly."

With that the doctor sliced into the area over the bullet, cutting through skin and muscle until he saw the little lump of lead through the gore. Using dainty forceps, he clamped onto the bullet and pried it free from its bony resting place. Owen tried to stay still, but the pain was like being stabbed with a red-hot poker and he wanted to leap off the table. Still, he remained controlled and calm. Smedley, having ensured the incision and the entry wound were free of debris, stitched them up and applied a damp cloth over them before making Owen sit up so he could bandage his torso.

"Well done, sweetheart," said Smedley, gently patting Owen on the shoulder, "all patched up."

Owen offered a weak thanks and got dressed before allowing Jack in.

Jack was given an examination on the table. The bullet in his shoulder was extracted through the same procedure as had been conducted upon Owen, and as the wound in his chest was already very clean it required nothing more than some stitches and a fresh bandage. The in his leg was also inspected for cloth and metal fragments before being stitched up and bandaged.

"You must be one lucky fellow," said Smedley, "the bullet went clean through. Nothing stuck in there, no damage to the bone, just a flesh wound."

"Hurts, though," said Jack miserably.

"Yes, I'm not surprised. Just be thankful they were using conical bullets and not round balls. Then we'd be singing from a different hymn book."

The head wound was stitched up, but Doctor Smedley was concerned about the signs of old injuries to his skull.

"You've had a few knocks to the head haven't you, darling? Tsk, tsk. Concussions are not good for you. Have you been getting headaches?"

"You mean apart from when someone hits me in the head?"

"Of course."

"Sometimes. I get dizzy, grumpy. Nothing too unusual."

"And what do you do when you feel this way?"

"I ignore it and push on. I don't have the luxury of bed rest."

Smedley leaned back into his chair and frowned.

"What exactly is it you do?"

"We're bushrangers."

Doctor Smedley chuckled. Jack remained impassive.

"It is no joke," Jack said.

Smedley's face dropped. He wasn't sure how to respond to the revelation.

"Don't worry. We will pay you. We'd also appreciate if you didn't tell anyone about our little visit."

"Alright," said Smedley. He got to his feet and showed Jack to the door.

"How much do we owe?" Jack asked.

"If you're telling the truth, I don't want your ill-gotten gains."

"Will you tell the police about us?" Jack asked while giving the doctor a hard stare.

"I won't say anything about this because I don't need the hassle. It is such a shame that strapping young men like you should take to a life of crime. Think of the good you could do with an honest living."

"Not all men have the luxury of gaining a good education and obtaining gainful employment. That's your prerogative, doctor. The rest of us merely survive by whatever means we can."

"My dear fellow," said the doctor, "if you choose to live like a wild animal, then you will die like one. I pray that you will make a better choice before it is too late."

This gave Jack a moment of introspection. He nodded and plucked ten pounds in notes from the pouch on his belt. He placed them on the doctor's desk as he left the office. He did not say anything as he took his leave.

***

While McKenzie and his men received treatment in the hospital at Goulburn, Mina Churchley and Anna had taken the opportunity to inform local police about what had transpired. Within the hour, information was telegraphed to all nearby towns describing the ambush by the bushrangers.

The news was so sensational that it made its way to the office of a prominent illustrated newspaper in Sydney. The editor was keen to capitalise on this event and had his top illustrator working on a large etching to appear in that month's edition of the publication, which was due to hit the presses by the end of the week. Such a turn of events was like music to the ears of the press. The fact that such brazen and dangerous criminal behaviour had spilled from Victoria into New South Wales was considered particularly newsworthy as it fuelled the toxic rivalry between the colonies. What made matters worse in the eyes of establishment types was that the Peacock Gang were making local police look incompetent; but in the minds of the lay people the longer the gang were at large, the more they posed a serious risk to the safety of the inhabitants of the colony. That would definitely sell papers. Bad news always sells papers.

Pressure was now on Henry Parkes, the premier, to do something. Parkes was a diminutive figure with a voluminous beard and long, flowing white hair. He also possessed the most astounding, heavy-browed eyes, which gave him the appearance of being perpetually furious. They were positively aflame with rage as he consulted with the relevant ministers about outlawing the gang under the Felons Apprehension Act that had been introduced to combat bushranging only a few years earlier. There had already been much discussion around whether 'wounding with intent to kill' was grounds to issue such a proclamation, but when the news of the murderous attack near Goulburn reached Sydney, the decision was made without hesitation. Thus, the wounding of John Memphis and Aoife Bradford, and the murder of Thomas Kaplan, gave the New South Wales government the green light to proceed with putting the wheels in motion to officially outlaw the gang.

***

With Jack and Owen injured, the gang proceeded more slowly than planned. It turned out to be ideal for the horses, as they had been so worn down by the relentless travel that they were beginning to misbehave. The frequent rests did them well. Every hour of travel ended with a rest in the bush, and it was during one of these rest stops that Ellen spotted a mounted trooper riding nearby.

She heard the hooves first and went to investigate. Through the trees she could see a man in a New South Wales police uniform. He was riding alone on a swaybacked nag, oblivious to the fact he was being watched.

Ellen's heart was beating fast and there was a dryness in her mouth. She drew a pistol and crouched in the scrub. The trooper stopped when he saw the tracks from where the gang had left the road to enter the bush. He stooped in the saddle and Ellen watched him closely as his gaze followed the trail. He seemed to think for a moment before deciding to continue on his way. Ellen relaxed and put the pistol away. It was an unpleasant reminder that nowhere was safe.

The gang continued towards the big city with its sprawling suburbs for the next day and a half after the close call with the trooper. To avoid suspicion, Lilly and Owen drove the wagon along the road while the other three followed close behind in single file. If the riders thought someone was coming towards them, they veered off the road to continue riding among the trees until the threat had passed.

It was on the morning of the third day when they had another unpleasant surprise. As Ellen was helping Lilly up onto the bench seat of the wagon, the younger woman halted and let out a gasp. Her free hand flew to her belly. She was feeling intense tightness in her abdomen.

"What's wrong?" Ellen asked.

"I don't know..."

Suddenly Lilly lurched, her eyes wide with shock. She looked down at Ellen with an expression of sheer terror.

"Ellen, I think the baby might be coming."

"Coming?"

"Help me down, quickly!"

Lilly was brought down, and she began to breathe with rapid, shallow breaths.

"Oh, my God, Ellen what do I do?"

Ellen tried very hard to remain calm for Lilly's sake and instructed her to take a seat on the grass.

"Are you in pain?" Ellen asked.

"N-no, but it's really tight here."

"Has anything happened down there?"

"Happened?"

"You know... Anything leaking?"

Lilly hitched up her skirts and spread her legs so she could feel between them.

"Nothing. Should there be something? Is there something wrong?" she asked, panicking.

"Nothing to worry about. I think it might be a false alarm. Do you still feel the squeeze in your belly?"

Lilly stopped for a moment and realised the feeling had stopped.

"It's gone," she said with something approaching relief.

"There you go," said Ellen, relieved, "it's just your body practising for the real thing. That's probably going to happen a few more times today."

Lilly nodded and her lips quivered. All at once the dam broke and she began sobbing and tears streaked down her cheeks.

"I don't want to give birth in the bush, Ellen."

"I know, sweetheart. Don't worry, we're not far off the town now. We'll have you in a nice house ready to go when the time comes. You just need to hold on a little longer. Yes?"

"Mmm hmm," replied Lilly.

Once again, Lilly was helped up onto the wagon and soon the gang were on their way. As they set out, Ellen could not help but think about how terrifying the prospect of having to deliver a baby in the wilderness was. For all of her births she had been safely at home. Not every birth was a success. As with many women, Ellen had suffered miscarriage and infant death. Her first baby was a little girl that she and Wallace named Mary, after Wallace's mother. She died at only a few months old from what would later be referred to as cot death. The local doctor had initially declared it a case of neglect, insinuating that Ellen had smothered the infant, but after the couple had shown him the way that they had put her down in the cot and pleaded their case, he simply declared it an "act of God" and registered the death as being from "natural causes". The subsequent pregnancy was a stillbirth, the infant coming into the world with the umbilical cord wrapped around his neck. When their daughter Catherine came into the world and survived, Ellen and Wallace finally felt like they had been blessed. Susie and Terry only added to their joy. Now Ellen was silently praying to a God she had long since abandoned that Lilly's baby would be born strong and healthy and in a safe place.

Seventeen

When Jack Cooper and his gang were officially declared outlaws in New South Wales by act of parliament, they were given fifteen days to surrender themselves to police so that they could await trial in custody. Refusal to surrender would be considered an admission of guilt, but the proclamation made it clear that the guilt was assumed regardless. Reward for their capture was set at £1000 by the New South Wales government, in addition to the reward already offered by the Victorian government. This meant that there was a chance that a skilled bounty hunter could earn £5000 for bringing them in – whether alive or dead was irrelevant.

Despite Kaplan being a Victorian native who was murdered by Victorians, as it was on New South Wales soil it was a matter for the New South Wales police. They began collaboration with police over the border to gather information on the suspects. The Victorian police were reluctant to send troops over the border again to look for the bushrangers, considering it a matter for the neighbouring colony to follow up, and they would handle extradition once the captures had been accomplished. The police in New South Wales were fully aware of this mentality. After all, they would have done the same if the tables were turned.

Senior-Sergeant Theodore Flanders was stationed at Berrima and keeping a close eye on the pursuit. He was a long-time member of the force and a veteran of hunting bushrangers. It did not take long for him to establish a pattern to the recent sightings of the gang.

Looking at a wall map of New South Wales, Flanders noted that the gang were going into townships, not sticking to the bush. He began to jab pins into the locations where they had been reported and stood back to take in the full picture.

"They're heading into the city," he said aloud to himself.

He immediately called out to his right-hand man, Constable Michael Vincent, who entered carrying a cup of tea.

"Sir?"

"Gather your things. We're going to head up to Sydney."

"Sydney?"

"Look at this map. The bushrangers have been spotted in these locations, which clearly shows that they are heading up towards the city. I will wager that they plan to gain passage on a ship there."

"Couldn't we just telegraph Sydney and let them handle it?"

"What's the matter, Vincent? Don't want a share of the £5000?"

"It's a long way out of our district. Who will take charge?"

"Well," said Flanders as he grabbed his coat, "Senior-Constable O'Rourke can do the job. I'm not expecting any urgent need for us to be here."

Constable Vincent was not convinced, but Flanders was his superior and that was all there was to it as far as he was concerned.

After some hasty preparations, Flanders and Vincent made their way to the train station at Mittagong and were soon on their way to the big city on the harbour.

***

Campbelltown was a grand municipality that had been long established and made prosperous by farming livestock. Around sixty years previous to the gang's arrival, the notorious squatter James MacArthur, who had engineered a mutinous overthrow of the government in what became known as the "Rum Rebellion", had taken up a 5000-acre run at a place known as the "Cow Pastures" where he began to breed merino sheep. This helped put the area on the map. Ten years later, the area was the venue of the slaughter of scores of men, women and children of the Dharawal nation, which would be known as the "Appin Massacre". The victims were rounded up and herded off the cliffs to their death to clear the land for white men to graze their sheep and cattle on. The official headcount was fourteen, but nobody cared enough to count them before they plummeted off the cliff. This bountiful region now belonged to the healthy, wealthy and white.

Since that time, the area had been renamed Campbelltown and subsequently built up to match the rising social status of the wealthier farmers. It was now home to numerous churches and a rectory, windmills, prosperous farms with mansion-like homesteads, popular public houses known as Bradbury's, Patrick's, the Jolly Miller, the Farrier's Arms and the Forbes Hotel. Of course, there was also the typical staples of larger, modern, towns: schools, post office, train station, town hall, courthouse, police station and gaol, plentiful shops and a range of tradespeople in residence. All of this greeted the Peacock Gang as they arrived in town in pursuit of Susie's home. They felt somewhat overwhelmed by the sheer amount of civilisation and modernity that surrounded them.

"I'm feeling a mite conspicuous," said Dan, desperately trying to hide his face. He wasn't the only one in the gang who was turning heads. They were all looking shabby in dirty and worn-out clothes, riding horses in poor condition. Ellen was, as per usual, dressed in men's clothing and riding astride, which was a risky move in such a populated place that valued the sense of propriety that defined the times. Owen and Jack were still wearing blood-stained garments and bandages. They could hardly have looked more out of place if they had tried. People stared but were unwilling to make a scene.

Ellen headed to the post office for assistance in locating the address written on the back of the *carte de visite* in her pouch. It was a handsome building and as she arrived a mail coach was departing to take a load of letters and parcels to their destinations. *Don't worry, you're safe in town*, Ellen thought to herself.

As she entered the building, she knew that she needed to maintain the illusion of being someone else. She was dressed as a man, and looking much rougher than usual, so she decided to impersonate a man. She altered her gait to a larrikin's swagger and sidled up to the counter.

"Can I help?" asked the postmaster.

Ellen puckered her mouth and in the deepest voice she could muster she mumbled, "Aye, I'm looking for Susan Baker. I have an address; I just need pointing in the right direction."

She slid the card across to the postmaster who nodded to confirm he knew the way. He grabbed a piece of paper and a pen and began to draw a rough diagram of the streets.

"Alright, this is the post office, here, and you want to go a little down that way, take a left, here, and continue on until you reach this intersection here. The house you're looking for has two floors and is made of stone with a lot of ivy covering the outside. She's a lovely young woman. Send her my regards."

Ellen nodded and took the diagram, tucking it into her jacket pocket as she turned to leave. At that moment she saw a calico reward poster on the notice board. She tried not to react as she passed it.

When the gang finally reached Susie's home, they discovered it was a rather large house in the Georgian style. Thomas had been making good money as a solicitor and had been working for his father, from whom he acquired the house as a wedding gift. "Long Tom" as his mates knew him, due to his towering height, had never questioned how his father had the money to buy such a house to give away. He believed very strongly in never looking the gift horse in the mouth.

The gang pulled up at the front of the house and Ellen dismounted.

"I think it is probably wise for me to go ahead and ease her in. I know well enough that uninvited visitors can be a mighty inconvenience."

The others remained on the road as Ellen walked to the front door. She knocked and waited anxiously. In a moment the door was opened and peering through the gap was a young woman with mousy-coloured hair and large pale green eyes set in a soft, round-cheeked face.

"Mum?"

"Hello, Susie."

The door flew open, and Susie rushed out with her arms wide to enfold her mother. Both women embraced and allowed their feelings of elation to overcome them.

"What are you doing here?" asked Susie. Her Australian accent was a strong contrast to her mother's Yorkshire twang, even watered down as it was after so many years in the colonies.

"I wanted to see you. I wanted to see the babies. I've missed you so much!"

Susie took a moment to give her mother a look up and down, finally registering her strange outfit.

"What are you *wearing*?"

"I have been riding long-distance. I'll be damned if I'm doing it on a bloody side saddle wearing a dress!"

"Won't you come in?"

Ellen hesitated.

"I have a favour to ask, sweetheart," she began, "do you see those people at the roadside there? Those are my friends. They rode up with me. Would it be a terrible inconvenience if they joined us?"

"Oh, uh... Well, alright. Come in and I'll do my best to accommodate everyone. I will put the tea on to boil. Try not to make too much noise as the twins are taking a much-needed nap."

"Thank you, my love," said Ellen.

*＊＊

Introductions were brief and awkward. Susie had no idea how to process the sudden appearance of these four strangers at her home, two of whom were clearly recently injured. They withdrew to a parlour which was beautifully furnished with couches and tables. The gang sat uncomfortably, conscious of the fact that the furniture was quite clean and likely expensive, and they were all dressed in dirty clothes stained with sweat and other fluids.

"So," said Ellen cheerfully as she sipped at her cup of tea, "where is Tom?"

Susie froze.

"He, uh, he passed."

"Passed?" Ellen asked incredulously.

"About two months ago. I had written to you, but I suppose you didn't receive the letter."

Ellen was ashamed. In all of her lawless escapades she had inadvertently severed communication with her children and missed crucial information.

"I'm so sorry..."

"It was quick. Barely two months after he started getting really sick, he was gone. He had time to get his affairs in order. He left us this house and no debts. I couldn't be more thankful for him."

The visitors were silent out of respect. Ellen, however, wanted to know the details and understand what her daughter and grandchildren had endured.

"In the last letter I received, you said there was another baby on the way?"

"There was... The strain of losing Tom took a toll."

Ellen was beside herself. There was an aching pain in her chest, like a massive knot right in the centre was being tightened.

"If I had known..."

"Don't trouble yourself over it, Mum. Life is fragile. You can't stop that whether you're here or not. At least the twins are alright. Tom left us enough money to get us through for a while. I'll need to find work soon, though. A nanny, too. I have no idea how I will manage that, but I will find a way."

At this, Lilly piped up.

"Mine is on the way and he'll be here very soon. If you'd have me, I would love to stay and look after the twins as well."

Susie looked to her mother. Ellen nodded.

"I was a maid... previously. I know how to keep a house in good order," said Lilly, "I know I look a fright in this old dress but if I had access to a laundry... At any rate, I thought I should just mention it."

"I can't afford to pay at present..." said Susie politely.

"I wouldn't dream of it. Your mother has been such a great support to me, and I want to do anything I can do to help."

"Lilly is a good girl," said Ellen. "She would be good for you. Owen, her husband, as well. It's always useful to have a man about the place. He's on the mend right now, but I promise he's useful."

Owen averted his gaze.

"I suppose. What about you?" asked Susie.

"Well, we have to keep moving," said Ellen.

"Why?" Susie looked at Jack and Dan suspiciously.

"I can explain," said Dan, "you see, we did some things we shouldn't have, and we're not proud of them, but it means we've got people following us. Owen and Lilly can go about their business here and help you out without being picked up, but the rest of us are well-known and the longer we stay here, the harder it will be to stop you from getting mixed up in it."

"Mum," said Susie, "can you come with me?"

Mother and daughter stood up and went down the passageway to the kitchen. When she was sure there was nobody eavesdropping, Susie pulled Ellen to one side.

"What the hell is going on?" she asked.

"What Dan said is true. I have strayed from the straight and narrow path and I'm a fugitive."

Susie reflexively clapped her hands to her head and began to pace around the kitchen. Everything seemed unreal, as if any moment she would snap awake and reveal it all to be some sort of nightmare.

"I don't understand, Mum. Help me understand."

"I'm a bushranger. We picked up Lilly on our travels. Her employer had made her pregnant and terminated her employment because of it. Owen has been steadfast in keeping us protected to the best of his ability and he is now Lilly's husband. He is smart and in control of his emotions. None of those looking for us know his name, and the descriptions of him are not good enough that people would recognise him from a hundred other men who have been on the road looking for work, so he is unlikely to raise suspicions. Dan and I look conspicuous, and Jack, well, he's made a name for himself quite independent of us. We made a pact to look out for each other. Owen and Lilly are good people, and they deserve a fresh start. If they're here with you, they can get one. It will also bring me comfort to know you've someone here to look out for you."

"And what was your plan if I refused, or if Tom was here and he refused?" Susie asked forcefully.

"We'd have moved on without a fuss. You'd be right to turn us away. The others never intended on staying, that was my idea. I just wanted a chance to see you and the little ones before I ran out of chances."

Susie began to cry, sinking down onto a stool to steady herself.

"I don't understand," she repeated, "why you? Of all the people in this world, how did this happen to you?"

"You don't realise how hard it was to keep going after your father died. You and Cathy flew off to start new lives abroad. Terry was my biggest support around the place but once he left to find work it was just me on my own to keep everything going. Then we had the drought, Terry vanished... There were so many things that pushed me."

"But you could have chosen not to do the wrong thing."

"You're right. I could have. But I didn't. There's a price to pay for that."

Ellen crouched next to her weeping daughter and placed a hand on her arm reassuringly.

"I have seen now just how easy it is to fall from grace. How tempting it is to just take what you think you deserve or need without thinking about the cost to others. You find all the excuses under the sun to justify doing the wrong thing for the right reasons, and I have done a lot of wrong lately, but it doesn't make it right. That's why I need to save Lilly and Owen and it's why I must leave to protect you from the consequences of my poor choices. Doing the right thing is hard, and a lot of the time it feels like God is punishing you for following the rules. I have not had an easy life, but it has taught me one thing: nothing worth having ever came easily."

***

It was not long before the twins awoke from their nap. The sound of banging on the railing of their cot let Susie know they were ready for trouble-making. She went to the nursery and plucked them out of the cot and placed them on the floor.

Ellen entered the room tentatively. She paused and looked down at the infants. They sat and looked up at her with a mix of awe and confusion.

"Look, Collie. Look, Maisie. Nana is here!"

"Nana?" said Ellen with a chuckle, "I guess I'm an old woman now."

Maisie got on her hands and knees and crawled to Ellen, who stooped to pick her up.

"Hulloa, Maisie. I'm your Nana Nellie. I am very happy to meet you for the first time."

Ellen held the baby close to her face and grinned. Maisie looked at the face before her carefully, her little eyes flicking around to take in the details, her brows knitting as she processed the information. Finally, she smiled broadly. Small nub-like teeth were visibly poking through her pink gums.

Susan picked up the other infant, Colin, and carried him over to Ellen. He was scared of the strange woman in bushman's clothes and tried to bury his face in his mother's shoulder.

"Oh, come on you. This is your Nana, say hello," Susie said.

"I'm sure he'll come around. Not all babies are as social as you were," Ellen replied.

"How long will you stay?" asked Susie.

"I'm not sure. Maybe a few days. I guess it depends on how well we can avoid being spotted and how long we have before we outstay our welcome."

"It's just me and the twins here in this big old house. Plenty of room for everyone. Tom's folks never visit. They never liked me much."

"Why is that?"

"Oh," Susie said with a sigh, "I wasn't what they wanted in a daughter-in-law. Tom's father wanted him to marry into wealth. He was very disappointed to learn I was a poor farmer's daughter."

"If I had ever met him before your wedding I would have given him a piece of my mind."

"His mother is worse. I think she blames me for his death, although she would be too cowardly to say it to my face. Talking about me behind my back is more her style. It was always false smiles and superficial hospitality when we would visit them. Anytime I would join in with the conversation she would change the subject, and she wouldn't give out a compliment unless there was a double meaning behind it. She never cared to talk about much other than gossip."

"How very middle-class of her," said Ellen. Susie giggled and placed Colin, who wriggled furiously, on the ground. Ellen did the same with Maisie.

"No doubt the old man was furious that Tom had left me the house and his money. I expect he was anticipating that it would all return to him when Tom died. He seemed to think Tom was a possession of his, not his child. I can't see how he turned into such a beautiful, considerate man given who he was the product of."

"If they wanted him to be like them, they should have raised him themselves instead of hiring a nanny to do it for them," said Ellen.

"Truth is," said Susie, "I'd give it all away this moment to get my Tommy back, even if we had to live in squalor. It's too hard without him here."

No sooner had the words escaped her mouth that Susie crumpled and sobbed. In that beautiful town with all of its stately Georgian buildings, its abundant population, Susie had found no connections, no friends or family to confide in. She was completely isolated and trapped in that big house with her babies, mourning a man who had plucked her from the middle of nowhere to give her a better life, only to lose him just when that life was starting to manifest.

Ellen looked on. She knew this feeling well. Seeing her daughter experiencing such agony made her queasy and her heart began to thump hard against her breast. She got down on the ground and hugged her daughter as tightly as she could. Suffering seemed to be their lot in life.

Eighteen

It was fortunate that Susie's house had a rather large yard in the back, but it was insufficient to hold a wagon and four horses, not to mention the lack of available food for said animals. Instead, the gang's mounts, except Old Tom, were taken by Ellen and Owen to a boarding stable to be housed. Owen was dressed in some of Susie's dead husband's clothes, which fit rather well but their formal style was at odds with his long hair and beard. Ellen wore her one good dress, which was looking rather shabby by this point.

"Good grief," exclaimed the groom as he saw the beasts for the first time, "what have you been doing to these poor horses?"

Owen looked ashamed.

"We've been riding from Victoria and were lost in the bush for a while. We tried to get them stabled as often as we could, but it was a long journey and we were short on coin..."

The groom shot Owen and Ellen a dirty look. He didn't believe for a minute that there was a good excuse for underfed and saddle-sore horses.

"I'd suggest keeping your judgement to yourself," snapped Ellen, "your job is to look after these horses, and we will pay you handsomely for that. Or would you prefer we had put a bullet in them?"

"You'd better keep your woman in line," said the groom to Owen.

"Let's not make a scene," said Owen calmly.

As much as Ellen felt justified in putting the judgemental groom put in his place, there were no other stables nearby they could go to, and they needed someone to look after their horses. She heeded Owen's directive. The groom was paid and the pair left Tombstone, Diana, and Sancus in his capable hands.

As they walked through Campbelltown, they noted how very different everything was here compared to most of the places they had been. Given they were closer to the big city, they sensed the change in atmosphere. It wasn't so painfully dry and dusty, and the town seemed alive with activity, like the aperture of a formicary.

"You know, if we weren't on the run, I would be happy to live here," said Ellen, "if I had known about poor Tom before I took up with you, I very probably would have moved up here to be with Susie. I had plans to look for a place to buy while we were here but given how things have escalated in the past week, I don't think that would be reasonable. Besides, I have less money than I thought I did."

"I wish there was an easy way to erase the past and start fresh."

"Well, there isn't. We made those choices, and we must pay the price for them. If that means that I can't live a quiet life as a grandmother, so be it."

"You don't really believe you deserve that, do you?" said Owen.

"Of course I do."

"Why?"

"There must be consequences. How would you feel if somebody robbed you or shot your spouse? If you hurt someone, what's to stop you doing it again if there are no consequences?"

"Well, I think a better question is why we should suffer so much for our crimes when there are men with great power and position sending others to kill and rape and pillage in their name with the only consequence for themselves being that they gain more power and property?"

"I never said consequences should only apply to us."

"What did you ever do wrong to deserve to live in poverty on your farm? You worked hard, you raised children, you were a dutiful wife, and I suppose you were a church mouse too, weren't you?"

"I did attend church, yes. I thought it was the right thing to do. I was raised in the faith."

"And God is meant to reward his followers?"

"Yes, with eternal life."

"After a life of torment?" Owen asked pointedly.

"Well, nobody ever told me that was part of the contract, as such, but based on the evidence it must be the case."

"What kind of loving God tortures those who are faithful to him and allows those who are godless to prosper?"

"Faith requires us to overcome the challenges God puts in our way so that we are rewarded in the afterlife."

"Then faith makes us no better than a dog that you kick and beat but it keeps coming back to you hoping that one day you'll be kind to it instead," said Owen, his voice growing louder. "If that's what it takes to be a good person, then I see no sense in being good. I'm not going to just let life beat me down in the hope that when I die it might get better as a reward for my suffering. That's why you joined us. You saw the folly in that life. You know it's all just a cruel joke. Nobody ever got ahead in life by being good and Godly."

Ellen halted and spun on her heel, tears in her eyes.

"Shut up, Owen! I know it's not fair. I know, I know. Do you think I'm heartless enough to look at my poor widowed daughter and see it as a blessing from the Lord? The cruelty of life is not an excuse for us to be cruel in kind. We have to be better. Consequences are what stop us from plummeting all the way down until we're just animals killing and fucking and shitting where we sleep."

Owen was wordless as he stood, frozen, looking at all the people staring at them.

"Alright, I apologise. Let's just head home. Yes?"

Ellen was trembling as hormones overwhelmed her body, preparing her for a fight. Her breathing was shallow, her chest tight, her hands balled up into fists. Owen flicked his eyes left and right to direct her attention to the crowd. Realising they had an audience helped her snap out of her rage.

"I'm sorry," said Owen, "I just don't believe you should accept bad things happening to you. You're a good woman. I don't believe you deserve to suffer misfortune."

Ellen hugged Owen and the pair continued to walk briskly back to the house in silence. Luckily for them, the onlookers were too perplexed by the hideous language to even think of going to the local police to have Ellen arrested for it. They didn't recognise the words, but assumed they were vulgarities.

Once the pair reached the safety of the house, Owen took Ellen through the side gate and into the back where Old Tom was munching hay in a shelter. He guided her to a wooden bench, and they sat.

"Owen, I'm sorry about all of that…"

"No, I'm sorry. I should have realised how you might be feeling. If you would like, you can tell me about it?"

Ellen took a deep breath and allowed herself to relax. This was a safe place.

"I have a lot of regrets, Owen. I feel like such a fool for having allowed myself to be led down this path, but it's nobody's fault but my own. You see, the thing is," she said, leaning forward and squeezing her arms into her belly in a self-soothing gesture, "I know I should be angry at myself for committing crimes, but I'm not. I'm angry that I didn't get away with them. I'm angry that I can't just leave it behind me and come up here to live with my daughter and her beautiful children. The rest of my life, however long that might be, I will have to be constantly outrunning those who want to put me on the gallows, and all because I let myself slip in a moment of desperation. How many more women are out there that have been in my place, doomed to a life of infamy because, like a trapped animal, they took the only way out they could see?"

Owen listened as all those bottled-up thoughts and feelings that Ellen had been too afraid to speak of came pouring out: her fears, her self-flagellating impulses. By the time she had run out of words she was weeping and rocking herself gently to try and settle herself down. Owen simply put his arm around her and held her close.

"Owen," said Ellen, "I want you and Lilly to stay here, look after my girl and her babies. You'll be safe. Nobody knows who you are. She has agreed to it. This is a chance for you to have a life I can't."

"What were you saying about consequences?"

"You and Lilly are good people, and it won't be too hard for you to avoid suspicion. You deserve a chance to have a life. This is something I can do to balance the scales a bit."

"Lilly and I are wanted as much as you are."

"Yes, 'Lillian Brook' is. But you're married to Lilly Brady, remember?"

Owen cringed.

"I don't think that's going to work."

"Well, what would you suggest?" asked Ellen.

"We could ask her," Owen replied.

"I suppose so. What do you think Lilly?" Ellen asked looking over Owen's shoulder. He whipped his head around and saw his wife standing barefoot in the garden with her hand massaging her round belly.

"Susie already asked me to stay while you were out. I accepted."

Ellen got up and hugged Lilly warmly. There was a little kick from inside Lilly's belly.

"Oh, the little so-and-so kicked me," Ellen exclaimed.

"So, what of the name?" Owen asked.

"My father used to call me 'Babbling' when I was little because I talked so much. He had an awful sense of humour. I've always rather liked the name Dorothy. Dodo for short. It was the name of a cousin I had."

"I like the sound of that," said Owen, "should I change my name?"

"Nobody knows who Owen Brady is. I think you'll be fine," Lilly replied.

"Owen and Dodo Brady. Not a bad sounding couple," said Ellen.

***

In the evening after supper had been cleared away, the group retired to the parlour. A fire burned in the hearth, and everyone enjoyed a glass of tawny port, except for Lilly and Susie.

"This is a sweet treat," said Dan, who was allowing himself a little indulgence, just one small drink. The sticky, mellow, sugary taste of the port was comforting to him.

"Tom was always adamant that he needed a glass of port before bedtime. He wasn't one for the harder drinks like rum or whiskey, but he enjoyed wine of all sorts. Sherry is more my poison," said Susie.

"So, have a drink with us," said Jack.

"I haven't touched a drop since I had the twins. At first it was because I was feeding, but then I just lost the desire for it."

"Is it bad to drink when you're feeding?" asked Lilly.

"I know plenty of women who didn't let their babies get between them and the bottle. I can't say I'd want my little ones turning out like that, and I'll say no more," said Ellen.

"Who do you know that drank when they were pregnant?" asked Susie.

"Mary Ann Talbot."

"Mrs. Talbot! I always thought her boys were a bit strange. Hughie Talbot was always getting into trouble at school."

"Yes, he didn't get any better with age. He's in the Ballarat Gaol now."

"Oh, my God! What for?" asked Susie, wide-eyed.

"He got caught with some stolen horses and tried to fight the policeman that arrested him."

"That makes perfect sense," said Susie, "Once at school Miss O'Brien caught him trying to look up girls' skirts and caned him so hard that he couldn't sit for the rest of the day. He had a real gutter mouth too. He called Miss O'Brien a strumpet. He didn't know what it meant but he heard his uncle call his mother that and decided he liked the sound of it."

The group chuckled. Ellen drained the rest of her drink.

"Well," she began, "there's something to that. Leigh Talbot was a bullocky and he was off herding cattle for months at a time, yet he and Mary Ann had twelve children. Now, unless he was spending just about every waking moment he was at home in bed with his wife, I don't think they were all his."

"I always said that Merritt Talbot looked a lot more like Mr. Barlowe the baker than Mr. Talbot," said Susie.

"Everyone knew that there was something happening between Mary Ann and Mr. Barlowe," said Ellen, "Well, everyone except Mr. Talbot, I suppose."

It gave Ellen a sense of calm and security to reminisce on the community she had left behind. She also became quite conscious that her baby girl was now an adult. The way she spoke was not so different to how she spoke as a child, but here she was as a mother herself and, unfortunately, a widow. They had more in common now than at any other time in their lives. When she looked at Susie, she could see a younger version of herself, with a dollop of Wallace mixed in. Susie had her father's round face, and when she smiled it made Ellen feel like Wallace was in the room with them. She had already used up her daily allowance of tears, so instead of allowing her feelings to rise to the surface, she drowned them with another glass of tawny port.

A short while later, Owen and Lilly dismissed themselves and re-tired to their room. This left Ellen, Jack, Dan and Susie.

"So, Jack," Susie began, "tell me a bit more about yourself. What did you do before you dragged my sainted mother into a life of crime?"

Jack bristled at the suggestion that he had seduced Ellen into a criminal lifestyle, but admitted to himself that there was, perhaps, some truth to the claim.

"Well, my dear Susan, I was a miner. I went from place to place trying to make my fortune with a mate of mine named Dick McFeely, but I gave up on that when the big mining companies made it impossible to get a good yield."

"What a name," Dan muttered to himself.

"What then?" Susie asked.

"That's what I asked myself at the time. The answer for Dick was to become a butcher. He was always a bit sly though, and a lot of the meat that he handled was less than legal. He figured out very quickly that it helped you avoid unwanted attention if you slipped the local constable's wife a little extra meat when she did the shopping. For me, though, I turned my hand to whatever I could find a quick shilling in. It then occurred to me that there were plenty of rich folks around who had enough to share, so why slave away trying to get their table scraps when you can prompt them to give charitable contributions with a little prompting from a pistol aimed where their hearts should be?"

Susie was not so impressed by Jack's description of his descent into the world of crime as her mother had been. She also did not like the way he sat sprawled across the sofa like he owned the place. It seemed that in his mind he was holding court and everyone else were his sub-jects. She could not for the life of her understand what her mother saw in him. Ellen had not said aloud that they were lovers, but she suspected it. At the very least, she suspected that Jack had his eye on her mother for one nefarious reason or another and it made her un-comfortable.

"So, what do you plan to do now? If the police are looking for you, will you stay in the colony?" Susie asked.

"I think leaving Australia is the only wise decision," said Jack, "If we head to New Zealand, it might give us enough space to avoid pursuit."

"New Zealand?"

"Well, Susie, that's one possibility," said Ellen.

"We'd need more money before we can leave the country," said Jack.

"Where will you get the money?" asked Susie.

"There's a small amount I have hidden away, but to get it we need to go back into Victoria."

"When were you planning on telling us this?" asked Dan.

"I had to be sure there was no other way," said Jack.

"How much money are we talking about here?"

"About £1000."

The others gasped. Ellen glared at Jack.

"You didn't think that money might have been useful before we left the colony?" she asked.

"I know, I know. It was an oversight. The thing is it wasn't hidden in a place that was on our route."

Dan folded his arms and sighed.

"Where did you hide it?"

"There's a cave I used to go up to before I met you and Owen. It's in the east, well, essentially in the east."

"Where?" Dan asked again, this time less patiently.

"Beechworth. It's in a cave near Beechworth. It's one of the places where I tried to find gold back in the day. If we can get back to the cave, I can get the money and that will pay our passage to New Zealand. We just need a bit more after that to make sure we have enough to establish ourselves when we get there."

"If you're sending us on a goose chase, Jack Cooper, I will kill you myself," said Ellen.

"When have I ever lied to you in the past? Have a little faith, Nellie."

"Don't call me that."

Susie cheered her mother on internally.

"Fine, whatever. Just trust me. Please."

There was a moment of stony silence as Ellen and Dan looked at each other. When the moment passed Dan gave a nod to say he was okay with the plan.

"Very well, you have our trust," said Ellen, "We will stay here for a few days more and then we start making our moves. Understood?"

"Clear as crystal. You won't regret this."

"Make sure that I don't," said Ellen with more than a hint of venom in her tone.

Nineteen

Sergeant Flanders and Constable Vincent had found no satisfaction in Sydney. They made the decision to start moving back towards Goulburn, following the route the outlaws were most likely to take. The journey back took them through Bankstown and Liverpool, and by the time they arrived in Campbelltown they had very low expectations.

They split up to wander the streets, hoping to come across something of use. Both were equipped with handwritten notes of the descriptions from the proclamation, just in case they needed a refresher. It proved to be remarkably difficult to single out a blonde middle-aged woman, a man with dark hair and a bushy beard, a tall man with lighter coloured hair and beard, a black man with a deformed hand, and a pregnant teenager, in amongst all the people clogging the walkways.

Flanders went into a clothing shop where he pretended to browse. He noticed a man of average height looking at the coats that were being modelled on mannequins. He had long hair, almost black, tied back with a strip of cloth. He had a beard of the same colour, but it was fairly short. Most remarkable was how threadbare and dirty his clothing was. Flanders watched him carefully. Nearby was a woman, on the taller side of average with blonde hair and a worn-out dress. The two were clearly shopping together as they would occasionally ask the other's opinion on a garment. Flanders was almost certain this was Jack Cooper and Ellen McReady. He wished Vincent was nearby for backup.

He sidled up to the man and got his attention.

"Do I know you?" the suspect asked.

"No. But I know you, Jack."

The man screwed his face up with confusion.

"What are you talking about?"

"Jack Cooper. You're a wanted man," Flanders replied.

"That's not my name. I'm Frank Burgess."

"The jig is over, Jack. You won't be leading me a merry dance," said Flanders with a confident smirk.

The blonde woman approached them.

"What's the matter?" she asked.

"This fool keeps calling me Jack," said the rough-looking man.

"Sir," the woman said with an Irish brogue, "you have him mixed up with someone else."

Flanders turned to the woman.

"Don't worry, I'm taking you in too, Mrs. McReady."

"My name is Maria," the woman replied, "Maria Burgess."

The shopkeeper, who had been keeping an eye on the situation, decided to intervene. He was a small man, but his quiet confidence helped him dominate the situation.

"Sir, can you please leave my customers alone?"

"They're fugitives."

"No, sir, they are not. Mister Burgess and his wife are locals. They have a farm a little way out of town."

Flanders was on the back foot. He had little option but to cut his losses and take off. He apologised sheepishly and left the shop before he accidentally escalated the situation and lost face.

Meanwhile, Constable Vincent was strolling along the shopfronts, examining everyone he passed. He had no success finding anyone that matched the descriptions but had a gut feeling they were definitely somewhere in the town.

When he reunited with Senior-Sergeant Flanders, he suggested they stay a while.

"I can't explain it, but I just have a really strong sense that if we linger here for a day or two, we will find them."

"So, your intuition is telling you to stay?" said Flanders who was fiddling with his tobacco pouch in anticipation of loading up his pipe.

"Just for a day or two. If we get no result, then we move on. No harm done."

Flanders mulled over the suggestion. It was not an unreasonable proposition. After all, if Vincent seemed convinced the outlaws were in the town there had to be something to that. He had selected Vincent for his strong intuition and sharpened observation skills as much as his capability as a policeman. He nodded to himself and cleared his throat.

"Very well, we'll stay. I'll get us a reasonably priced room at one of the public houses. If we cannot find them in the next day, we'll need to head back to headquarters. Any more time spent out here gallivanting and our absence will be noted."

***

Susie was going about her chores, washing dishes in preparation for that evening's meal. As she was scrubbing away, Dan entered the kitchen. He was looking much better presented than when he had first arrived, having dug out the best of his clothes from his swag. He wore a blue Crimean shirt with a red grid pattern; the collar was held in place with a magenta neckerchief. His trousers were brown corduroy and made a soft zipping sound when he walked. His maimed hand was looking properly healed now, and the scar tissue was pink and glossy. Now that he was feeling more comfortable in the big house he had stopped covering the wounds with a bandage.

"Mr. Thatcher," said Susie, noting his arrival with a glance over her shoulder.

"Missus Baker," Dan replied.

"Is there something you need?"

"No, I came to see if there was anything you needed, actually. A hand, that is. I still have one good one left."

"Well, if you really want to help you can take the rag there and dry up these dishes."

"Right you are, missus."

Dan took up his position next to Susie and began wiping the plates down with the scrap of fabric. As he did so he noticed there was the letter T embroidered into the cloth.

"There's a letter stitched into this one."

"Yeah," said Susie, "It used to be one of Tom's handkerchiefs."

"Why are you using it to dry dishes?"

"Well, there is a story behind that. Tom was a big fan of cricket, and he played locally on weekends. One day he was hit in the face with the ball, and it broke his nose. Blood everywhere and his nose was kind of misshapen afterwards. Anyway, one day we were in the study, and he decided he wanted to rearrange the books on his shelves. He got on the step stool, and he tried to dislodge this big leather-bound book of laws, but it was wedged – the shelves were tight. So, this book is stuck, and he begins wiggling it, and really giving it what for when all of a sudden, the bloody shelf gives way!"

Susie began to laugh as the visual was conjured up in her mind.

"All the books came pouring down on him and the big old book of laws hit him right in the face correcting the crook in his nose. Blood everywhere. The only thing we had on hand to catch the blood was this monogrammed handkerchief his mother had made him as a present when he became a solicitor. Needless to say, it was not very presentable after that, so he cut out the stained bit and I started using what was left as a rag."

Dan watched Susie carefully as she recounted the story – the way her eyes sparkled as she spoke of her husband, followed by a deep sorrow as she realised that she was not just talking about events of the past, but of a person she loved who was now also no more than a memory.

"He was special, eh?" Dan said.

"Very special. I've never met a man like him. He gave me everything I ever wanted. A beautiful house in a lovely town, two beautiful children. But the most wonderful thing he ever gave me was himself. Have you ever had something like that, Dan?"

Dan averted his gaze.

"I can't say I have, missus."

Susie extracted her hands from the water and dried them on her apron. She turned to Dan and grasped his arm.

"I hope someday you find someone like my Tommy. Someone who will make your dreams come true."

Dan struggled with the lump in his throat, and he tried to look away.

"Men like me don't get to have our dreams come true."

"Why ever not?"

"I came from the gutter. I never knew my father. I have robbed and fought to keep myself alive. Those things are hard enough, but to top it off I had the misfortune to be born into this skin, which is a crime in itself to many of the people out there."

"What are you talking about?" Susie asked, confounded.

"Every day of my life I have had to try and ignore the looks of scorn and disgust, the names that get hurled at me, the abuse and the attacks for the crime of being different. A beautiful white woman like you has never had to face that and I hope you never do, because nobody should have to."

Susie was dumbfounded. She had never seen a person treated poorly because of the colour of their skin, although she confessed to herself that she had never seen anyone with such a complexion before. She had thought nothing of his appearance when her mother had introduced him except for the bedraggled manner in which he was dressed. She figured that if her mother liked him, she must have her reasons, and that was reason enough to accept him in her home. What's more, in the handful of days since they had been staying with her, Dan had shown himself to be quiet and considerate, unlike Jack Cooper who had a thinly veiled arrogance that got under her skin.

She wrapped her arms around Dan and gave him a tight hug. Although taken off guard by the action, Dan reciprocated. He was not used to such affection and knew that it was a good idea to savour those moments when they arose for fear that he forget what affection felt like altogether.

***

In the afternoon, everyone stayed indoors relaxing. Dan sat on the floor of the parlour playing with the twins, Lilly joined the other women on the couches where they quietly discussed motherhood. Owen and Jack wandered out to the back of the house where Jack smoked his pipe. Wind was starting to pick up and the clouds were looking dark and heavy.

"Rain coming," said Owen.

"Yep."

"I reckon winter's coming up pretty quickly. I wonder if it'll be wet enough to fight back that damned drought."

Jack folded his arms and puffed thoughtfully.

"Hard to say, but I'm not confident it can make a mark in it," said Jack. "At any rate, we'll be in New Zealand before long and then it's green pastures as far as the eye can see."

"Are you sure it's a good idea to head back over the border?" Owen asked.

"I've got my buried treasure to find. Once we've got the money, we can find our way out of Australia. There's nothing for us here."

"For you, perhaps, but did you ever consider Ellen having to leave her family behind?'

"If Ellen was worried about that she would have said something," said Jack, "but she has not, so I think it fair to say she doesn't see it as a problem."

Owen did not respond, although he wanted to rip through Jack for either being wilfully ignorant or indifferent. He couldn't understand what made him so incapable of considering the impact his choices had on those around him. He was glad that he would be staying with Lilly and Susie, because in the past few months he had been shot and chased and starved too often for being Jack's associate. Now he had a chance to start fresh and it filled him with a sort of inner peace he could not remember feeling for a long time.

"Well, I 'm sure you'll get all of the green pastures you deserve," said Owen as he turned and hobbled back into the house.

Later that same evening, once the twins were asleep, Owen, Lilly, Dan and Susie occupied themselves by playing card games. Ellen, in no mood for games, wandered up to Tom's old study with a hurricane lamp and browsed through the shelves. They were packed with all sorts of books, and there were stacks of books on the floor beside the shelves where new tomes had been acquired but did not have a home. There was a defined space for Tom's legal books, which he would have used in his work as a solicitor, but on the opposite wall was a separate case where they had stored their more frivolous books — the novels. Ellen ran her finger along the spines and paused when she spotted some familiar ones. These were the old books that belonged to Susie when she was a girl growing up on the farm in Myers Flat.

Susie had been an avid reader and could often be found under a tree with a novel, the romantic stories were her favourites, or with her nose buried in a book of Shakespeare when she was supposed to be doing chores. She would occasionally sneak a candle into the partition where she slept with her brother and sister so that she could read in the dark before her parents turned in. Her books were so frequently read that many were falling to bits. One of her favourites was *Madame Bovary* and it now sat on the shelf in the study nestled between Susie's other prized books. Ellen stroked the broken spine and smiled. She thought about all the times Susie would follow her around with the book, which was entirely inappropriate for her age, giving a run-down on the story and the characters. She would sometimes find Susie wiping away tears as she read.

"I promise I will never become dissatisfied and loose like Emma, Mummy," she had told Ellen after reading the book for the first time. Ellen would simply nod, never thinking for a moment that her sweet-hearted daughter might be capable of spinning out of control into a lifestyle of hedonism and unsatiated sexual appetites. Susie spoke about how she understood why the character Emma wanted to have an exciting life away from the boring old farm, but would tell her mother, "I know that it is wrong to throw away a good husband because he's daft and boring, even when there are so many handsome and exciting men out there in the world. When I marry, I will be like you with Daddy." Ellen wasn't sure it was the compliment the teenager had intended.

She wondered if there was a bit of Madame Bovary in her since she had allowed herself to be seduced by Jack because he was handsome and exciting. Was he truly a man who captured her heart, or was she so desperate for a companion that she threw herself at the first man who showed interest?

There were footsteps on the landing behind Ellen and as she turned around, she saw Jack leaning against the doorway. He seemed very cocksure in the casualness of his pose. She rolled her eyes.

"What do you want, Jack?"

"I thought I might have a chance to speak to you alone while the others amuse themselves with silly games."

Ellen adjusted the lamp on Tom's desk, and planted herself in his old, padded chair. Jack stood opposite her in the gloom, barely lit by the glow of the lamp.

"What is there to discuss?" Ellen asked.

"Us," Jack replied. "More to the point, I want to know what I've done to keep you so cool towards me. I helped get you here safely, isn't that the test you set for me to prove myself?"

"Jack, I can't tell if you're a fool or take me for one. I told you that if we were to try again that you needed to prove yourself. Yes, you helped me get here but I don't think that you have actually made any serious attempt to shake off those parts of you that seek trouble. Your temper has gotten you into trouble a few times since we crossed the border. Your arrogance certainly seems to be unimpeded."

Jack sneered.

"I did not realise you thought so poorly of me, Nellie."

"What have I told you about calling me that?"

"You're being unreasonable. Have I put us in jeopardy even once since we had that argument?"

"You don't recall that fight you started in Deniliquin?"

"Do you mean when those tosspots attacked me because I was defending my friend?" Jack snapped.

Ellen folded her arms and leaned back in the chair.

"What about your set-to with Power?"

"That didn't put us in jeopardy, it was him falling asleep that was the problem!"

"Perhaps, but it did show me that you're still making the same poor choices about how to handle situations. Whatever romantic feelings I once had for you are no longer there. I cannot give my heart to a man who is not mature enough to care for it. Once we have the money to get out of Australia, you will go your own way, and I will go mine."

Jack's face became twisted with anger, his upper lip curled, and the bridge of his nose became creased.

"If you think I'm going to beg for you to take me back, you've taken leave of your wits. I could have any woman I wanted, Ellen. I've had so many women throw themselves at me I've lost count. How many suitors have come knocking at your door?"

Ellen leaned forward and rested her elbows on the desk then interlocked her fingers carefully.

"Jack, I don't care how many whores you have bedded. Frankly, that I haven't contracted a horrific venereal disease from you is nothing short of remarkable. I will admit that I had fun at the beginning, but I need more from a man than a stiff cock. I need a man who will be at my side and who will protect me when I can't do it myself. Someone who I can trust, and who is capable of being selfless. Looking at how you handle yourself, you're just a little boy playing at being a man." Ellen smirked. "It is driving you mad that you can't strike me right now without everyone else in this house being ready to skin you alive if you do."

Jack went red in the face and clenched his jaw. He huffed like a bull about to charge but restrained himself. Without a further word he left the room and Ellen relaxed.

Jack did not stop when he left the study. He quietly let himself out through the back door and marched around the house to the street. Still enraged, he wandered through the streets for the next hour. As he walked, he ranted in his own head about Ellen and threw every disgusting epithet he could think of at her. He wondered how long it would take the others to realise he was absent and come looking for him. *The imbeciles*, he thought, *how dare they insult me!*

Eventually, he came to a small bark-slab hut in a spot fairly close to the Georges River on the outskirts of town. This was clearly not an approved structure, and behind it could be seen a quintet of dirty, yellow coloured tents. In the window of the hut, a faint red glow could be seen. Jack sneered. Without hesitation he strode to the door and knocked. There was movement on the other side and a tiny beam of light poked through a peephole as the occupant looked out at the new arrival.

"Yes?"

"I saw the light. Can I come in?"

"You police?" the voice on the other side replied. There was a faint accent on it, Jack couldn't quite place it, but he figured it was probably Welsh.

"Me and traps don't get along. No, I'm not police."

The door opened and Jack entered the one-room hut. He looked around at the walls papered with newspaper, the makeshift tables and chairs, and the wooden bed in the far corner. He turned around to get a look at his host. She was short, thin and appeared to be around middle age. Her black hair was frizzy with lashings of silver streaked through it and her face was plain. She was dressed in a knitted shawl and nothing else, which left nothing to the imagination. Jack took inventory: *small breasts; soft belly; wide hips; thick thighs; thick, curly thatch obscuring the tender parts — not exactly 'deluxe'.*

"Like what you see, handsome?" the woman asked, doing a twirl to give Jack a chance to take full inventory of her body.

"What's your name?" Jack asked.

"Caitlin. Yours?"

"Jack Cooper."

The woman gasped and halted with her mouth agape.

"*The* Jack Cooper? The bushranger?"

"The very same."

The woman suddenly seemed to revert to an excited schoolgirl, clapping and doing a little dance.

"What are you doing here at my place? Surely there's something better to be doing than visiting a whore in a shanty on the edge of town?"

Jack smiled at Caitlin as she guided him to her bed.

"Sometimes a man has needs he can't drink away."

Caitlin began to help Jack shed his clothing, handling the items carefully and with a strange reverence, draping them over a rickety chair that had been carved crudely from a large tree trunk by an enthusiastic amateur.

"You're pretty famous around these parts," Caitlin said, "it's been a while since we had an honest to goodness outlaw to talk about. Ben Hall and Johnny Gilbert have been dead for a few years now and the Clarkes are gone. Thunderbolt is supposed to be somewhere up in Queensland, but he's not a patch on you. Me and the girls read about you in the papers. I even got the illustrated paper because they had a portrait of you. I clipped it out and keep it by the bed."

Caitlin reached over to her bedside table and grabbed a piece of paper on which was printed a woodcut of a fierce-looking man with long hair and a big beard, dressed like a miner with a row of pistols in his belt.

"I have to say they didn't do you justice. You are far more handsome than I could have expected. The girls will be so jealous when I tell them you visited!"

"Are there many of you out here?" Jack asked.

"Oh, not too many. There's about five of us and we try to keep things quiet except for Tess. She gets drunk and starts fights. She makes it hard for all of us because the local troopers get called up to sort her out and we nearly end up getting nabbed for plying our trade. Silly bitch."

Jack nodded politely while the prostitute rambled. He was curious about how quickly the word would spread about his visit, although he was more preoccupied with the spread of his reputation rather than the risk of news of his visit to the prostitute filtering back to the police and exposing the rest of the gang's presence in town. As he pondered, Caitlin began to stroke his body.

"My word," she said, "you are a specimen. Look at all these scars! You've been through it, I can tell. You know, we really appreciate someone taking a stand against those bloody traps and the snobs. It's just a shame it comes at such a cost to such a beautiful body."

She stood before him and sank to her knees.

"Let's see if we can get the Private to stand to attention, eh?"

Caitlin spat into her palm and began to use her freshly lubricated hand to stroke Jack's penis. It soon had the desired effect, and Caitlin gave a little giggle of delight as it twitched and grew to its full potential.

"Now," she said as she pressed Jack gently down on the bed, "just you let me do the work. I know the way to put a smile on a fella's face. Plenty of experience. You're lucky you got me and not one of the others because I know a few tricks that will make your toes curl."

Jack closed his eyes and let Caitlin do her thing. He hoped that there were no head lice on the pillow.

***

Despite Jack's hopes that his absence would arouse, at a minimum, curiosity about his whereabouts, the rest of the gang and Susie barely noted it. When Ellen emerged from the study, she announced that Jack had thrown a tantrum and left. The others simply nodded and returned to their game.

There was, however, the nagging thought in the back of Ellen's mind that Jack might cause them trouble just like he had done in Rochester. He was petty and childish and reckless, which was not a good combination. As she sat watching Susie play cards with the others, the nagging grew louder until she could not ignore it.

She got up and walked to the table where the game was wrapping up. She gently tapped Dan on the shoulder and gestured for him to join her.

"What's the matter?" Dan asked.

"It's Jack. I'm getting worried that he's going to do something stupid."

"Where do you think he's gone?"

Ellen paused and considered the places Jack usually went when he was in a bad mood.

"The pub?"

"Nah," said Dan, "pubs are closed on Sundays. If I know Jack, I will say he's found somewhere to slip his shoes under the bed, if you catch my meaning."

Ellen frowned. She didn't care if he visited prostitutes. They were no longer together, so it was of little consequence to her what he did with his penis. The problem was that she knew him well enough to know that now his name was starting to be recognised he would hardly be capable of shutting up around booze and loose women. There was nothing for it but to track him down before he could do something that would bring about unwanted attention. She and Dan grabbed their coats and hats and headed to the front door.

"Sweetheart," Ellen said to Susie, "we're going out to find Jack before he does something stupid, if we're not back within an hour don't come looking. You are not to arouse suspicion. If anyone thinks for even a moment that you are linked to us, bad things will follow."

Susie nodded and gave her mother a hug. Dan and Ellen ventured out into the crisp night air, disguised in their wide-brimmed hats and coats, determined to drag Jack back to the house if necessary.

They spent the next half hour wandering along the edge of town, figuring that the sort of house of ill-fame that Jack would be looking for was unlikely to be in the middle of the town. Eventually, the determined pair reached the small shanty by the river with the red light in the window, where the sounds of chatter and laughter were plentiful. They knocked on the door and the peephole was opened. On the other side a pair of woman's eyes peered out at them.

"Yes?"

"We're looking for someone," said Ellen, "a man."

"What kind of man?"

"A man named Jack. He has long dark hair and beard..."

"He's our mate," Dan chimed in.

The eyes behind the door squinted suspiciously then the peephole was closed. A second later the door swung open. Dan and Ellen squeezed inside where they saw Jack seated at a wooden table surrounded by women who were completely undressed except for their stockings and shawls. Jack was dressed only in his trousers.

"Ah, here they are. I was wondering when you'd come looking for me," he said, slurring slightly. In his hand was a dirty tankard from which he slurped whiskey.

"We've come to take you back home," said Ellen.

"Ladies, may I introduce the notorious Mrs. McReady and the almost-as-infamous Danny Thatcher? These are my mates. Ellen, Dan, this is Caitlin, Mary Ann, Tiffany, Tess, and you've already met Agnes. Come and have a drink."

"No, we're not staying. It's late and we need you to come back with us," Ellen repeated.

"Oh, come off it. Have some fun. The girls are very professional. They don't discriminate. It's not a problem that you're a woman. They know their way around that area too."

Ellen screwed up her nose.

"Although," Jack said as he gestured for the prostitutes to lean in closer, "Danny doesn't much care for women. Maybe you can change his mind, Tess?"

"Oh, you are a card, Mr. Cooper," Tess cackled. She was an awkward-looking woman of twenty years who was missing several teeth, some of which had rotted due to her excessive drinking, some of which had been knocked out during one of her many brawls.

Agnes, a girl of nineteen, approached Ellen and began removing her coat. Ellen shrugged her off.

"No offence meant, Mrs. McReady. I just wanted to help you get comfortable. The girls and I would love you to stay and join the conversation. We've been following your stories in the periodicals, and we quite admire you all."

"If you've been following the stories, then you'll know that we can't afford to make a scene and attract the police."

"No fear of that," said Caitlin, who was draped over Jack's shoulders and nuzzling his neck, "The local police won't get out of bed on a Sunday night for anything less that the rapture."

"Please join us. Please," the women said entreatingly.

Dan and Ellen exchanged looks.

"Maybe one drink wouldn't hurt?" Dan said. Ellen sighed.

"Alright. But... just a little conversation. None of the other stuff," she replied.

As they handed their coats and hats to Agnes the women cheered. Ellen and Dan were directed to the table where they sat on a wooden form. Tiffany prepared drinks for the new arrivals.

"Here you go," she said, "this is our best brandy. We save it for special occasions."

Dan and Ellen thanked her for the drinks and sipped politely.

"So," said Ellen, "what has this rogue being telling you in our absence?"

"Well, he speaks highly of you, Mrs. McReady," said Tiffany, "He told us how you rode through the bush like lightning to find his hideaway and warn him about the police who had been spying on you, and they chased you but you shook them off, but then your horse took a tumble and he found you hurt in the bush and rescued you. It was very romantic."

Ellen cackled.

"Is that how he tells it? Let me tell you, ladies, he did not *rescue* me. I shook off those troopers on my own and, yes, my horse took a tumble, and I was pretty badly beaten up by it, but I got up and I walked that horse all the way to his cave on my own. He and the others didn't even know I was coming!"

The women were spellbound.

"Now, Mr. Cooper, you shouldn't be making up stories like that," said Mary Ann. She was a woman with curly red hair and pretty features that were sprinkled with freckles.

"Ah, now, come on, it was only a little embellishment, ladies," said Jack, slightly flustered, "sometimes you have to spice your story up to make it more exciting."

"Do you have any other stories?" Tiffany asked Ellen.

"Oh, we have plenty of stories. It has been a very eventful time since I joined up with these rascals."

"Do tell us more," said Tess with enormous enthusiasm.

The warm reception made Ellen and Dan immediately comfortable, and Ellen quickly found herself being whipped up in the excitement of it all. She was starting to see why Jack craved attention so much.

"Hey, tell them about the coach robbery we did," said Dan.

"Oh, yes," said Ellen, "It was the first time I had ever done a robbery. Now, being of the fairer sex, I needed to look more like a man to be taken seriously by our victims, but all I had were my dead husband's clothes and they were far too baggy, but I wore them anyway. On this coach there was this portly little fellow in fancy duds, so when we bailed up the coach, we lined everyone up and I took him into the bush. He was standing there trembling like a leaf in the wind and I ordered him to strip."

Ellen looked around at the group of women absolutely riveted to the spot as they listened to her recounting her adventures.

"What happened next?" Tess asked.

"Well, he knew that I was the one with the barking iron, so he starts undoing the buttons on his coat as slowly as possible, the whole time begging me not to hurt him. Off comes his coat, then the rest until it's him there in the bush, bollocks out, trembling like a foal taking its first steps. I don't want to rob him of his dignity entirely, so I give him his shirt back and march him back to the others. The clothes fit me splendidly. In fact, these are his trousers I'm wearing."

The women giggled. It was such a strange feeling for Ellen who had never been the centre of attention. As a girl she mostly kept to herself, and as an adult she only really saw other people when she did the shopping or went to church. Nobody ever seemed to really notice her, but now there was a whole room full of people giving her their undivided attention.

As the hours wound on, Ellen held court with Dan occasionally adding his own parts to the stories. Jack quietly stewed when the attention wasn't on him. Eventually Ellen ran out of steam and asked the women to tell her about themselves.

"What do you want to know?" asked Caitlin.

"Tell us a bit about where you're from, how you ended up in this life," Ellen replied.

"Well, I came out as a bounty migrant with my family in the '40s," Caitlin began, "We were from Dublin originally. My father died when I was a girl, and we were not well established, so I had to go out and find work to avoid being sent to an industrial school. I wasn't suited to being a maid and I was told I wasn't pretty enough to be working in a shop. When I was at my lowest, I fell in with an older woman named Marge Thompkins."

The other women nodded at the mention of Marge's name. As the stories went on, it became clear that Marge was a brothel madame who had brought them into her world and trained them in the carnal arts, binding these women together like sisters and her as their mother figure. When she died the "girls", as they dubbed themselves, made their way to Campbelltown together hoping to find work.

"Opportunities were not as abundant as we had been led to believe," said Tiffany with a sigh.

"When we first heard about your adventures over the border we were appalled," said Mary Ann, "but the more we heard, the more we realised that you weren't monsters. You were like us. You know what it's like to suffer because of the cruelty of men with power. The thing we heard so often was that the Peacock Gang never robs the poor or harms a person with a pure heart."

"Guilty as charged," Jack replied with a smug grin.

"We ain't heard of a lady bushranger except for Mrs. Thunderbolt, and she's been out of the game awhile," said Tess. "You and Miss Brook are my favourites. I heard that she is with child, is that true?"

"As true as anything can be," said Ellen.

"I do hope the babe is safe," Tess replied. "Is it true that she chopped off that old man's truncheon and kept it as a souvenir?"

Ellen's jaw dropped at such a horrendous suggestion.

"Certainly not! Lilly did kill Jim Churchley, and she crippled Churchley's wife, but it was only because they had ill-treated her. She had worked for them, and they hurt her very badly. Jim Churchley broke a lot of promises he made her."

"Is the baby Jim Churchley's?" Tiffany asked. Ellen nodded and the women all nodded knowingly in response.

"Reminds me of that banker fellow that put little Jacqueline in the pudding club," said Mary Ann. "Such a shame. She was too young to be carrying a babe, and it killed her bringing it into the world."

"I'm sorry to hear that," said Ellen. "So, you don't have anyone here to protect you from men who act inappropriately, or to stop the troopers making life hard?"

"We're women of ill-fame. In the eyes of those toffs down the road we're not worth protecting. We look after ourselves," said Caitlin.

Agnes unbuttoned Ellen's blouse, pushing her clothing down to expose her shoulders and chest. Ellen was relaxed enough by this point from the alcohol she had consumed to allow this. Agnes then began to massage Ellen's neck and shoulders. She closed her eyes and allowed herself to enjoy the sensation of the hands rubbing her tired and aching muscles.

"We are all we have. When one of us gets sick, we all pitch in to help until they're better. We help each other relax like this," Agnes said swooping her hand over Ellen's collarbone and across her chest. It was a soothing sensation. "People don't realise that it's not as simple as laying down and parting your legs. It can be a very vigorous and dangerous occupation with some customers."

"Would you care for a rub down, Mr. Thatcher?" Tess asked.

"Not for me, thanks. I'm just conscious of the time."

The ornate clock on the mantle of the fireplace, the only expensive piece of furniture, indicated that it was close on midnight.

"You're right, Dan," said Jack, "we should be heading off."

The women protested, begging them to stay. The men stood and gently rejected the request. Reluctantly, Ellen did the same.

"Ladies, it has been a pleasure to meet you all. I hope we shall see each other again someday," Jack announced with a lazy bow.

Jack and Dan exited the shanty, but Ellen lingered. She looked at these poor women who had been so generous to her even when they had nothing. She felt a tightness in her chest and throat.

"Before I go, I want to leave you something. It's not much but I hope it will go some way towards repaying your kindness and hospitality. You are all fine, beautiful women who have weathered the harshness of life like desert flowers. I wish there was more I could do," she said as she produced a stack of banknotes from her coat pocket and laid them on the table. She wasn't sure how much it was, but she suspected it was somewhere in the region of £80. It was a considerable chunk of the money she had left over from the robberies.

The assembled women gazed at the stack of money in awe. As Ellen turned to leave, they all rose from their seats and rushed over to hug and kiss her. It was overwhelming and Ellen felt tears streaming down her face. She knew how much even a small amount of money could have changed things for herself in those dire days before she joined the gang, and she saw from the reactions of these five women that it was a shared reality.

The walk back to the house was quiet. Ellen was still too overwhelmed to speak, and Dan was not in the mood to discuss the situation with Jack. As for Jack, he was fuming that Ellen had stolen his thunder, especially given that it had started as a way of getting back at her for demeaning him earlier. He swallowed his pride and let it pass, knowing that if he stood any chance of successfully going back into Victoria and retrieving his treasure, he needed Dan and Ellen with him.

Twenty

The morning of the departure had arrived, and it was decided that the trio would travel light. The plan was to go back into Victoria via Albury, grab Jack's treasure and return to Campbelltown before departing for New Zealand. With a bit of luck, it wouldn't be more than a week or two. The more time they spent travelling, the higher the risk of being intercepted, so it was vital that they avoid as much time on the road as they could.

While Dan retrieved Sancus from the boarding stables, Ellen and Jack knew that they needed new horses. Old Tom and Tombstone were not young enough or fit enough for the long distance riding they needed to undertake anymore, and Diana belonged to Lilly. Ellen decided Old Tom should remain in the family as the property of Susie.

Ellen and Jack enquired about whether the local animal pound had unclaimed horses for sale. After some negotiation, and a little financial incentive, the pound-keeper agreed to sell them two horses that had been waiting to be claimed for a little over a week.

"Now," said the pound-keeper, "I have to keep this quiet as legally I can't sell them unless it's at an auction."

"Just pretend we were the only bidders," said Jack.

"Well, the way things are around here at the moment, I wasn't expecting them to sell, if I'm being honest. Anyway, I've got these five here for you to choose from."

"I reckon that mare over there will suit me. What about you, Ellen?" said Jack.

Ellen studied the collection of horses. Nearly all of them carried the same brand and had similar colouration. She settled on a slightly smaller mare. Both animals were large, muscular and had dark brown glossy coats with black manes and tails.

"They're damned hardy horses, these ones. They are those waler horses that some of the farmers have been breeding around here."

"Walers?" Ellen asked.

"Yeah, mixed breed. A bit of Arab, a bit of thoroughbred, and a dash of Clydesdale. Gives you a big horse that works hard and doesn't struggle so much in the heat."

"That will do nicely," said Jack.

Having acquired their new mounts, Ellen and Jack walked the animals back to the house, guiding them with halters and lead ropes.

"You seemed to catch on with the women last night," Jack said.

"I suppose it helped that I wasn't there for their services. They're good women who have been dealt a poor hand in life. I can sympathise with that. They deserve some respect."

"They idolise us," Jack replied.

"Is that what you want? To be idolised?" said Ellen disdainfully.

"It wasn't my intent, but it goes to show how standing up for an ideal can inspire others."

"What ideal are you standing up for?"

"We represent the poor pushing back against tyranny and unfairness. Isn't that worth looking up to?"

"Be honest with yourself, Jack," said Ellen, "what have you ever done that hasn't been primarily out of self-interest?"

"We need to look out for ourselves or we're no good to others."

"Even if the good you do for yourself harms others?"

Jack went to snap back that he had never harmed anyone but before the words left his mouth, he caught himself. For once, Ellen had made a point that landed with him. He could not escape the reality that not only had he deprived people of their property, but he had taken lives. The harm he had caused to his friends did not even rate a mention in his mind as he considered that to be an occupational hazard that they should have been prepared for. He now began to understand that he needed to make changes or else irreparably damage his reputation.

"You know, you're right, Ellen. I need to try harder to do no harm. I will do that. You have my word."

"Don't make promises to me. I don't care a fig what you plan to do. We have one more adventure together to get us all out of the country and then we part ways."

"Understood," Jack replied, but he did not actually understand. He felt hurt that his relationship with Ellen had crumbled away, but his pain was not because he loved Ellen and she did not love him in kind. Rather, it was because he could not understand why she had turned on him. Like a dog that could not comprehend why it was being scolded for biting, Jack had merely acted as was his nature and it was other people that had the problem. Nevertheless, he was certain that there was some angle he could use to wheedle his way back into Ellen's good graces.

***

By the afternoon the horses had been prepared for the journey and the trio were saying their goodbyes to Owen, Lilly and Susie. Dan found Owen and Lilly in the parlour where they had been quietly chatting.

"Well," he began, "we're just about to head off. I wanted to come and say farewell because I don't know if I shall be able to return here before we make for New Zealand."

Owen rose and walked to Dan but halted just in front of him. It was in moments like these that Dan was reminded of how much taller Owen was. He looked up at his companion and the two began to tear up. All the mayhem they had been through together, all the times they had rescued each other, and now it was time for their journey to end. Owen said nothing but embraced Dan as tightly as he could, encircling him in his arms. Dan returned the gesture.

"It shouldn't have ended like this," said Owen with a sniff.

"We both should have been dead by now, but fate smiled on us at least a little," Dan replied.

"I suppose. She must have something else in store for you."

"I would like it if she had something nice for me for a change."

They broke their embrace and Lilly stepped forward to say her goodbyes.

"Missus," said Dan.

"Sir," replied Lilly.

They hugged. It was a far cry from their early interactions. Her relationship with Dan had taught her a lot about herself and he had come to feel protective of her.

"Now, don't you be bossing my darling here about while I'm gone," Dan said.

"Me? Bossy? Never!"

Dan knelt and kissed Lilly's belly.

"Goodbye little one. You be good for your Mum and the old man there. I'm sorry I never got to meet you properly."

The infant in Lilly's womb wriggled and kicked.

"I will do my best to write to you both," said Dan, standing, "but it will mean I have to learn how to write first, so it might take a while."

The three of them laughed, but they knew that it was only the kind of laughter that stopped them from sobbing. Dan kissed them both and left to mount Sancus.

Meanwhile, Ellen had been in the nursery with Susie and the twins. She had not said much after they got back from buying the horses. The past few minutes had been spent silently watching Colin and Maisie playing on the floor with some wooden toys.

"Mum," said Susie, breaking the silence.

"Yes?"

"Why are you doing this?"

"How do you mean?"

"Why are you going back to Victoria with Jack? You know you can't trust him. I'm terrified that something awful will happen and I will lose you."

"Oh," said Ellen, distracted, "I understand."

She returned her gaze to the children.

"I used to watch you like this, you know? You had a little wooden horse that you could have played with in the one spot for hours. So much has changed."

"Mum, can you promise me that you will stay safe?"

Ellen reached across and clasped Susie's right hand with her left, squeezing reassuringly.

"Susan, you know as well as I do that there are no guarantees in life. Your whole world can collapse in a moment and there's nothing you can do to stop it. The only thing we can do is find a way to dust ourselves off and march on. I can't promise you that I will always be safe, but I can promise you that I will do my best. I want to be able to come and see you and the twins, but I can't do that until I find a way to shake off this outlaw business."

"I understand that, Mum, but I just can't help this feeling that something awful is going to happen," Susie replied.

"You know, your father had a gift. He'd call it his 'intuitions'," said Ellen. "He would get these remarkable dreams, and these messages would linger in his mind the whole day and there were times where it seemed that they were warnings about the future."

"How do you mean?"

"Well, do you remember that time there was a fire in the barn?"

"Yes," said Susie.

"Well, your father had one of his intuitions the night before. He said to me that he would have to get the hay out the next day because he had been told that it was going to go up. Unfortunately, he didn't get to it in time and sure enough it went up like tinder."

"You never told me about that."

"I think you have a little of your father's gift. What is your intuition telling you?"

Susie leaned back in her seat and thought to herself.

"I feel like you're going to be shot."

Ellen nodded. She tried to downplay her reaction, but the prediction troubled her.

"Well," Ellen replied, "I shall just have to make sure I avoid anyone with a gun, won't I?"

The remainder of the conversation was fairly superficial. Neither wanted to dwell on the gloominess of the imminent departure, but neither could they forget about it. The chiming of the grandfather clock in the parlour indicated that it was time to go.

Everyone convened downstairs and the intrepid trio walked their horses out to the street. They mounted, and looked down at Susie, Lilly and Owen.

"Now, Susie, keep those babies of yours on the straight and narrow path," said Ellen, "Look after Old Tom, he's been good to me and deserves a bit of quiet from now on. I will write. Keep your eye out for letters from Mrs. Gunn, they'll be from me. I can't afford to use my real name. Owen, *Dodo*, you have a second chance now. Good luck with the baby, stay out of trouble."

Dan and Jack said nothing as Ellen gave her farewell address. Dan was trying hard to keep his emotions in check and distracted himself by adjusting the glove on his left hand, making sure the padded fingers were sitting in the right position to be convincing. Jack occupied himself with surveying the street for any potential dangers.

"Alright, gentlemen, let's go," Ellen stated with authority. With a little wave the trio started off on their journey. Susie, Lilly and Owen waited until they were out of earshot and returned to the house.

As Ellen, Dan and Jack reached the high street, they became conscious of the increasing amount of people around them. They dipped their hats lower to shield their faces.

On the opposite side of the street, mounting their horses, were Senior-Sergeant Flanders and Constable Vincent. They noticed the trio trying to look inconspicuous, which only served to make them stand out more.

"What do you make of that, Vincent?" Flanders asked his colleague.

"Looks like three out of five."

"Three fifths are good enough for me, let's follow them and see what they're up to."

The police crossed to the other side of the street and began tailing the outlaws on horseback with all the subtlety of a bright yellow cathedral in the middle of a forest. Naturally, the outlaws noticed this and without needing to verbalise they spurred their horses on. The animals snorted and took flight, bolting down the street, dodging wagons and pedestrians. The police followed, doing their best to match their speed.

"Halt, in the name of the Queen," Flanders screamed.

"Bugger the Queen," Jack shouted in return.

"Stand, three times," Vincent called out as he produced his revolver. Without further word he began firing at the fugitives. Not a shot hit its mark, and the three riders split up, Jack and Dan going in opposite directions into side-streets to shake off the pursuers.

"You go left, I'll go right," said Flanders.

"What about the other one?"

"We'll catch them soon enough," Flanders replied.

The police forked out, Flanders in pursuit of Dan, Vincent in pursuit of Jack. Ellen continued riding to the edge of town and did not stop until she knew she was clear of the police.

Dan hurtled down a narrow street between houses looking for somewhere to turn off. He looked over his shoulder and spotted Flanders gaining on him. He reached a cart that had been carelessly left in the middle of the street and realised it was now a dead end. Knowing he was short on viable options, he turned around. Staring the trooper down, he stayed motionless. He put his hands up to show he was unarmed. Flanders slowed and dismounted. He kept his pistol out and approached Dan.

"You a peeler, then?" Dan asked.

"I'm a member of Her Majesty's police force."

"They only giving out single-shot horse pistols still?"

"What are you talking about? This is a revolver."

"Your bulldog is out of bark."

Flanders hesitated and looked at his weapon. The distraction was just enough for Dan to spur forward and brush past Flanders. The trooper lost his footing and tumbled against a wall. He pulled the trigger with lightning speed, but it jammed. Without looking back, Dan galloped ahead and tried to find Ellen.

As for Jack, his new horse was proving to be a little harder to control. Vincent was hard on his tail, and even though Jack's mount had the speed, it would not follow its rider's steering. The spooked animal took a hard left without warning and almost threw Jack off. He stuck to the saddle like a limpet and hunkered down. A little more riding showed him an opening that would lead him to the train line. He spurred on, hoping to gain some room to move.

Vincent began to recover ground and fired his revolver. The shot clipped Jack's shoulder, ripping his coat but leaving his flesh unscathed. Vincent knew he had two shots left, so he rationed them. Jack reached into the boot on his right foot and withdrew a small pistol from the pipe. It was a brass barrelled Belgian "Manstopper" pistol. A single shot was loaded and ready in the weapon. Jack waited for his horse to find a steady rhythm and he looked back, cocked and aimed at Vincent. He pulled the trigger and there was a huge puff of smoke from the tiny pistol as it snapped like a great firecracker. The ball lost momentum quickly but still reached Constable Vincent with enough power to injure him in the leg. The ball struck just above the knee and lodged in the flesh. He cried out; it felt like being whipped with a cane by a circus strongman.

Now there was a bit of space, Jack rode near to the train tracks then took a hard left towards where he anticipated the others would have made their rendezvous point. Constable Vincent wasn't so quick to give up and he fired again as Jack rode in front of him. This time the shot went wide and completely missed.

"Bastard," he shouted. He cocked and fired his last shot and as the smoke cleared, he could not tell if he had hit his target.

In fact, the bullet had struck Jack in the left upper arm, punching a hole clean through the flesh, but not hitting any bones and almost miraculously missing the brachial artery. It bled freely but not copiously. Jack's body was so pumped full of adrenaline he barely felt it. Onwards he rode, pushing his mount as hard as it would go. A peek over his shoulder showed him that Constable Vincent was still in pursuit, despite having used up his ammunition. He tucked the ironically named "Manstopper" — that had not, in fact, stopped the man pursuing him — into his belt and pulled out his Beaumont-Adams revolver, the hefty double-action weapon that had gotten him into so much trouble back in Rochester. He held the reins in his left hand, although his grip was weak, and aimed with his right. He squeezed the trigger and fired at his pursuer with a boom, and the shot struck true. Constable Vincent was hit in the chest just above his heart. The trooper knew he had been hit, but he wasn't sure until a deep burning pain in his chest told him to stop and check. He brought his foaming horse to a halt and pressed his right hand to the wound. He saw blood on his fingers and realised that it was serious. Unfortunately, it was the last thought he had before he passed out and slid off his horse.

Seeing the daring constable tumble reassured Jack that he was in the clear and he continued riding, smug that his aim had once again proven him to be the superior marksman. After only a matter of minutes of waiting on the Appin Road, Dan and Jack caught up to Ellen. Both men's horses looked spent, and Jack was clearly injured.

"What happened?"

"We got clear of them, that's all that matters," said Jack clasping his wounded arm.

"Where do we go now?" Dan asked.

"If we double back, we can trick anyone who is trying to follow us along the road here. Then we head into the forest and that should help us stay out of sight until we can safely come back onto the road," said Ellen. The men agreed it was a sound proposal.

They rode at a decent pace, not pushing the animals hard but not inviting disaster by dawdling. They meandered back up past Campbelltown and decided to find a place to rest the horses and sort Jack's arm out. Eventually they came to a rocky outcrop where a natural cave could be seen up a sandstone slope. They rode as well as they could towards it and dismounted when they reached the aperture. They hobbled the horses near the scrub and went inside. Jack slumped down and gingerly removed his coat and shirt. The bullet had entered laterally and pushed all the way through the bicep and out again. It was a fairly clean wound, but there was no way to remove any foreign particles that might have entered it with the limited tools at their disposal. Instead, Ellen fished a bandage out of Jack's saddle bag and bound the wound. He winced as she tightened the bandage around his upper arm.

"Do you think you could go longer than a week without being shot?" Ellen said, annoyed.

"It builds character," Jack replied.

"I think we've lost the peelers by now. I think we ought to put our minds towards figuring out where we are and where we're going," said Dan.

As he put his clothes back on Jack noticed something odd on the walls of the cave.

"What's that?" he said.

The others got a closer look. The walls were illuminated through the west-facing mouth of the cave by the descending sun, revealing that they were festooned with paintings: outlines of hands, a boomerang and what seemed to be a depiction of two cattle, one of which was clearly a bull from the distinct sexual organ depicted. These were paintings left by the first people to inhabit this area. The Dharawal, the Dharug and the Gundugurra all moved through this patch of land, and this was the first record they had made of the strange European creatures that signified the beginning of the end for their people and way of life.

"My goodness," was all Ellen could say.

They began to feel like they were trespassing on something special, something that was perhaps sacred, and the notion gave them itchy feet. They wasted no time in getting back on their horses. They headed deeper into the bush and eventually reached the Georges River, which they followed until they could find a point to cross. The anxiety they felt about being found and captured meant that the three bushrangers could not appreciate the natural splendour around them, but when they reached a spot where the river narrowed and the cool waters flowed over smooth, brown-grey rocks just deep enough that they wouldn't have to force the horses to swim, they took a moment to assess their surroundings. In another context they might have taken time to stop and relax by the water, maybe even strip off and go for a swim, but such an indulgence in this moment would have possibly doomed them all. They pushed on, crossing the narrowest part of the stream as best they could, then disappearing into the wall of trees on the other side behind the embankment.

They rode until it became dark. The bush was thick with box gums and peppermint trees, giving the area a fresh, minty smell infused with the tang of eucalyptus. They found a clearing and established a camp. Their first day of their last great adventure had been a disaster and now they were considerably off-course. Their fire was a piddly affair, barely enough to boil the billycan over, which was just as well because none of them was prepared to go looking for a creek to fetch water from. Instead, they drank from their flagons and turned in early so that they could get moving at dawn.

**

Dawn came and with it came the cackling of the masked lapwings and laughing kookaburras. The three bushrangers arose and kicked dirt over their fire before they packed up and mounted. Jack's arm was in considerable pain by now, but he pushed through it.

As they packed their swags onto the horses, Dan's eyes widened upon seeing something unwelcome and eight-legged resting on Ellen's shoulder.

"Don't move, Ellen!"

"What? What is it?" Ellen asked with terror in her voice. She froze stiff.

"You've got a friend on your back. Don't move, I'll get him off."

Dan grabbed a stick and moved cautiously towards Ellen, hoping not to frighten the large huntsman spider splayed out on her shoulder blade with its legs forward-pointing in a crab-like formation. He reached out with the point of the stick and tried to flick the creature harmlessly off but only succeeded in spooking it. The spider did not arc up in an aggressive way but rather scuttled with baffling speed over Ellen's shoulder onto her breast. She did not feel the movement, rather she spotted the grey blur on the edge of her vision. She was paralysed with fear and wanted to scream but only a tiny squeak could escape. The spider settled its plump, fuzzy body against her chest, twitching its pedipalps as it waited for another attack from the pointy wooden implement.

Jack, seeing this ridiculousness, strode over to Ellen and gently extended his hand towards the spider. It recoiled slightly, but Jack stayed still and calm.

"What are you doing?" Ellen whispered.

"Hush now," Jack replied.

After a moment he gave the critter a soft tap on its abdomen, and it wandered onto Jack's outstretched palm. The span of its legs was enough to cover the width of his hand, but he remained calm and gentle as he relocated the spider to a log on the ground. It dismounted and scuttled into a crevice. Jack stood up and grinned like the cat that got the canary.

"When I was prospecting with Dick McFeely, we'd get them in the hut all the time. They keep the pests under control. I've never been bitten once."

"Well," said Ellen, "that's reassuring." It took her another five minutes to get her fight/flight reaction under control, by which time they were mounting the horses and working their way towards some kind of road or trail that would lead them out of the forest.

They reached a rough track that followed the Woronora River and began to travel along it southwards, figuring that it was their best bet to find a settlement. When they reached a fork in the road, they stopped to take a vote on whether to take the path to the right or the left. There was very little discussion, and the decision was reached based on feeling rather than anything observable. The result was a unanimous decision to take the path to the right, which took them further inland.

Having spent the whole day on horseback with only a few moments of rest, they decided to camp again before continuing. Ellen and Jack had been quite impressed with the endurance of their horses but were glad to find a spot near a creek where the horses could drink and graze, and they would be able to fill their billycan and flagons.

As night settled over their camp, they tried to fill the time before turning in with chatter. Ellen still felt a degree of discomfort with Jack after the nastiness of their argument in the study but knew that the key to this mission being successful was cooperation. Jack, in the meantime, had given no further thought to his relationship with Ellen, instead he had spent the bulk of the journey so far trying to remember how to reach the treasure he had hidden near Beechworth.

"So," said Dan, "what are you going to name your horses?"

"I hadn't really thought about it," said Ellen, "I guess, having had her for a couple of days, she seems a reliable, calm and tough kind of horse. What's a name that makes you think of those qualities?"

Dan stroked his beard thoughtfully.

"I had an aunt who was named Esmeralda. She was like that," he replied.

"It's a nice name, but I'm not sure that is the one."

"I might call mine Rocket."

"Rocket?" Ellen said with confusion.

"Like Stephenson's Rocket. The steam engine. She goes fast and seems to have good endurance."

"Rocket. That's a good one," said Dan.

"I think I will call mine Alice," said Ellen, "I have always liked that name. Alice, yes. That will do."

***

The following day they rode along the track and finally reached civilisation in the form of Appin. It was a busy town full of sandstone buildings that mostly dated back to when the place began to boom from wheat and dairy farming around the '30s and '40s. It had taken two days through some of the thickest bush they had traversed, but they were finally back on track.

They did not linger in the town and made their way along the road to the Cataract River. At Broughton's Pass they crossed the deep ravine on a bridge constructed from logs with iron railings. There was a strange feeling of terror that seemed to rise up in them as they rode over the gushing waters. If they had known that it was in this very river that scores of Dharawal people were sent plummeting to their deaths from the gorge by British soldiers and their dogs half a century earlier, they may have given the feeling more attention.

After the extermination had been concluded, Governor Macquarie ordered the corpses to be strung up in the trees as a warning to other Aboriginals, and many of the deceased were decapitated so that their skulls may be studied by professors in England to see how the black man might be proven to be inferior to the white man. The fate of bushrangers in that time was no different. There was a belief among the 'respectable' classes that criminals must have some malformation of the skull that showed they were sub-human and explained their behaviour. In either case, the key message behind such actions was always that any attempt to push back against those with wealth and power would be met with swift and unforgiving vengeance, whether you had the gall to break their laws or the temerity to live on the land that they wanted to possess.

Times had changed, of course. A white man's remains had not been publicly hung in chains since 1837, only a few years after the Ribbon Gang's corpses were hung in chains along the streets of Bathurst to demonstrate the fate of rebels. But in the western colony it was barely over ten years since the last Aboriginal men had received such indignity. The thought creeped in once in a while that the powers that be might make an exception for the Peacock Gang and bring back this barbaric behaviour when they met their fate. Ellen, Dan and Jack pushed thoughts of this sort of thing to the back of their mind whenever they bubbled up from the depths of their psyche. It did them no good to lament over their potential fate if their plans failed. No, they were resolved to staying in the moment and keeping several steps ahead of their pursuers.

As they rode, they stayed three abreast. This allowed them to converse without straining their voices or their hearing.

"Where do we go from here?" Dan asked.

"We need to cross into Victoria, so we head south as best we can," said Jack.

"Where do we cross?"

"I believe the best place to cross will be at Albury. That's where I used to go when I was hopping between the colonies back in the day," Jack replied.

"Any idea how to get there?" asked Ellen.

"Not at all. But we can find out."

***

Mina Churchley had returned to her farm without further incident after the fatal confrontation that had left the majority of the posse either injured or dead. She and Anna had departed from Goulburn without the men and made no apologies for it. In Mina's mind, the men in their company had demonstrated arrogance and ineptitude, and their wounds were the proof of these character flaws.

In her absence, the remainder of her workforce had continued their labours looking after the sheep, and the task of doling out the weekly pay had been allocated to her maid, Marie Ronan. What Mina was unaware of was the mischief they had gotten up to in the house while she was away. Of a night, instead of returning to their quarters in the outbuildings, the men were invited into the homestead by the maids where they would get drunk, sing bawdy songs and engage in all kinds of lewd behaviour in various rooms. Some of the men had made it a challenge to have sex with the maids in every room of the house at least once before Mina returned. The maidservants made sure to clean up afterwards and ensure everything was spick and span in preparation for any unannounced return of their mistress.

Upon Mina's return she announced her decision to leave the farm and take up residency in Melbourne, where the Hahn Textiles factory that she had inherited from her father was. She had developed a severe distaste for the place her husband's father had built up and hired her cousin to take over the property for her. The cousin in question was Leopold Hahn, a man of barely nineteen years of age with no experience in agriculture. This was not a problem for Mina, who had selected him purely because he was easily manipulated. Leo was, in the colloquial sense, 'simple'. Whatever Mina told him to do, he would obey. Thus, Mina reckoned, she could run the operation from afar exactly as well as if she were there by using Cousin Leo as a puppet.

Once Leopold arrived from Adelaide, Mina would take her leave and head to the town house in Melbourne where she intended to live with Anna. She could hardly wait to turn her back on the wretched chapter of her life that had cost her so dearly.

***

In the parlour of a Bendigo hotel, Senior-Constable Frederick George Haigh smoked a cigar and nursed a glass of brandy. He reclined in his chair and gazed at the fireplace. Draped over the arm of the chair was a newspaper, open to a report of the Peacock Gang's murderous attack on police in Campbelltown. Admittedly, neither of the police had actually been murdered, but "injurious attack" had less of a ring to it.

He thought about how the bushrangers had slipped through his own fingers months earlier. He often ruminated on the embarrassment of having been unable to nip their criminal career in the bud, but he knew that the moment they crossed the border back into Victoria, he would be there to bring them to justice personally. He would never be satisfied until he could see Jack Cooper dancing on the lid of a coffin or with his brains blown out.

He sucked deeply on the cigar, filling his mouth with peppery hot smoke. He blew it out slowly, watching the plumes curl and waft towards the ceiling. He believed it was only a matter of time until he could attain his desired outcome.

***

With her mother, Jack and Dan gone, Susie had been tidying up the house and adjusting to her new life with "Dodo" and Owen. In the process of cleaning the room where Jack and Dan had been sleeping, she discovered a haversack that Jack had left behind. It was a filthy, calico thing full of all kinds of bits and pieces. Her curiosity got the better of her and she opened it up to look inside.

Among the bullet moulds and smoking paraphernalia, was a book. It looked fairly worn out. She opened the leather cover and saw a bloody thumbprint next to the shakily written inscription:

Ellen McReady
Myers Flat
Love
Terry

Susie felt her heart sink. She put the book to one side and looked in the sack again. She spotted a locket and withdrew it. She pried the halves apart and saw inside a portrait of her mother. She ran her finger over the outside of the piece and felt an engraving – the letters T and M. She didn't want to entertain the thought that was screaming inside her head, but she had no choice. She clasped her hand to her mouth and sobbed. There was no way that her mother could have known this and still tolerated Jack's existence.

She flew downstairs and found Owen and Lilly in the dining room. She produced the journal and the locket.

"Have you seen these before?" Susie said with a trembling voice.

"Never," said Lilly.

"No, I can't say I have. What are they?" Owen asked.

"They were in Jack's belongings."

"Alright," said Owen, "but what's the matter? What *are* they?"

Susie opened the locket and placed it on the table, then opened the journal to her brother's final inscription. As soon as the others realised what they were looking at they went pale.

Owen began to weep.

"I'm so sorry," he said.

"What do you know about this?" Susie asked.

"I don't know where he got those, but I know Jack Cooper well enough to know that if I ever see him again, I'll kill the bastard myself," Owen replied. His face went red, and he clenched his jaw. He had rarely known such rage, but there was no denying that Jack Cooper had done something utterly deplorable. There was no other answer.

"Is this why you went to my mother's place?"

Owen shook his head.

"Jack told Dan and I that someone he had met had recommended your mother as somebody that would help us. That's all we knew, he refused to tell us anything else."

"Tell me," Susie said, "is my mother safe with that man?"

Owen took a breath and collected himself.

"As long as Dan Thatcher is with them, your mother is safe."

***

The last three members of the notorious Peacock Gang were now on the road to their final adventure. They had crossed the Nepean River and were heading into the highlands where they were greeted with rolling hills, looming mountains, steep cliffs and deep valleys lush with trees. The long journey back to Victoria would give Ellen McReady plenty of time to reflect on what had led her to this point and how she was going to find a way to get back to her family in spite of the proclamation that had declared her to be no more than vermin for extermination. She was an outlaw, yes, but before all else she was a mother and a grandmother, and she was not going to give that up in a hurry.

She looked at Jack Cooper. She barely recognised him as the man who had swept her off her feet and sent her on this bizarre and tragic path. She then looked to Dan Thatcher, a man she had come to admire. For all of the cruelties he had endured he had remained optimistic, loyal and most importantly self-controlled. She was glad to have him by her side.

As she gazed out on the majestic ridge of Mount Gibraltar, she wondered what that rugged road would have in store for them. She would find out soon enough.

To be concluded...

ABOUT THE AUTHOR

Aidan Phelan is an independent writer based in Melbourne, Australia. In 2020 he published his debut novel, *Glenrowan*, and is the writer and historian for *A Guide to Australian Bushranging*, which has been bringing Australia's outlaw heritage to a worldwide audience since 2017. Since 2020 he has released two editions of his novel *Glenrowan*, *Aaron Sherritt: Persona non Grata*, *Bushranging Tales: Volume One* and his edit of William Westwood's autobiography, published as *William Westwood In His Own Words*. He has also written and published two children's books about the outlaw Ned Kelly: *Ned Kelly the Bullet-Proof Bushranger* and *The Story of Ned Kelly*.

He is a member of the Australian Crime Writers Association, and in 2025 he co-wrote the upcoming feature film *The Sundowner* with acclaimed director Matthew Holmes, which is currently in production.

Also by this author

The Kelly Gang have been on the run for months and are the most wanted men in the British Empire. No expense has been spared in the hunt to bring them to justice. With the introduction of highly specialised trackers to hunt them and rumours of treachery amongst their supporters, the outlaws are desperate. Soon their leader, Ned Kelly, will hatch a plan that will not only bring an end to the pursuit, but will leave an indelible mark on the history of Australia. *Glenrowan* is the story of how one man's burning obsession can have far reaching consequences, and how a tiny town between towns became as iconic as Gettysburg or Waterloo.

Bushranging Tales: Volume One depicts real cases of Australian bushranging through a series of short stories, biographies, original illustrations and archival material. Discover thrilling and horrifying true stories of robbery, prison escape and murder, featuring events from the lives of Michael Howe, Matthew Brady, Martin Cash, Daniel Morgan, Johnny Gilbert, Harry Power, Captain Thunderbolt, Captain Moonlite and Ned Kelly.

Aaron Sherritt: Persona non Grata explores a perspective of the hunt for the Kelly Gang, and Sherritt's role in it, that has been rarely examined. You will learn how internal politics led to Aaron Sherritt's tragic demise. In popular perception he has been portrayed as a traitor, a double-agent, or a victim of false accusations through over 140 years of slander, myths and misinformation.

Did Aaron Sherritt really betray his friends for money?
Were there others who were more deserving of such scorn and suspicion?
How did Aaron Sherritt go from everyone's mate to *persona non grata*?

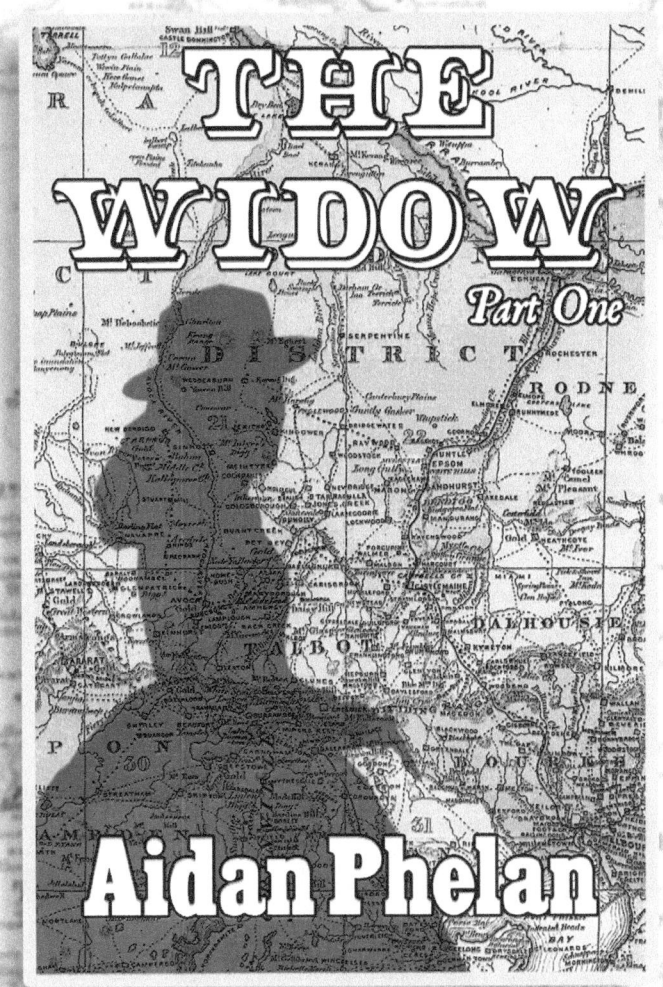

Ellen **McReady** is just a lonely widow struggling on her drought-stricken farm, but when Jack Cooper and his band of bushrangers turn up on her doorstep it will lead her on a journey that will turn her life upside down.

THE WIDOW is a rollercoaster of crime, found family and romance set on the backdrop of colonial Australia.

www.ingramcontent.com/pod-product-compliance
Lightning Source LLC
Chambersburg PA
CBHW020005140726
47904CB00018B/1890